W9-BTS-169

The Obsidian Dagger:

Being the Further
EXTRAORDINARY
ADVENTURES
of
HORATIO LYLE

Catherine Webb

www.atombooks.co.uk

ATOM

First published in Great Britain in 2006 by Atom
This edition published in 2007 by Atom
Reprinted 2007

A CIP catalogue record for this book
is available from the British Library.

ISBN 978-1-904233-79-4

Papers used by Atom are natural, recyclable products made from
wood grown in sustainable forests and certified in accordance with
the rules of the Forest Stewardship Council.

Typeset in Fournier by M Rules
Printed and bound in Great Britain by
Clays Ltd, St Ives plc
Paper supplied by Hellefoss AS, Norway

Atom
An imprint of
Little, Brown Book Group
Brettenham House
Lancaster Place
London WC2E 7EN

A Member of the Hachette Livre Group of Companies

www.atombooks.co.uk

INTRODUCTION

London

London, 1864

It is said that there are forces beyond any mere man's control. Some call it magic, some call it God, some call it luck, some call it fate. Very few know what it really is. And they're the few who it, whatever 'it' may be, will never change.

It is said that, when everything else is sleeping, the stones of London Town whisper to each other. The old cobbles of Aldgate murmur to the new of Commercial Road, telling them what a world they have inherited, what a place, what a hunger, pouring out their history, whispering with the changing tide as the Thames rolls gently from here to there and back again, bringing with it little pieces of the world outside, which are quickly lost and consumed in the city.

It is said that, when every footstep is silent, the city is alive, aware, breathing, warning its brief inhabitants of danger coming from afar, and fighting it with the experience of centuries.

Except, perhaps, tonight.

Winter.

In Heron Quays the last coal-carrier looks up as he heaves the final sack of black, lumped will-be-soot up from the base of the barge, just a small shape in a city of ships clinging to the side of the river, and sees, a long way above, the first few specks of snow caught briefly in the moonlight, as they drift towards the river, which shimmers in the dark corners where sunlight never reaches, still and frozen.

In St Mary's Church, Cheapside, the priest stops hacking at the long icicles hanging from his once-white spire, now almost black with soot, as the first snowflake touches gently on the brass bell of the tower, which seems to hum an old, forgotten tune picked up by the bells of St Paul's and St Pancras, which whisper to each other:

> *Hark, hark, the dogs do bark,*
> *The beggars are coming to town.*

The snow is trodden under the feet of the costermongers calling out in Brick Lane and Chapel Market and Whitecross Street and along Poultry and down Maiden Lane, until it is black and slushed and clings to the black ice that hides between the rounded cobbles for protection against the onslaught of hob-nails and chipped leather and baked suede and rolling wooden wheels and iron hooves and bare toes turned blue.

It falls across the light of the single lantern burning in the darkness on the deck of a ship, old and unusually tattered, rigging hanging down as if it has just sailed through a storm, its mast one branch in a forest of ships that sit, creaking to each other about the places they have seen, the spices and silks and sailors and smells that they have carried from Aberdeen to Zanzibar. The snow settles on the deck, where even the salt water, that has seen more oceans than the moon, begins to shiver and whiten in the cold.

The snow falls outside a tall window, through which yellow light spills, eclipsed only by the black outline of a man. For a second the light warming the snow turns red as it catches a slurp-ful of port, swirled absently in a crystal glass, and the glass hums in sympathy to the voice that says, 'One would have thought, that if they wished to avoid this situation, they would not have permitted him to be moved. It is unfortunate when our allies' failures inconvenience us.'

'Yet it may work to our advantage, my lord.'

The owner of the voice regards the black and white landscape, pinpricked with yellow lamps and dirty candlelight, blurred behind the still-falling snow that blends at knee height with a grey-green fog rising off the frozen river, and wears an expression which implies that here is a phenomenon which, if it knows what is good for itself, won't come anywhere near *his* shoes, and says in a voice colder than the icicles on every uneven roof and tortured drain, 'I will not underestimate this . . . person.'

'Is your agent not competent? Mine is.'

Yellow light turning red, port swirling in a glass, settling again. For a second the moon tries to make itself known over one of the clouds, but if the snow doesn't eat up its light before it can touch the cobbles, then the smoke does. 'He is competent. But . . .'

'My lord?' A voice, not entirely familiar with the sound of English, raised in polite enquiry.

Yellow light, turning red, port swirling in a glass, drunk, gone. A little sigh, appreciation of the finer things in life, and nothing else besides. 'He has an unfortunate inclining that we really cannot countenance.'

'Which is, my lord?'

'Scruples, *xiansheng*.'

The snow builds up against a long window in a tall house that overlooks a steep hill, inside which a voice like marble warmed in the sun whispers to itself, 'So soon.' The owner smiles, and thinks of a time when the snow was heavier, whiter, colder, and there weren't nearly as many fires to drive it away.

And the snow falls on a tall, dark-haired man half-caught in the light of a ship's dull lantern, who says, 'You should not have brought him here, captain. He will cause no end of trouble!'

A voice, fast, scared, teeth chattering in the cold, coming out of the darkness, across the loose rigging and old, battered, salt-stained wood, 'He's safe! I make sure! He go nowhere!'

'He came *here*.' A voice like stone, like the stones around, baked London clay, white Portland stone, granite and scarred limestone, yellow sandstone and chimneys of old, blackened brick. 'You brought him here after he had waited alone for so long, you brought him *here* and now we are all in danger.'

'I not know, I not know, the man he say . . .'

'Which man?'

'The man! Who come with the letter and say he was priest, and he say he go and see that cargo ready and . . .'

'He's here? Now?'

Horror in the voice, horror and fear, a deep-down true knowledge of what is to come. And still the snow falls on the crooked roofs of Bethnal Green, on the tight, winding alleys of St Giles, on the high peaked roofs of Mayfair, on the carriages of Belgravia, on the dome of St Paul's and the steel slope of Paddington, on the trains of King's Cross and on the barges of the Thames, which gobbles up each snowflake and grows fatter, whispering always the old stories that run from Bromley to Barnes, from Swiss Cottage to St James, from Highbury to Holborn, and say,

> *Hark, hark, the dogs do bark,*
> *The beggars are coming to town.*
> *Some in rags, and some in tags,*
> *And one in a velvet gown.*

And the snow falls between the pillars of the Royal Institute and through the cracks of the collapsing slums of Whitechapel and Bow, on the carts of the costermongers, the laden carts from Dover, the snorting train to Edinburgh waiting for the last passenger to save his top hat from a savage vent of steam, on the top hats and frilled bonnets, on the tinker, tailor, soldier, sailor, rich man, poor man, beggar man, thief, on the lass selling roasted nuts in Drury Lane, on the man setting up his stall of dark green watercress while the bells ring out across Old London Town, each in their own little temporal universe that will never agree with its neighbour, telling stories of when the city was smaller than it is now, and the people crowded into the garrets of Holborn, and the world stopped at Hyde Park, where the murderers were taken to die, and the snow falls on an old ship, just one tree in a forest of masts, and on a dark-haired man who's just felt horror and fear for the first time in his life, and realized that, again for the first time, he is standing with his back *against* the light.

And from the darkness of the thick London night, something rises up, looks around, and for the first time in the city's memory, hears its song, and remembers an older time, and looks down into two terrified faces and remembers the fear and the anger that has been burning inside for too long. And it says, '**You would have tamed me. Learn, even changed with the dark, I cannot be tamed!**'

And, somewhere close, Old Edgar, king of the beggar men, wakes from a shivering, frost-touched sleep under the pier, where the sewers give a little warmth against the cold and the wind can't quite reach its pale blue finger, and hears a scream – and another – above the whisper of the snow and the lapping of the water, which in the places where the sunlight never reaches has already started to freeze. The shrieks are cut off, as if the air that should be rushing by in a high, tight wail has suddenly found itself with nowhere to go. He shivers, and knows that tonight he'll have nightmares to contend with, as well as the cold.

And there is a carriage, snow still heavy on the roof, and a voice, like rich maple syrup, like an autumn tree bending in the breeze, murmurs, 'Welcome to London, your grace.'

And a man taller than most men, who walks with bare feet on the ice and feels no cold, looks round, hears the hum of the street and smells the darkness and the history pouring out of every crooked alley, off every slanting rooftop, climbing up from every broken cobble and drifting away from every cooling, toppling chimney and says, like a man coming home, *'Yes.'*

CHAPTER 1

Heath

Morning after snowfall was, for a very brief moment, before the feet and the smoke of the city corrupted it, fresh and clean, or at least as fresh and clean as the city of London was likely to get, all things considered.

The bells proclaimed the hour to be eight of the morning, and grey sunlight, embarrassed to be up this late when most folk of the city had been working for a good three hours already on a breakfast of cress, black bread and dripping, seeped across the white fields of Hampstead Heath. It crawled through the old trees, where pigeons nestled against each other to combat the cold; it slid past the high mansion walls of the very rich, which looked down on the black and grey city sprawled higgledy-piggledy below.

The light drained the colour out of a brown and white dog with huge ears trailing in the snow, that lay, wrapped in a tartan blue blanket by a black tree heavy with snow, and slept.

As it slept, it snored. Loudly. One long ear twitched in time to the tail, the very end of which flexed between the snores in a rhythmical sequence that would have impressed even the most stringent of conductors.

Somewhere, just below the verge of the hill, voices, too lively for the black pall of smoke that rose out of the chimneys below and the heavy, snow-weighted clouds above, drifted into the air.

'I said put it *there*.'

'You said left!'

'*That* way!'

'That's *right*!'

An embarrassed pause. 'Oh.' Then, just in case, '*Is* it?'

'I think you'll find it is.'

'Are you *sure*?'

The dog in the thick blue blanket, which itself seemed greyer for the monochrome landscape, stopped snoring, opened a single lethargic eye, and regarded the world over the end of its large brown nose. Unimpressed, it closed the eye again, and snoozed on.

A man appeared from behind a thicket of leafless twigs, carrying a box of heavy tools and a large watering can smelling of oil. He strode past the dog, oblivious to anything but his task, humming under his breath. His head was bare, despite the cold, revealing sandy-red hair, looking as if it couldn't decide whether to be entirely yellow or entirely ginger and had settled for a reluctant compromise. His face was young enough to still be deemed handsome, and old enough to be deemed respectable, though he had always suspected that respectability was just another way of paying tax. Grey eyes blinked at the grey landscape, and found themselves uninspired.

There was the sound of feet crunching snow, accompanied by voices, rapidly getting closer. The man stopped to listen, head on one side, as if trying to understand an eccentric social ritual.

The voices drifted closer.

'Well, if you *will* light the fuse what do you expect?'

'I was going to attempt to put it out . . .'

'By steppin' on it?'

'I'm sure it could have worked and I feel sure that if you'd given me the opportunity, rather than just grabbing me in that undignified manner . . .'

Two shapes appeared over the rise of the hill. One, a tall, skinny boy with yellow hair, wore a greatcoat that was clearly designed to give him a certain aged gravitas, but flapped embarrassingly around the wrists and ankles. The other, a girl somewhat shorter and younger than he was, bounded along at a lively pace, and was wearing so many layers of thick clothes in so many faded and stained colours, it was hard to tell where one garment began and the other ended. When the boy spoke, it was as if he had stolen all the vowels from her, so that each syllable dripped good diction, while she often stopped short of a full word, as if expecting any intelligent listener to surmise immediately what it was she could be talking about.

Today, and not for the first time, the girl was dragging her elder companion by the sleeve and, sighting the sandy-haired man, she called out in a sing-song voice, 'Mister Lyle? That ain't a clean coat what you're wearin'?'

The man addressed as 'Mister Lyle' looked down at himself, as if he hadn't given the idea much thought. 'Well, I suppose it's relatively –'

Somewhere, just below the hill, something exploded. The noise sent birds, sleeping a second ago, racing for the sky, and set dogs barking all around. The shock wave caused trickles of snow to run off the branches of the trees, shook what few withered leaves still remained from the bushes, swirled the powdered snow in eddies and, in the direction of the actual blast itself, lifted up a fat, mammoth-sized spoonful of black earth and white snow, threw it twenty feet into the air, pushed it outwards, and then slowly dropped it down again with a *squishplopsquish* noise.

The dog, snoozing in the blanket, twitched its nose disdainfully, and kept on dreaming of biscuits yet to come.

There was a long silence, while everyone and everything waited for something else to happen. When it didn't, Horatio Lyle picked himself up from where he'd dived on to the ground, brushed the worst of the snow and dirt off his front self-consciously, ran a hand through his hair in a nervous gesture that belied his deliberately calm face, and surveyed the crater below.

When he spoke, his voice had a weary alertness and lilt that softened some vowels and gave some consonants a crippled edge, so that every costermonger in the street would touch their hand to their forehead in respect for a gentleman, and every gentleman would retreat a little polite pace, in suspicion of a man who couldn't quite be of *their* class. It was a hard voice to place, so most people identified it as 'not mine' and left it at that.

He said, 'Now, do you think it was a problem with the chemical composition and ratios, or with the packaging?'

The three regarded the crater a little longer. In his blanket, the dog made a contented snorting noise. Finally the boy, brushing snow out of his hair and off his greatcoat that barely disguised the thinness of his frame, said hopefully, 'Do you think we can . . . have it filled in?'

Lyle didn't answer. His eyes had settled on a dark shape beyond the crater, that was slowly getting closer, and a frown had started to draw together across his face.

The girl, however, turned and stared at her companion. 'Uh?'

'No one need ever know . . .'

'It's a hole in'a ground, bigwig!'

'Perhaps it could serve as an ornamental fishpond?'

'A *pond*?'

The boy shuffled, his feathers rumpled. 'Well, what would *you* do with it?'

The girl didn't hesitate. 'We walk away, all polite, and if any bigwigs send the bobbies after, we can hide out in this place I know 'til the cry's gone down an' then . . . and *then* . . .' she was warming to her topic, '*then*, 'cos you see, I've been thinkin' about this, *then* Mister Lyle can take us to see Paris and Venice and that place with the big castles . . .'

'Where? Specifically.'

'. . . an' when we come back it'll all be better an' no one will ever know.' She beamed, pleased at her idea, and waited for everyone to agree.

Lyle didn't reply. His eyes were fixed on the dark figure who had clambered nearer and was now fairly distinct in a huge black cloak lined with silk, a top hat so tall and shiny it seemed almost a pity to expose it to hair on one side and rain on the other, and a walking cane, topped with ivory. Behind him trailed a couple of men who had the detachment of people hired to be respectful, but only to one man, and downright offensive to everyone else. As they drew nearer, the dog's nose twitched and both eyes opened. It stared at the man and started to whimper, trying to crawl, if such was possible, further into the blanket.

The girl followed Lyle's eyes, saw what he saw and immediately, without seeming physically to move, attempted to shuffle round behind Lyle and pretend she wasn't there. The boy looked up, saw the man, brightened and exclaimed, 'Why, good morning, my lord, is it not a fine morning for a ramble across . . .'

Lyle put a very firm hand on the boy's shoulder, and he closed his mouth hastily. The man didn't seem to have noticed any of them. He stopped on the edge of the crater and peered down into it. Still examining it, he said mildly, 'Crisp morning, is it not, Mister Lyle?' Somehow, Lyle was always *Mister* Lyle. No one had worked out why, but then, no one had ever dared question it either.

'A little cold, Lord Lincoln.'

'I see you've been conducting . . . experiments.'

Now the boy too began to edge round behind Lyle, and pretend he wasn't there.

'That's right.' Lyle could have been talking about the weather for all the expression he showed.

The man shifted ever so slightly, leaning on his ivory-capped walking cane and looking as pained as his limited range of expressions would permit. 'I wonder,' he began, voice clipped with vowels so precise they could have taken a job as an acupuncturist, 'was it entirely necessary to conduct these experiments in the memorial flower bed of Lord Wessex's third cousin killed in the Crimea?'

A flicker of something uncomfortable started at the edge of Lyle's eyes, though he tried to hide it. 'I'm sure Lord Wessex's third cousin would have been only too pleased to give of his flower bed for the sake of scientific endeavour.'

'What, pray,' only Lord Lincoln could give 'pray' so many teeth, 'is this scientific endeavour?'

Lyle hesitated. Lincoln raised one – just one – eyebrow. In Lincoln's case, Lyle was willing to believe that the cold menace distilled into that single look was genetic, rather than acquired through the usual hard practice all people secretly undertake to learn how to raise just one eyebrow, and felt his toes start to go numb. 'I'll show you,' he said dully, and led the way.

A few minutes later, when everyone else was gone, the dog untangled itself from the blanket where it had been snoozing, stood up, looked at the crater, regarded the path its master had taken up the Heath, considered its options, and then very calmly claimed a little bit of Hampstead Heath as forever part of its domain.

When that was done, it trotted after Lyle, and wondered what mess he was going to get into today.

Hampstead Heath, which was gradually becoming the ambling grounds of the city rich who sometimes felt the need for a little 'untamed' space, but without straying too far from their clubs, had recently acquired a new addition to its usually austere hillside. Half-hidden under the night's snow, a straight stone path dropped rapidly through the heath towards the sprawled grey city below. Someone had driven several large roman candles into the earth beside this path, and filled over the many pot-holes with rickety wooden planks, to create an even surface. Standing at the top of it was a large wooden shed, looking as if a gentle breeze might knock it over, with half the main door open.

Lyle stood just inside this structure, and beamed at the thing it held.

The thing was a monster of struts and strains, a body of stretched canvas and wood carved so thin you could almost see the ground through it. The wheels underneath the main body were harsh metal things that gleamed, the two seats were criss-crossed with nailed-down ropes, the back wing stood up at least as tall as the boy, and the mess of ropes and pulleys and struts that pushed at the various crudely attached gears and flaps gave the impression that the thing was merely a prediction of what would happen when the shed that housed it collapsed.

Peering out from behind Lyle, the girl examined it. Teresa Hatch, though she always insisted that she only ever worked on the thing because Lyle paid her three shillings a week and gave her a place to stay, food and, unless she found a particularly good hiding place, regularly enforced hot baths, had to admit a certain attachment to the monster. There had come a point a few months after the night when she had first met Mister Lyle, during an attempt which had gone wrong to . . . *relocate* . . . some of his property, when she had realized that not absolutely everything he said was nonsense.

To Tess the thing was known, if only in the privacy of her imagination, which understood when it was best to be silent, as 'the big flappy thing with wings'.

To Lyle, who believed very firmly in precision with regard to scientific endeavour, it was 'the pressure-differential-velocity aeronautical device' and never anything else, however difficult it was to say in a hurry.

To the boy, whose dream it was and who, as if that wasn't enough, secretly had a poetical vein, it was and would always be 'Icarus'. He wasn't sure why he'd chosen this name, and had the sneaky suspicion not only that it had unhappy mythological con-notations, but also that if he dared tell the other two labourers on its production, they would give him *that* look, that two-pronged attack of two pairs of eyes that always managed to make him feel like a five-year-old and want to curl up in a hole and whimper. So he said nothing, and kept his poetic inclinations to himself.

The three of them waited for Lincoln's reaction. Even the dog, who generally showed nothing but disdain for the work of any creature foolish enough to think that two legs were better than four, waited. Tess idly reached into her pocket, and gave him a walnut. He ate happily.

When Lord Lincoln finally spoke, it was so suddenly that Tess almost jumped. 'Tell me – are those things wings?'

'Yes,' said Lyle in the same voice the inventor of the wheel must have used when asked if it rolled.

'Do they . . .' Lincoln searched for an appropriate word, '. . . flap?'

'They do *not*!' Indignation was plastered across Lyle's face. 'They'd have to . . .' the word seemed acid in his mouth, '*flap* far too fast or be far too large to push a sufficient amount of air to create lift. The wings are shaped,' he said, warming to his topic as he saw the potential to enlighten the ignorant, 'in order to allow for a faster acceleration of air *above* than below, thus reducing the pressure above and creating a difference in the forces acting. You see,' he bounded towards the wings, eyes sparkling, 'the curve of the wing, which I refer to as an "air splitting and differentiating curve", for the simple way it . . .'

'Does it work?' There was a gleam of shrewdness in Lincoln's eye that Lyle didn't like. It was almost hungry, like a starved snake.

Lyle swallowed. 'Well, theoretically.'

'You haven't tested it?'

Silence. Tess said quickly, 'We was testing the prop . . . propel . . . the thing that blows up and makes it go faster, this mornin'. That's why you mustn't arrest Mister Lyle and chop his head off in the Tower for treason, 'cos he was only blowin' up your heath for scientific things and . . .' She saw Lincoln's expression. Her voice trailed off. She ate a nut as a distraction, and gave another to the dog, as if she'd never spoken.

There was no hint of that hunger now in Lincoln's eyes, as the ice settled, suggesting it had never left. 'Mister Lyle. A word, if I may.'

Lyle followed him dutifully outside. Not even the two body-guards followed, as Lincoln led him into a little grove of dead trees. Lyle was feeling, for the first time, the intense cold of the whitewashed morning.

'Mister Lyle, can you surmise why I'm here?'

An expression of consideration, slightly larger than life, settled on Lyle's face. 'Yes?' he hazarded.

'And are you prepared to renew your services to the Crown?'

Horatio Lyle thought about it. 'Do people still get executed at the royal behest?'

A very tight smile that was an answer in itself. 'Last night in the docks the captain of the *Pegasus*, Captain Fabrio, and one of my own employees, Mr Stanlaw, were killed and the *Pegasus* was holed and is taking on water. She is in quays and the water is nearly frozen, so she does not sink all the way. But her lower decks are flooded.'

'I can't afford to take time out from my experiments at the present moment –'

'I see,' said Lincoln, 'that you persist in having those . . . children . . . assist you. You care for the thief who on one occasion tried to break into your own home, and the young lordling who once nearly killed you. There is much confusion as to why you permit their presence. Is it truly because she can crack any safe in London and he is the next Faraday of his age? Or are you merely a bastion of care and charity?'

Lyle said nothing.

Lincoln smiled. It was always a surprise to Lyle, whenever Lord Lincoln revealed any teeth, that none of them were fanged. 'You are obviously aware of the great benefits in working for me again. The prestige, for one. But naturally a man of your reputation needs a better reason to act, and here is one – there is a murderer on the loose, Mister Lyle. A killer who strikes people down in the dark and doesn't care who they are or what sins they've committed. A killer who is a threat to us all, even the children.'

Lyle didn't move. Lincoln's smile widened ever so slightly, though humour had never entered it. 'Kindly inform me when you've found him, Mister Lyle.'

And Lord Lincoln nodded once, with the same command as the starting gun at a race, turned, and strode away.

Lyle stared after him, and wondered exactly what property of Lincoln's shoes let him glide easily across the snow, where mere mortals would have sunk. Perhaps the snow itself knew better than to cross *this* aide to Her Majesty?

Somewhere, the bells of London started tolling the hour, each in their own, very private world that couldn't agree quite with that of any other clock and argued that 'seconds' were just such an arbitrary imposition on time.

Lyle reached a sudden conclusion. His eyebrows drew together and his lips curled into a scowl. 'Damn,' he muttered. 'Damn damn damn.'

The boy and girl appeared, with the dog in tow, drawn by this mysterious utterance from the trees. The boy, practically saluting, said, 'Sir, I trust that Lord Lincoln is in tolerably good hea—'

'The evil bigwig what does all the evil murderin' and schemin' gone away, 'as he?'

'Yes, Teresa, he's gone.'

'He ain't a good person, Mister Lyle.'

'No. I don't think he is.'

'Sir! He is the Queen's personal aide, a servant of the Crown and the Empire . . .' began the boy.

Tess rolled her eyes. Lyle gave the boy a wry, sideways glance and said, 'Exactly.' He let out a long sigh, looked once more into the distance as if trying to see all the way to the sea, miles to the south, clapped his hands together to bring himself back to the world and said, 'Right! Get your coats!'

'Where we goin'?' demanded Tess as Lyle turned and began stalking through the snow.

'To look at a ship. Just quickly, then we can have some lunch, and maybe we can go down to Greenwich and see if the hill there is long and steep enough to merit our attentions in terms of a sufficient downward velocity . . .'

The three walked through the snow.

Voices drifted back. 'Mister Lyle, 'bout lunch . . .'

'You can't be hungry already.'

'Tate ate my walnuts.'

'You shouldn't spoil him. He'll get fat and lazy.'

'Aw, but he's just a little doggywoggy, ain't he? Yes you are . . . yes you are . . .'

Together they walked towards the city.

If Lyle had doubts about accepting a commission from the man once responsible for his near-death who he regarded, if not as the root of all evil, then certainly as a branch of the tree, he kept them to himself. After all, there was a murderer on the loose. And Mister Horatio Lyle always liked a challenge.

CHAPTER 2

Docks

Travel across London.

Fog rises up from the river, thick and white and heavy, like suspended ice that almost jangles when you push through it, muffling sound and sight and smell, and making familiar streets an alien land. Hansom cabs, flagged at Liverpool Street and heading west towards the marble of Mayfair or the ballrooms of Belgravia, jostle with coaches caught at Dover, rattled up the old mud road that runs from the southern ports through the hop fields and past the oast houses to the southernmost suburbs beyond Victoria Station, where the great trains snort and belch like sleeping iron giants after a bad meal of coals, and the black smoke rises up to meld with the black smoke from the chimneys of Battersea and the fires of Clerkenwell, and the still blacker clouds above, laced with waiting snow that, just as soon as the last cart from the Norfolk fens has unladen its bucket of live, writhing eels on to the cobbles of Bermondsey, sloshed with salt and smelling of the mud, these clouds will empty their weight of snow and ice on to the steeped roof of Covent Garden, the towers of St Pancras, the dome of St Paul's, and the carts and carriages and coaches and trains and horses and feet that dare clatter so inexorably, so fruitlessly, against the streets of Old London Town.

On Commercial Road, a hansom cab rattles, from the coffin-like recesses of which can be heard voices.

'So . . . we goin' to the docks?'

'Yes.'

''Cos the bigwig asked?'

'Yes.'

''Cos the bigwig *paid*?'

Embarrassed silence from the depths of the carriage, followed by an almost despairing, 'Oh, Mister *Lyle*.'

Up Pall Mall, where the Horse Guards parade, in a grander carriage, bearing all kinds of official insignia and two frozen grooms clinging to the back by the tips of their white-gloved fingers, someone else says, 'I have sent Lyle. He was not eager to go. But I have no doubt that his curiosity, not to mention over-developed sense of the moral side of things, will decide the argument.'

'Is Lyle enough?' A voice not English, speaking the language with the flatness of a tongue that has never met such strange syllables before, and doesn't think much of them.

'He was last time. He prevented a disaster, *xiansheng*. Besides, Her Majesty had great satisfaction demanding that Mr Gladstone find the money from government resources.'

'My agent was involved too, my lord.'

'Your agent didn't fall from the top of the cathedral. And his grasp of Newtonian mechanics is, I'm told, quite lacking.'

Elsewhere, in a room untouched by sunlight, colder almost than the ice outside, a man with a maple-syrup voice says, 'Is anything lacking, your grace?'

Silence from the darkness, except, perhaps, for the gentle scrape of something hard against stone, like a rusted blade dragged across chalk, or rough crude bricks creaking against each other in a storm.

The maple-syrup voice doesn't seem to mind the dark or the silence. 'I think you will find everything provided for. There is a young lady, an heiress, who has placed her fortune entirely at my disposal. She is most Christian in her views and actions. You shall want for nothing.'

When the other voice does come out of the darkness, it is like a slow, rumbling earthquake, heard with one ear pressed to the ground. 'What do you want for my liberty?'

'What makes you think I want anything, your grace?'

'All men want. You free me from the island, you protect me from the sun and the view of men. You want. It is written in your eyes. You cannot hide your face from me.'

There is the creak of new leather shoes bending slightly under a change in the weight on them. Then the voice launches into a prepared speech. 'I have a vision, your grace. Sent by the

Lord to serve His purpose upon this city. I know you have seen this city, your grace, but I assure you it has degenerated beyond all imaginings since your prime. I am here to change it, to wipe away the *filth* of its past and make for it a *glorious* future, untainted by the darkness that has seeped into the very stones. But I need your help.'

A brief consideration; then, in a voice heard through the feet as well as the ears, though it hardly rises above a contemplative whisper, **'Why should I help you?'**

'As you say, I set you at liberty. And you are still weak. Those of my kind who kept you before were unimaginative, did not realize the true calling that God has set down for men like you and me. Perhaps you have sinned in the past. Perhaps that is why you are punished by God in this way.'

'It is no God that has done this to me.'

'I will not argue pre-determination nor even the most elementary theology with you, your grace. Aid me, and I will give you the power that clearly should be yours by right and by divine ordination.'

'Do you believe your own words, priest? Do you think you can control me? Tame me?'

'I think I can aid you in an alien world. Be your guide, counsellor, protector. Maybe even a friend. What do you say?'

And the other thought about it, and it was good.

Horatio Lyle had a dog, and that dog was, for reasons unknown possibly even by its, for want of a better word, 'master', called Tate. The true biological origins of Tate lay lost in the mist of space and time, and those few experts in animal breeding who had ever examined the floppy-eared creature in any great detail had all come back concurring that, whatever had happened, it probably wasn't ever going to happen again, and maybe that was for the best. Quite what it was that upset these animal experts so greatly about the basically well-meaning creature, they never said and could never really explain. Probably it was just a sense of inferiority.

A moment, to share perspectives . . .

Welcome to the Docks, Symbol of Britain's Greatness! Come stretch your paws, little Tate, and savour the smell . . .

Millions of lives moving in and out of each other on the way to a better place; a million rough coats brushing against a million rough jackets; a million hob-nail boots trampling a million yards of damp, pale mud turned silver-black with the overnight ice and squashed, kicked snow now so much liquid filth; spices, silks, salt, stone, statues, ships, sails, sailors, slime, smoke; a hundred different ways of saying 'hello' and 'goodbye'; a hundred different definitions of crumbling shanty roofs sporting five hundred yards of downward-pointing icicle; a hundred different weaknesses of beer; a thousand different ladies of the land looking for a thousand and one sons of the sea; a hundred cats; a million rats; a dozen ways into the sewers, two dozen men and boys competing to get into them – one silver spoon somewhere inside, catch it if you can; two changes of the tide; three new quays; four new companies; ten former slaves startled to find freedom; twenty former freemen startled to discover slavery and a one-way ticket to Australia; thirty soldiers of the Queen's Navy trying to recover the familiar swaying of the sea by a shilling's worth of rum; five convicts hoping to sneak overseas;

two bobbies knowing what they're trying; one physician convinced that it was a mistake to restrict opium, now forced into selling morphine as an alternative; one nurse back from the Crimea at long last, who suspects that clean hands are more useful than the juice of a poppy plant when it comes to amputation; black skin, yellow skin, white skin, red skin, pink skin, beetroot skin with a lumpy nose made of whisky, brown skin, tanned skin, pampered skin, cracked skin, smooth skin. Welcome to the Docks, Symbol of Britain's Greatness! And where would *you* like to go today?

'The thing is,' Lyle said absently, eyes dancing on the face of every man and woman and shadow who drifted out of the fog, hands buried in his pockets, 'there are so many people here, and so many in and out every day, that the police hardly bother with watching it any more. Easier by far to track down the killer of a rich society lady who moved in a circle of five good friends and fifty expedient ones, than it is to find the man in a million who murdered an unknown, shunned and lost street girl in a part of the city where English is spoken in thirty different accents that are unintelligible to the average city-bred copper.'

'So . . . what we doin' here?' demanded Tess, glancing round at each passing face with the uneasy expression of someone coming back to an old haunting ground, and hoping its ghosts won't remember her.

'Well, we're . . .' Lyle hesitated. He looked round for inspiration, and saw Thomas's eager face lit up in expectation. 'We're doing our duty as good citizens of Her Majesty.'

Thomas's face could have guided ships into port on a stormy night. Tess scowled at Lyle, who had the decency to look sheepish. Tate sneezed. The four walked on, while the fog grew thicker, and the narrow walls of the street, all makeshift and already crumbling houses, warehouses and shop fronts, smelling of the seas, threatened to vanish behind the fog's endless white wall. It was hard to tell the hour, but Tess half-thought she heard a church bell ring out ten a.m., a long way off.

Thomas, idling along, head turning like a pigeon's as he squinted through the fog from one wonder to another, whether it was the cripple calling out for alms or the sailors scowling at all who passed them by, stepped forward, into empty space. He tottered for a second, back foot sliding out behind him on the thick ice mushed into a deadly black sheen by the dozens of boots which had passed by, then teetered forward. A hand grabbed him by the collar and gracelessly pulled him back from the edge of the quayside, visible only as a long line where the white pavement stopped and white fog began, with a hint of thick black water a long way below. Lyle steadied Thomas and said quietly, 'Ah! Well done. The waterside. Just what we were looking for.'

Lyle was always surprised at how much free time the average London spectator could find to stand around and watch a spectacle. He'd seen thousands gather for a really good fire, never helping to put it out, but generally agreeing that it was a damn good blaze and well worth watching. He'd seen hundreds join in the enthusiastic chase of a pickpocket one day, and the crowd had just kept on picking up people as it moved, until half the pursuers seemed convinced that it was a rush to a fair or for a pot of gold, and the pickpocket was long gone, dived into a rookery alley or up a drainpipe.

Despite having seen all these things, Lyle was surprised at quite how large the crowd was that had gathered round the tattered remains of the *Pegasus*. A representative of every part of society seemed to have magically appeared, from a collection of officious-looking men in top hats with the air of people who dabbled secretly in insurance when no one was watching, to the smallest street urchin whose interest was engaged more by the gold fob-watch of one of the top-hatted men than by the actual ship. A line of bobbies had formed a semi-circle round the quayside and wharf that led up to the side of the *Pegasus*, which even to Lyle's inexperienced eye and through the blanket of fog didn't look well.

Tess tilted her head thoughtfully on one side as they approached, until the *Pegasus* seemed to be standing upright again, and said, 'Mister Lyle?'

'Yes, Teresa?' Lyle already sounded resigned to what was coming.

'It ain't normal for no ship to look like that?'

'No, Teresa. That is what's known, I believe, as listing.'

'You mean . . . kinda leanin' the wrong way?'

'Technically,' chimed in Thomas helpfully, 'there is no such thing as "the wrong way" when a ship is listing, owing to the fact that any motion in a plane other than the forward one is a highly inefficient transfer of . . . ow!'

'Sorry,' said Lyle, hastily taking his foot off Thomas's. 'All this ice is very slippery.' If Thomas's upbringing had been a little less restrictive and his natural disposition a little more flexible, he would have pouted all the way to the ring of bobbies. As it was, nothing but a concerned frown plastered itself across his face, as he wondered whether there was anything he could do to give Mister Lyle's shoes a little bit more friction against the ground.

Lyle faced the first bobby, fixed his features in a serious expression, and proclaimed in his deepest, most authoritative voice, 'Erm . . . hello.'

Icy eyes stared back. The confidence drained from Lyle's face. 'You're not going to believe me if I say I'm here by royal appointment, are you?'

It seemed unlikely for anything to be colder than the fog, but this man's expression managed it. Lyle started patting his pockets. 'I'm sure I've got something official-looking here . . .'

And a voice exploded out of the shadows. 'Coo-eee! Horatio!'

It took Lyle several seconds of squinting to spot a familiar red-headed figure appearing through the white fog, the grin so broad and bright it seemed to emerge from the gloom before anything else. 'Charles,' Lyle said, looking relieved. 'What are you doing here?'

'Oh, I got transferred,' the other man said. 'You know, it's the strangest thing, but for some reason my bosses weren't happy about the Old Bailey being stormed on my watch by a crowd of madmen.'

'Ah.' Lyle's face was unreadable.

'And then, you'd never believe, they weren't pleased either with the fire that broke out and the gun battle in the street outside and they recommended, after that little battle in St Paul's Cathedral – bullet holes are hard to get out of stone, you know? – they thought that my dazzling personality might be better deployed elsewhere.'

He waited for a reply. Lyle thought about it. 'Ah.'

Charles rolled his eyes. 'You, Horatio Lyle, are about as useful as a herring in an iron foundry. I see you've still got your pets.'

Tate, Thomas and Tess avoided each other's gaze.

'Yes, Charles. Can you tell me what's been happening here?'

A shrug. 'Two murders, one witness of sorts, if you believe him, which the Inspector doesn't, saying that he ought to be in the workhouse, not contaminating the streets; that's the Inspector, though . . .'

'Which Inspector?'

'Inspector Vellum,' said Charles, pulling a sour face.

The reaction was instantaneous.

'I say! How rotten!'

'The stupid potato-man!'

'Oh, *no*.'

Even Tate offered a growl, wrinkling his nose up until the tip nearly touched the point between his eyes and his ears almost seemed to rise up on end.

'Can't you convince him that there's a *clue* somewhere else?' said Lyle weakly. In all the history of investigation, only Horatio Lyle could make 'clue' into a dirty word.

'Like Chelsea,' added Tess. 'Or the big place over the sea to the left with the funny people an' big hair.' Four pairs of surprised eyes stared at her.

She glared back. 'America!'

Lyle shook himself and said, 'I'd like to look at the bodies, please.'

'*Examine* them,' added Thomas helpfully, eyes wide and bright.

'Erm . . . yes, examine them. In an investigative manner.' Lyle took a deep breath. 'Yes. I think that's what I'd like to do.'

CHAPTER 3

Pegasus

The cold had not only preserved the bodies, but frozen them solid. They practically clunked when the bobbies pulled the blankets off them, revealing a dark-haired, clearly foreign gentleman whose salt-seared skin looked an unhealthy shade of off-white where the effect of too many years under the sun had clashed with a short time in the cold. He wore what Lyle thought of as default, 'yea-wise-captain' outfit: tough clothes designed to withstand fifty-foot waves, but heavy with the kind of ornamentation that is both a flashy indicator of rank, and unlikely to blow away at embarrassing moments. In death, the man's hands had swollen, which was probably the only thing that had prevented a fistful of shiny gold rings from having been stolen. 'You found him in the water?' murmured Lyle. It wasn't really a question, and Charles's brief, 'Yes,' was hardly heard.

Tess recognized this expression. It was the look that came over Lyle's face when he was trying to calculate the forces on a steam engine piston, or on a couple of magnets in each other's fields, or a conker on the end of a string being whirled horizontally, or sometimes even on the side of a glass full of swirling liquid. When he wore this face at supper, you would have to remind him every few minutes to keep eating, otherwise he would sink into intense and prolonged musings about the nature of a pork pie, usually ending with an announcement like, 'I wonder if they use combustive organic oils in the upper Andes between May and October?'

You did not interrupt Mister Lyle when he looked like that. It wasn't that he'd get angry, he just wouldn't be able to process human speech.

She avoided looking at the bodies. True, she had seen bodies in her time, abandoned in the street for someone to clear away like litter in the morning, but she had always found the dead immensely creepy, ever since, at an early age, she had sat with other children of her profession and heard ghost stories of the workhouse gutted by fire, from which voices could sometimes be heard at night, or the orphanage where the children were never seen except as shadows in the window, or the cemetery where the lady always sang her little nursery rhyme, *Hark, hark, the dogs do bark*. Now the dead were not just the dead in her imagination, they were the once-alive, and at any moment they might open their empty eyes and stare like fishes at her accusingly, as though to say, *did you do this?*

She had once, almost, considered explaining it to the bigwig, but Thomas regarded the bodies as an experimental subject; sometimes she suspected he regarded all life as a giant experiment. As for Mister Lyle, when he worked ... something professional and shut away from common observation seemed to take over the usually childlike enthusiasm of Horatio Lyle, and something very small and angry whispered, *what a waste*.

So Tess didn't look at the bodies. She didn't even look at Mister Lyle. She stood as far back as she could and tried to look at the water, dedicate all her thoughts to it, try to ignore, among other things, the unpleasant odour which had lingered on even after the first sewer had opened and the river no longer seemed thick enough to walk on. In the shadow under the wharf, ice was forming, dirty brown ice dusted with white snow left over from the cold of the night before, and slowly thickening and spreading. Ice clung to the side of the ship too, and icicles hung from the masts; it pressed against the hull, crawling into every chipped and battered wooden crack. She remembered something about ice and salt water, but it was a vague haze against the all-present distraction of ... two *once-alive* people lying on a cart.

Lyle was saying something, but it was a something that he didn't realize he was saying, and which no one really took seriously, so Tess only listened with half an ear.

She heard him say, in that distant voice he always used when thinking aloud or trying to remember something or occasionally talking to himself about electronic cations and anions after he'd dozed off by the fireside, 'Necks broken, just like that; incredible strength, considering the thickness of the spine, extraordinary, right-handed; look at the bruising here, the fingers have pressed right down into the windpipe; he must be fast to get them both too; but this one has bruises around his hand so was probably killed second, at least he had time to put up a fight; I wonder if . . .'

Tess stared at the crowd, and let her mind drift. She thought of the time she'd first met Mister Lyle, that fateful night a few months back when a rich gentleman had offered her a whole sovereign to sneak in and steal any papers she might find . . . had it rained that night? She couldn't remember. She couldn't really remember much before that. It was as if something had switched in her mind, and the person before that night was another person, whose actions she could remember, but not the thoughts that had driven them. She couldn't remember thinking before that night, though she was sure she must have. It took thought and dedication to spot a mark, to eye him up, to move with the rest of the street and match paces with the mark and, when he least expected it, to . . .

'No drag marks on the boots. They weren't dragged across the deck, they must have been bodily carried and thrown into the water. No bruising on the legs either. Dead before they hit the water, of course, and an interesting ring on this man's – Stanlaw I presume . . . yes, coat from Savile Row, what a waste – hand. Two cogs, one inside the other, made of iron, and clock hands inside them, the larger outer cog indicating the hour, the smaller cog indicating the minute – one minute to midnight. How prophetic, considering the condition of the bodies and probable time of death. Very different. Very unusual. Perhaps if . . .'

And there it was, the little thing that had been bothering Tess. A flash of colour in the crowd, brighter than the blacks and greys of the thick fog, shining through for just a second, like Constable Charles's smile. Gone to the left, re-emerging for a moment to the right. At her feet, Tess realized Tate was sniffing the air, shuffling slightly towards the crowd, nose wrinkled up and eyebrows scrunched down in an expression of concentration. Deep burgundy red, a scarf, possibly, drawn over nose and mouth against the cold, fading into the fog. It reminded her of something which she couldn't put her finger on, something from a time when she wasn't sure if she'd been thinking or not.

If she'd had Tate's sense of smell, she could have added to the general impression a faint and sudden odour of ginger biscuit, that faded with the flash of red, into the fog.

Lyle straightened up. 'Even with my natural inclination for continued self-preservation and the many adventures a prolonged life might bring,' he declared, 'I think it's fair to say that *no one* would like to meet this murderer in a dark alley at night.' Having made this announcement, he looked down into Thomas's shining eyes, to see what reaction this statement received. He sighed. 'Except, perhaps, one.'

'I'm sure, sir, that between us we could contrive a method of the killer's downfall and passage into the hands of custody and Her Majesty's justice . . .'

Lyle put a kindly hand on Thomas's shoulder. 'Lad, have we ever had a serious discussion about slippers and a decent ham omelette by the fire?'

'No, sir.'

'How about . . . the curious physical properties of inertia?'

'No, sir!'

'No.' Lyle let out another profound sigh, and stared away. 'I thought not.'

'Should I research the subject, sir? Would it help?'

A look almost of dread flickered across Lyle's face. 'Maybe not right now . . . Charles!' He grabbed at the first escape he saw, taking everyone, especially Charles, by surprise. 'Did I hear mention of a witness?'

As they turned to go, Lyle half-turned back to look at the two bodies, Captain Fabrio and the mysterious Mr Stanlaw, employee of Lord Lincoln and thus instantly suspect, and hesitated. Very quickly he leant over and, with a speed and dexterity that would have surprised and impressed the expert eye of Tess, pulled the iron ring off Stanlaw's finger, slipping it into his pocket and walking away with the most innocent expression.

He had a bad feeling about the ring; but then, he had a bad feeling about anything which might have to do with Lord Lincoln.

Old Edgar was a beggar apart. Long ago, when perhaps he was merely middle-aged Edgar and just seemed a bit worn by time, he had perfected the art of leaping out in front of sailors newly arrived from the furthest land across the furthest ocean, clinging to them and screaming, 'Let me save you, the plague is here! I can save you, the plague is come an' all the metal that you carries will be dust by the morn. Turn back now before the plague is spread any further; you ain't goin' to die if I can't save you. For God's sake and your men's get rid of your metal now before it contaminates you all!'

Regardless of the native language of the person who heard

this, the effect was usually dramatic – sometimes more so for a small piece of soap Old Edgar kept in his mouth, just in case foaming was required. In the docks there were thousands who daily held out their hands in a desperate plea for survival, but, as the bobbies sometimes noted on their way back to the station, Old Edgar hadn't yet been broken as the others had, and as a result, he could suffer with *flair*.

Which explains why, when Lyle approached the bollard where Old Edgar was sitting counting a very small pile of pennies from a very large collection of pockets, the old, stick-like man took one look at him, threw himself flat at Lyle's feet, clung on to his knee and started whimpering, 'You shouldn't have come here, good sir, the place is death, good sir, ain't for the likes of you. They breathe the death here, it is on every coin you have been given by anyone what comes here. You'll take the metal contaminated with their death back to your loved ones, sir, an' it'll kill them all. Oh, the death is come . . .'

Thomas looked shocked, Lyle looked a bit embarrassed. Tess rolled her eyes and said, 'If there's one person gettin' money here, it's gonna be *me*.'

Lyle slowly turned to look at her, eyebrows raised.

She coughed. 'For charity?'

Lyle turned back to Old Edgar. 'Good sir, there isn't a plague.'

Edgar took this reassurance in his stride. 'You mayn't have seen it yet, sir, but believe me, it stalks the streets at night plucking at every new-born babe and . . .'

'I'm a policeman.'

Edgar backed off. He looked Lyle up and down. His

expression suggested that he wasn't very impressed, but in a far more normal voice he said, 'Oh. New, are you?'

'No, just professionally misguided. May I ask a few questions?'

The beggar man, who in many ways took pride in being the most dramatic of all who were forced into his trade east of the Tower and south of Bethnal Green, considered and said, 'I already spoke to the Inspector.'

'Would this be Inspector Vellum?'

'That sounds 'bout right.'

'A man with a potato for a face, a turnip for a brain and a shameful attitude towards all in need?'

'Could be.'

'I imagine he wasn't keen on supporting you in your hour of need.'

'He weren't the most comfortable customer I seen.'

'Ten shillings in exchange for the truth. Not whatever you told Vellum: the *real* truth.'

Edgar managed, just in time, to force a considering expression on to his face. 'I can speak a dark tale, mister, a story of doin's in the night and —'

'Sir,' said Lyle in an impatient voice, 'your beard is filthy on the surface but not below the newest growth, implying regular washing and only a superficial application of dirt. Your nails are long and curved, but the ends are worn down in straight lines, and there is a degree of abrasion across these lines at the points, suggesting regular filing. Your boots are torn but the socks you wear inside the boots are not only socks, but supported with leather and wool so that, in effect, you are wearing two pairs of boots, not one. Your jacket is slashed and filthy, but the lining has a seam here,' he snatched at the astonished man's coat, 'and here, where stuffing has been sewn inside by a careful seamstress who knows how to leave an exterior ragged but the interior warm, not to mention three extra pockets lined with sawdust to prevent the rattling of coins when you move. You are, in short, not just a beggar man but a thief, and you are taking money at a rate to anger the most serene starving textile worker or any frost-bitten old maid struggling to keep out of the workhouse. Now, I could go to all your starving, diseased, and broken colleagues on the street, the ones who die in corners and are never noticed until they start to smell of the death that killed them, all the true cripples who are too weak to dance and sing a merry tune for any passing stranger with a weak eye and a weaker pocket lining, and tell them the truth about good Old Edgar, king of the beggars. Or I could pay you ten shillings and hope my conscience doesn't keep me awake at night. Please tell me now which you would find more useful towards the rendering of an accurate witness statement?'

Five minutes later, Edgar sat by the fire in a local tavern that stank of cheap ale, cheap tar and, very faintly, cheap opium, nursing a bowl of porridge and a small pot of ale. Lyle sat wearing the expression that Tess had secretly marked in her mind as 'you *will* have a bath, Teresa, or you will *not* have supper'. It was an expression that brooked no argument.

Edgar talked, while the world moved around them.

'I was woked by the bell, ringing one. It were a cold night, last night, the river were starting to freeze, like it do today. I were under one of the piers, near where the old sewers used to drain out at high tide, 'til they built this new pumping thing, but it were still warmer there, out of the wind. You ever heard the wind, when the river is just startin' to freeze? You hear waves an' you hear stone all at once – they say the river will be all froze over by tomorra mornin' too, like stone. But it weren't just the wind what I heard.'

'What *did* you hear?' Lyle's impatience was gone, replaced by the same tight determination Tess had seen when he looked at the bodies.

'I heard someone on that ship – the *Pegasus*. The lantern was lit. Two men, talkin'. And their footsteps.'

'Could you hear what they said?'

'No. Not those two. One sounded foreign . . . I don't know why I say so, but his voice were all . . . bendy, not like the other fella. Like he were one of them circus clowns doin' a silly foreign accent. The other fella always talked lower than the foreign man, like he was threat'nin' or scared or something. Then there were this sound like a door or something banging 'gainst the wood, something *really* heavy, an' then this foreign man was screamin', but it got cut off with a real nasty crack, and the other man was runnin' but I didn't see 'im and then there were this other crack and then someone said something and someone else answered an' I ain't never heard no voice like that voice.'

'What was it like?'

'It was like . . . like what the earth would sound like if it talked, or . . . or like a rumble, deep down. An' then this other man says something in a more normal voice, and then there's these two splashes, quick after each other, an' then more foot-steps, and then a carriage, goin' away.'

'A carriage? As in a hansom cab?'

'No, I heard 'least two horses an' it sounded all heavy.'

'What was the more normal voice like?'

'Like . . . well, it was almost like . . . Like honey. It was all brown and smooth and warm but cool all at once, like it was . . . honey. Like maple. Can't say why I say so, but that's what I think.'

Edgar hesitated.

'And?'

Edgar kept hesitating.

'I like irrational impressions and utter honest frankness,' said Lyle quietly. 'It relieves me of my doubts and fears whenever I contemplate the human race. And?'

'It'd may be my imaginings.'

'But?'

'I'd've sweared the other man, the normal man with the honey voice, I'd've sweared he was American.'

Lyle sighed. 'Thank you, sir. You've been very generous with your time.'

Another place, an equal time.

A knock on the door.

'Enter.'

A voice like maple syrup. Warm and cold all at once. Speaking fluent English, but not quite as it is spoken in England.

'Sir.'

'Henton. Does her ladyship require my attention?'

'Her ladyship, sir, appears to be absent this morning.'

'She appears to be absent many mornings. A night-owl, her ladyship. But I am sure she spends her day in piety enough. What, then, Henton, is the concern?'

'A servant has just returned from the scene of last night's arrival, sir.'

'And? If you have news, speak it quickly.'

'There have been complications.'

'Such as?'

'A witness.'

'What kind of witness?'

'A beggar heard voices in the night.'

'It hardly seems a concern.'

'Her ladyship might disagree. She was very clear – her aid comes at a price, father; it is necessary that no end is left . . .'

'Her ladyship will not make a problem of it. Was there anything else, that you are so halting in your news?'

'Lord Lincoln has sent Horatio Lyle to the docks.'

'This should cause me concern?'

'Her ladyship has mentioned him. He was involved at the incident at St Paul's Cathedral, and it is rumoured that . . .'

'We do not listen to rumours, do we?'

'No, father. Forgive me. I merely thought that you should be made aware, as it might pose a threat to the Marquis if . . .'

'It does not. If her ladyship should appear before sunset, inform her.'

'Yes, father.'

A door closing. A sigh. The creak of a chair as someone leans back into it and considers, and relaxes. For now. And a brief thought, looking for a receptive brain to call home, sees the man with the maple-syrup voice and the eyes like the auburn leaves of autumn. Just for a second, doubt raises a cautious eye above the lip of the trench, before it is overwhelmed and forced on to happier hunting grounds, far, far away.

Inspector Vellum was in the wrong job. No one was entirely sure why he was a member of the Metropolitan Police, although it was rumoured that he was discharged from the army after a brief and fairly disastrous career in India, and had simply fallen for the police uniform and its shiny buttons. The Commissioner had been won over by the Inspector's ability to spout proverbs, albeit at inconvenient moments, and regarded the Inspector's knack of getting other people to do the work – probably how the Inspector regarded it too – as merely encouraging latent talent. The Inspector's robotic nod to all colleagues he passed in the corridor eloquently expressed both his inherent nobility of character in merely acknowledging these lesser beings' presence, and the necessity of him being Somewhere Very Important Immediately. When Mister Lyle talked about the Inspector, Tess was always slightly surprised to hear not just a new tone in his voice, but a whole new accent take over, as his mother's East End sharpness competed with his father's Yorkshire lilt, the power of opinion overwhelming the refinement of adulthood in his speech.

Tess knew that bad news awaited them as they returned to the *Pegasus*, because as they approached, Charles said not a word, but stood up straight and gave Lyle a single, crooked look of warning. Lyle took a deep breath and started down the wharf towards the ship. 'Tess,' he said quietly as they walked, 'I want you to take Thomas and find a very long flexible watertight pipe, a pair of smithy's bellows, two tins, a couple of pins, and any sulphur and saltpetre you can find.'

Tess thought about this. 'You ain't goin' swimmin', Mister Lyle?'

Despite himself, Lyle smiled. 'That's my lass.'

As the two children scurried off, a voice that could have come from Pinocchio's nose during a bad fit of hay fever said, 'Ah. *Mister* Lyle. What brings you here?'

'Two legs and a hansom cab.'

'A good way to travel, I've always believed; although I'm told,' with a sound half-way to a cough, but which in any other man would clearly have been a snigger, 'that your recent studies show an interest in more aeronautical activities. Tell me, are you familiar with Lord Byron's view on—'

'No.'

'A man of the mind really must read Lord Byron, or His Lordship as he is fondly known in my family. It enhances perception, allows for a clearer interpretation of—'

'Inspector Vellum, have *you* ever paused to consider the effect of air travelling at different velocities above and below a shaped fixed object of surface area "A" proportional to the downward force "F" of a construction accelerating through the air at velocity "V", the effect on pressure and consequently the forces acting and so on that might be induced above and below the differential curve?'

'I can't say I've felt the need.'

'One day, try.' Lyle sidled cautiously up the plank leading on to the slanting deck of the *Pegasus*, and glared at the Inspector. 'Until then, *I* have a royal commission to investigate and *you* are disturbing the evidence.'

The Inspector turned red. 'Very well. I shall leave you to the tasks of a constable while I attempt to find a criminal. *But at my back I always hear Time's wingèd chariot hurrying near* — is it not so, Mister Lyle?'

'Indeed, Inspector. I believe it was Lord Byron who once remarked to Ruskin, *Caesar adsum jam forte*,' replied Lyle brightly, as Vellum skulked down the steps.

Alone in the fog, on the *Pegasus*, Lyle noted how much snow had fallen in the night: enough to leave a good inch over the ice on the leaning deck. Only a little, however, had built up on the lower side, where the ship leant unevenly. He tried to remember when it had stopped snowing the night before.

Footprints were dotted across the deck. He took his shoes off, flinching as his bare feet touched the snow. The deck sloped so severely it was hard to walk on and he had to pick his way across by clinging on to the mast, and the loose rigging which hung down from the neglected spars. The *Pegasus* was not a healthy ship. The sails were made of so many patched pieces, it was hard to tell which was the original fabric. The mast was scarred, and what little paint had survived the *Pegasus*'s life at sea was thin and peeling.

The ship creaked. Lyle made his way carefully over to the lower side of the slanting deck, and peered at its surface. It wasn't hard to recognize the regulation shoeprint of the police-men, too recent even for a faint covering of snow, and his own footprints hardly made a visible mark. Which left four sets of prints, older and slightly snowed over, but still clear enough to follow. There was a confusing mish-mash on the plank up to the deck, but then they spread out. He identified the captain's footprints, and followed them. From the gangway, with Stanlaw's footsteps just behind, they headed towards the cargo hold, stopped on the threshold into darkness, and shuffled round in a mess of snow to face Stanlaw's footprints. These were deeper and slightly disturbed, but still less fidgety than the Captain's where both men had stood still. The footprints then moved together away from the cargo hold, stopped once more, and changed again.

There was the faintest drag mark, ending in a tiny point as if the Captain had literally been pulled up by the toes, besides a deeper, human-sized indentation in the snow where something had fallen, quite hard. By this time, the other set of footprints had changed, the stride growing narrower and the pressure of the toes increasing while the heel decreased to almost nothing: Stanlaw was running. These impressions abruptly ended just by the side of the ship, where there was a similar drag mark and man-sized impression.

Lyle followed a further set of footprints, which seemed to start at the top of the stairs down to the hold, move over to each impression of a body in the snow, pick them up leaving shallow drag marks, move to the edge of the deck, turn, and stop in a little shuffle. There they faced the fourth and final pair of shoes, fine shoes too, but no pair that Lyle could immediately recognize. There were deeper marks here as the two sets of prints faced each other, with a tiny ridge around the edge of every mark, as if the falling snow had built up when the men had stood and talked so long.

Lyle stared at the two sets of tracks leaving the ship and frowned. At the top of the plank, he could see the fourth pair leave, the pair that hadn't gone anywhere near the bodies, and he could also see it arrive. But there was no sign that the third pair of footprints, the set whose owner had dragged the bodies over the side and pulled up each man until just their toes touched the ground, had come on the ship. The footprints started at the cargo hold, nowhere else. And there was something *wrong* about the prints. Lyle knelt down by one and peered at it, leaning so close his nose almost touched the snow.

And he knew what was wrong. Five large toe marks, the ball of a heel and an empty space where the foot arched, that was what was wrong. The footprints were large and very, very heavy – too large to be a woman's, he decided, and the toes unusually long, but that wasn't what upset him. What upset him was that this person who had left with the pair of leather shoes that Lyle couldn't recognize had had bare feet, and had been on the ship before it even started to snow.

Lyle turned and looked at the dark drop into the cargo hold, tight narrow stairs going down as close to vertical as possible without actually turning into a ladder, and heard again the creak of the dying ship. In a worried but conversational tone, he rubbed at his hairline nervously and, addressing the ship, announced, 'I've got a sinking feeling about you.' Then felt just a little embarrassed.

Thomas Edward Elwick, only son and heir of Lord Thomas Henry Elwick (Order of the Magpie, Cross of the Sallow Oak,

Knight of the Daffodil and devout believer in the quality of your hounds as a proof of intellectual and spiritual endeavour), was in culture shock. And had been for a number of months. How he had met Tess was obvious – where Lyle went, the short, wild-haired and frequently larcenous Tess was never far behind. How he had met Mister Lyle was more of a blur. He remembered something about strange men with a Plan; one of those Plans that wasn't just any old mish-mash of vague aspirations and a decent railway timetable, but a real, heart-stopping Plan. He remembered something about a thunderstorm and a cathedral. He remembered seeing Mister Lyle fall. But there were other things which he remembered, and didn't quite understand, things which, at the time, had seemed to make sense. But the more he tried to analyse them logically, the less plausible they became.

He remembered a time after, too, when he'd looked up at his father and for the first time in his life, realized that his father didn't understand. He remembered the moment when Lyle had turned round and said calmly, 'Have you seen Da Vinci's sketches working on the principle of forcing air downwards to create a lower area of pressure above the craft rather than below?'

Which was an improvement on his father's 'If God had meant us to fly, he *never* would have invented the pheasant! Let that be a warning to you, m'boy!'

Somehow, at the end of it all, he was here; following Teresa Hatch as she darted through the maze of toppling streets that made up the docks, all sprawled along the riverside as if some great god had got bored and just thrown them down with a shrug and a splatter. The roads, Thomas realized, weren't roads at all, just gaps that houses hadn't yet colonized, getting pressed tighter and tighter by the weight of human life in every possible form, but mostly a squalid, deprived, starving one, pushing down on the streets themselves. Tess seemed to know every alley, and Thomas wondered if it was his imagination that made her eyes gleam every time she saw a bulging pocket, or made the few loose coins on the smithy's desk vanish as her hand passed within a foot or two. He knew that Tess was what his father would have called, '*Not* One of Us,' or quite possibly, 'Reprobate,' or, if he was really pushing, 'Socially undesirable,' but at the same time . . . she *was* very good at what she did. Thomas had heard Lyle say this in almost an embarrassed voice several times, usually with a warning not to let Tess know on pain of instant insufferability.

So Thomas trailed along behind, senses overwhelmed by everything he saw, smelt, heard. He had never realized faces could come in such variety: not just a mixture of a dozen noses with a dozen chins all juggled up together to make a few hundred combinations, but each face stamped with its past as well as its biology, marked by the lines of its trade or seared by far-away sun; skins and colours and eyes and scowls and smiles – few of those indeed – in such diversity that Thomas almost wanted to touch his own face, just to feel what it was like, wondering if it too could look like that, had the potential to be so rough or scarred or burnt, or so black or pale, or so pinched or old.

In the fog, there was no way of keeping track of where they were as they darted from place to place, getting everything that Mister Lyle wanted and, to Thomas's quiet disapproval, a whole suet pudding too. ('So as we don't starve of neg . . . negl . . . of bein' all starved.')

They ate the suet pudding quickly on one of the bollards by the riverside, and Thomas, to his guilt, enjoyed it immensely. Then the two of them walked up uneasily on to the crooked deck of the *Pegasus*.

Lyle was nowhere to be seen. Thomas cleared his throat and opened his mouth to call out, when a voice drifted up from almost underneath his feet, echoing in the cold and gloom: 'Did you leave me any pudding?'

Thomas turned bright red, but Tess leant past him, peered down the tight stairs into the deck below and called out, one loud, deliberate word at a time, 'It ain't good for you, Mister Lyle. We had to eat it 'cos if we didn't you might've made yourself *ill* an' then how'd you've cooked supper?'

'As always, Teresa,' said Lyle, head rising up suddenly from the darkness of the deck, 'your care for my well-being is heartwarming.' His eyes turned to Thomas, and he broke into a grin. 'I see Teresa got you to carry everything.'

'Yes, Mister Lyle. I mean, naturally, it was my duty to ensure that the lady –'

Tess almost laughed. Lyle's smile trembled round the edges with the effort of self-control. Thomas felt the tips of his ears burning. '– naturally . . . didn't have to suffer any inconvenience . . .'

Lyle clambered out of the deck and patted him on the shoulder. 'Well done, lad. That was very thoughtful of you.' Tess beamed. 'Now, I don't suppose you speak Italian?'

'Erm . . . no, sir.'

'How about Latin?'

Thomas's face lit up with excitement. 'Oh, yes, sir. I have had the pleasure of studying the ancient and noble languages of the classics, and I must say I find them fascinating both for their development in various European languages and for their natural, even original –'

'Good. You can come and help me translate a few things.'

'What shall *I* do, Mister Lyle?' demanded Tess with a pout.

'Take all the tins, saltpetre and sulphur you have, and make me a torch.' He dug into his pockets and came out holding a handful of small, frosted glass spheres, which he passed to Tess. 'Add as much magnesium as you can, stir well and allow near no naked flame.'

On Tess's face, for a second Thomas saw a strange, thoughtful expression.

'You are plannin' on goin' swimmin', ain't you, Mister Lyle? Only it seems to me you got this oxygen source an' this rapid burner and initial combust . . . thing for startin' the reaction an' how you're all containin' it . . .' She frowned suddenly. 'What we *really* need is phosphorus, Mister Lyle.'

Thomas looked at Lyle when he didn't answer, and saw the older man's face beaming with an almost childish expression of pleasure. His voice was as quiet as ever, but his eyes lit up proudly as he said, 'Could be, lass. Definitely could be.'

Lyle put a hand on Thomas's shoulder, and guided him away, leaving Tess and Tate sitting together on the deck. Tess smiled, staring after their shadows in the fog, lost in her own contentment. At her side, Tate lay down, ears trailing across the deck. She scratched him idly behind the ears, head on one side, thinking. Really thinking; not the usual quiet thoughts of every-day life, but thoughts which had words she could almost hear, like a little voice in her mind, and pictures too: thoughts which felt bright and real. She could almost feel how things worked, almost stand up and announce to the fog and the lost sunlight, *this is what will happen.*

She picked up one of Mister Lyle's little glass balls, and knew that inside there was a slither of a magnesium compound that would burn for a few minutes with a bright, intense white light. She smiled, and kept smiling, as she picked up a tin and thought about fire and light. And for a second, just a second, Teresa Hatch heard something beneath normal hearing, something that drifted into her mind without consulting the ears, rising up from the old cobbles and the trapped water underneath the thin, trans-parent ice, to join the thoughts that had been slowly bubbling away ever since Mister Lyle sat her down, many months ago, and said, 'Teresa, that letter is the letter "a".'

Tess realized she was humming.

> *'Oranges and lemons,' say the bells of St Clement's.*
> *'You owe me five farthings,' say the bells of St Martin's.*
> *'When will you pay me?' say the bells of Old Bailey.*
> *'When I grow rich,' say the bells of Shoreditch.'*

Teresa Hatch almost laughed and, for a second utterly lost in thoughts beyond normal expression, began to hammer together a scientific marvel. It seemed perfectly obvious what had to be done, when she thought about it. Inexpressible, unutterable. Simply . . . perfect.

CHAPTER 4

Sinking

The captain's cabin was cold, grey and lit only by a couple of candles and whatever light managed to crawl through both the frost-covered glass and the fog outside. It was almost entirely bare. Not a picture hung on the wall nor a book lay on a table to suggest any personality inhabiting it. The only exception was a very large shiny gold crucifix hanging above the bed. Lyle's eyes settled on it instantly, and his eyebrows went up.

'It's new.' Cautiously he picked it up, and surprise widened his eyes even further. He weighed it carefully in his hands before turning it over and running his finger up the back until it found a tiny mark.

'Good grief.'

'Mister Lyle?'

'It's gold all the way through. Not fool's gold – actual *gold*. With the mark of one of the Roman goldsmiths. It must be worth a fortune. This is the kind of thing a vain cardinal owns, not a hard-up cargo captain.' And a whisper almost below hearing, '*What a waste.*'

He sat down on the single bunk in a corner, head bent under the low roof. Frowning, he looked round at the sparse cabin. Thomas stood uncomfortably by the desk, waiting for an order. Finally Lyle said, 'Thomas, tell me this. What kind of seaman sails a ship quite as old and dilapidated as this, probably one of the slowest, weakest vessels on the seas, and yet has a possession that would make King Solomon himself blush from kneecaps to earholes?'

'A . . . very religious man?'

Lyle sighed. 'Captain Fabrio wasn't wearing a crucifix.'

'Not a very religious man, sir?'

'Try to see through the fact that you're standing next to an object that could . . . oh, I don't know . . . buy a substantial part of Warwickshire.'

'Actually, sir, I don't think that Warwickshire is for sale, not after the affair with Lord and Lady Randl—' He saw Lyle's expression. 'Yes, sir. Of course, sir. Perhaps it is merely the equivalent of a portable financial supply?'

'Then why hasn't it been spent?'

'You said it was new, sir.'

'That I did,' said Lyle, a grim little smile starting in the corner of his mouth. 'Perhaps the cross was payment? For a service rendered. Which probably means shipping.' He pointed with his chin at the desk just behind Thomas. 'Have a look.' Thomas looked uncomfortable. 'Go on. There aren't likely to be any traps or deadly spiders inside.'

Thomas slid the top desk drawer open, and pulled out a map. Lyle stood up and walked across, peering over Thomas's shoulder at the map spread out across the desk. The course last taken by the ship had been meticulously plotted as a thin black line across the feathery paper. Thomas traced it backwards from London, watching it shuffle round the Goodwin Sands, zigzag through the English Channel, then slip into Santander and out again. He saw it skirt the coast of Portugal and pass through the Strait of Gibraltar, blown briefly off course south of Malaga, before finally arriving at Venice.

He leant closer. There was a stop between Gibraltar and Venice, marked meticulously on the map, but almost too small to see with the naked eye. Thomas felt a tug on his sleeve and glanced round to see Lyle holding out a magnifying glass.

'Oh, thank you, sir.'

Lyle just smiled faintly, as Thomas took the glass and peered closer. A tiny island, marked with a faint cross to one side of its wobbly shape, and labelled Isalia.

Thomas stood back, frowning. The name seemed familiar. He tried to remember what little he knew about Italy and its islands. Though they were an increasingly popular tourist destination for the wealthy, for some there came a certain cap of wealth where anywhere overseas just wasn't interesting enough, and Thomas's family had passed that cap shortly after 1660. Uncivilized foreigners held no interest for members of the Elwick blood. Isalia, however, was a name that seemed to stick in his memory, though he had no idea why.

Lyle was watching him, reading Thomas's face as though his thoughts were written all over it. Finally, with a little smile and shake of his head, Lyle pushed the map to one side and opened the next drawer. A few loose coins, a handkerchief and a loaded revolver. He looked at the gun with an expression of dislike, and closed the drawer. The last drawer was locked. Thomas almost heard his excited intake of breath – locked drawers seemed to call to Lyle's sense of a challenge – and he stepped quickly out of the way as Lyle knelt down in front of the desk and dug into his copious pockets. Finding nothing satisfactory in his left jacket pocket, he tried his right, then an inner pocket, then another below that. Finally he seemed to find what he was looking for, in a third inner pocket that Thomas hadn't even realized was there, despite the way it had been meticulously sewn in with the wrong colour thread by someone who at least understood the principles behind sewing, if not the aesthetics.

He brought out a long and familiar roll of tools, wrapped in blue fabric. Thomas looked down at them, and realized that, although the majority of strange bits of metal with various hooks and loops remained a mystery, he could guess at the uses of at least five more than he had been able to last month. Lyle chose a couple of thin tools and slid them into the lock, eyebrows drawn together in concentration. He seemed almost disappointed when the lock clicked within a few seconds. Scowling slightly, he packed away the tools and opened the drawer a cautious inch. Seeing nothing sharp inside, he opened it all the way and pulled out a bundle of papers.

'Thomas?' He held up a paper, then passed it to Thomas. It had once been closed at the bottom with an old-fashioned red wax seal, in which a somewhat crooked cross had been stamped. Its neat black lettering was recognizable as Latin.

Thomas coughed, clearing his throat, and stood a little taller, pleased with his own importance. '"Captain Fabrio,"' he began, '"Thou . . ." well, "you" really, if you wish me to do a direct translation without –'

'"Thou" will be fine,' muttered Lyle, riffling through the other papers. He found one: a note written in English. 'From his London housekeeper, wanting to know how long he needs the property. I wonder if he had time . . .' Lyle's voice trailed off. He became aware of Thomas watching him, glanced up, smiled and said, 'I apologize. Please, carry on.'

'Well, then . . . "Thou art entrusted with a duty of most . . ." uh . . . "sacred" I think . . . "provenance, but heed the warnings of our brethren who have sent you unto our shores, for your passenger –"'

Lyle's head snapped up. 'A passenger?'

'Well, obviously it's not a literal translation; the word is more derivative from the Greek –'

'The ship is carrying a passenger?'

'Sir?'

Lyle's eyes had settled on a distant thought. 'The bare footprints weren't made getting on the ship, Thomas. They came up from the cargo hold; their source had to be on board already.'

'Bare footprints, sir?'

'A man weighing at least sixteen stone by the depth of the impressions, and judging by his stride I'd say he was at least six foot three and horrendously strong – he had no shoes when he went up on deck and attacked the Captain and Stanlaw, the man with the interesting ring.' Lyle's hand was in his pocket, feeling the iron ring he'd pulled from Stanlaw's finger. 'It's possible that the passenger and the killer are one and the same. What else does the letter say?'

'Uh . . . "heed the warnings of our brethren who have sent you unto our shores, for your passenger, though not of the power he once was when first he did come unto our sanctuary, hath yet the skill of the stone and may be of much danger unto you and your crew if he leaves his berth. Do not break the seal unless the good father is with you . . ." Oh, I think it means Roman Catholic priest, sir . . .' said Thomas, voice rising in a disapproving lilt of well-bred Anglican mistrust, 'rather than . . . a father, a . . . parent, sir . . .'

'I think I understand, Thomas. What else?'

'"God speed to your journey and may your passage be safe and undisturbed. Blessings . . ." I think this means priest or abbot or some such Popery equivalent . . .'

'Who signed it, Thomas?'

'Father Abbot Portare, sir. Oh, I say, I think if you literally translated the name it would mean Carrier, sir. I must say, it is ironic how the Roman Catholic Church has –'

'Lad?'

'Yes, sir?'

'I don't want to be the one to break many years of good Anglican upbringing, but you do realize that it's all the worship of a theological uncertainty with just a few little tweaks here or there that's led to centuries of bitter schism in Christianity?'

'Erm . . . yes, sir.'

'Well then, let's disparage the tragic decline of the Roman

Catholic Church and the weakness of Popery when we're feeling more religious and less pragmatic, shall we?'

'Yes, sir.'

'Good lad. Now, what seal do you think it means?'

'I don't know, sir.'

Lyle took the letter carefully and examined the seal at its bottom, with the slightly crooked cross. He frowned at an unspoken thought, then folded the letter again and put it on the desk. 'So . . . the *Pegasus* sails to Isalia, picks up an unknown passenger from a father abbot on the island, who gives the captain a warning that this man "hath the skill of the stone" and may be dangerous. Oh yes, and the captain of a struggling, ancient ship suddenly finds himself in possession of a new, all-gold crucifix for his trouble. On reaching London, someone, possibly the same passenger, emerges out of the hold of the ship, kills with his bare hands the Captain and Mr Stanlaw, an agent sent by Lord Lincoln – you know, he didn't tell me *why* he sent this Stanlaw; why doesn't he ever tell me *anything*?'

Thomas smiled wanly. 'Perhaps he didn't think it was important?'

Lyle glowered. '*After* breaking the necks of these two strong men, this mysterious killer leaves the ship with a man wearing expensive leather shoes and who may or may not have spoken with an American accent. *Why?* Why are two people dead, why is Lord Lincoln not telling me everything *again*, why is everything like this? This ship, this place, this time, these people? *Why?*'

'Because . . . *because* . . .' Thomas realized he'd started speaking, so might as well finish. He took a deep breath. 'This is all the work of foreign agents, sir, bent on disparaging Her Most Royal Majesty and bringing disrepute on the Empire of Gloriana Brita—'

He'd gone a bit too far. 'Thomas,' snapped Lyle, 'you have a gift for observation and logical thought, but . . . but . . .' He waved his hands in the air, struggling for the right combination of insult and tact, and couldn't find it in either his mind or heart. '*Urgh!*'

Snow fell. It drifted through the fog and landed lightly in Tess's hair where she sat on deck. Curious, she held out a hand and caught a fat feather of snow. Bringing the snowflake close to her nose, she could see each individual crystal that made it up. Tess blew gently, so that it rose from her hand and drifted back into the fog. She heard the sound of a door closing on deck and half-saw Lyle and Thomas emerge from the cabin, then heard Lyle walk to the edge of the ship, where he peered down. She said cheerfully, 'It's leanin' more than it was, Mister Lyle.'

'The ice is thicker too,' murmured Lyle.

'Ain't that a good thing?'

'I don't know. It doesn't feel cold enough. But I suppose that's just proof of how unreliable human instinct can be.'

The snow kept falling, more than just silent. It seemed to drain the noise out of the surrounding area, and make people talk in whispers. For a second Lyle thought he heard . . . something. He was aware of the gentle humming of the boat as it slipped further into the water, the distant buzz of the city, the creak of the ice as it pressed against the old, cracked timbers.

For a second, just a second, a ditty sprang to his mind, and he whispered, almost inaudibly, a tuneless chant, '*Hark, hark, the dogs do bark* . . .' He realized Thomas was watching him, and stopped, smiling weakly. 'Chin up, lad. How bad can things get?'

'I'm *cold*,' moaned Tess. 'It's *cold* an' it's *dark* an' I'm *hungry* an' it's *co-o-ld*.'

'Yes, Teresa,' sang out Lyle. 'Thank you for your observations.'

The four of them shuffled along a dark corridor that stank of tar, salt, rot and neglect. Lyle went first, followed closely by Tess and Tate, the dog having quickly worked out which human was most likely both to feed him, and to run away from danger. Last came Thomas, struggling along with the bulk of Lyle's newly purchased equipment, back pressed to the walls, head constantly turning as if he expected something to emerge out of the dark at a second's notice. The dark and cold here combined into something almost suffocating, shutting down every faculty except, worst of all, imagination.

A creak like Father Time rolling over in an old wooden bed made Thomas snap his head up with a sharp intake of breath, fingers tightening instinctively as he peered through the dark. Tess jumped. Lyle swallowed and forced a smile. 'It's just the ship.'

'Yes, Mister Lyle.' Thomas was white.

Another creak. It was the sound of tortured wood being pushed from every direction at once, by the freezing water inside and by the water freezing outside, ice slowly forming in every cranny and expanding, forcing the planks apart bit by bit. It was the sound of a thousand microscopic splinters ripping out of the ship itself with each second, amplified and deepened by the water sloshing around inside and out, until the noise rolled and rumbled down every corridor and made the rigging slap loudly against the mast above.

Lyle found a lantern, sniffed it, hung it up on a hook over the stairwell, pulled out a packet of fat, smelly phosphorus matches, struck one idly on the sole of his shoe and lit the lantern with it, while the match belched dirty smoke and dirty yellow light. The light didn't so much dispel the darkness as make it more obvious where the deepest darkness lay. It reflected off the black water that filled the stairwell below, lapping almost at their feet.

The silence that fell between the striking of the match and the rumble of the dying ship was almost painful. If Thomas strained, he could just hear the gentle slapping of the water, but even that was subdued by the ice slowly infecting it. The sounds of the usually roaring London docks seemed distant, like a circus heard far off. Even the rats were quiet.

'The rats are probably gone,' said Lyle quietly, as though reading Thomas's mind, if not his pallor. Thomas swallowed, and said nothing. Lyle smiled absently. 'Rats are very clever creatures. In many ways you have to admire them. They're the ultimate in survival.'

This didn't reassure Thomas in the slightest.

He heard a little gurgling noise and jumped back with a cry, banging his head against the wall as something cold and wet brushed his feet. He looked down and saw that the black water which had been crawling up the side of the stairwell had reached over and was now pouring in a thin sheen across the deck, rushing past his feet in silence. He could feel its cold through his shoes, but immediately flushed hotly at his own cry.

'This ship will go soon.' Lyle seemed almost sad, as if the ship was a living creature about to die, or a creation of his own. Standing ungainly on one foot, Lyle began pulling off his shoes, tying them together by the laces, and dipping his feet, a toe at a time, into the water, flinching at the cold. Thomas half-moved to take his off, and Lyle said, 'No, *not* you, lad.' Tess rolled her eyes and grabbed at the pipe and bellows slung over Thomas's shoulder.

'*You* can do the blowin',' she said happily. "Cos *I'm* a lady.'

'Yes, Miss Teresa?' He hesitated. When no more information was forthcoming, he hazarded, 'Forgive me . . . which blowing?'

Tess was jamming the bellows into one end of the flexible leather pipe. 'The blowin' what's goin' to help Mister Lyle do the swimmin'.'

Thomas glanced over at Lyle, who had stripped down to shirt and trousers, and was staring at the black water with an uneasy expression.

'Mister Lyle?' he squeaked.

'Yes, lad?'

'Are you sure this is . . . I mean, do you feel that . . . I'm sure that I could go without any difficulty, perhaps I ought to . . .'

'Not a chance, lad.'

'Oh. But I'm —'

Lyle raised a warning finger.

'Yes, sir.'

'Good lad. Now, just pump those bellows, all right?'

'Yes, sir.'

Lyle turned to Tess, who wordlessly shoved a long, round thing at him that Thomas realized was made of two tin cans hammered together. Peering down, he saw that the top can was empty, but that a small hole had been bored in its bottom, where it slotted into the second tin. Lyle took it in one hand and wrapped the hosepipe tightly round his wrist, so his end was closed, and a long slack ran from it to the bellows where Thomas stood.

Tess stepped back quickly as Lyle struck another match and held it over the two tins. His eyes narrowed suspiciously. She shrugged. 'I ain't *entirely* certain it ain't goin' to blow up, Mister Lyle. But if it does, it ain't my fault.'

'Thank you, Teresa. That's very reassuring.'

Lyle looked down into the dark water lapping at the top of the stairwell, took a deep breath, screwed his eyes up tight and dropped the match into the can. When the tins didn't blow up, he opened a cautious eye and let out a long breath. Something fizzed inside the can, hesitated and exploded with white light, almost too bright to look at. The tin immediately heated up until it was almost too hot to hold. Tate whimpered. Tess felt a smile start, an unstoppable grin of delight, which even her better judgement couldn't suppress. *London's burning, London's burning* . . .

Lyle shuffled forward into the stairwell, feeling his way down. The water rose up around his ankles, to his knees, and he started to turn white. 'My God,' Thomas heard him whisper. 'That's *cold*.'

He sank lower, shoulders vanishing under the black, murky water. He dragged the torch down – the light flickered, but kept on burning, strong and white. Lyle hesitated as the water lapped at his chin, took a deep breath, and slid down into blackness.

There is a kind of cold that isn't felt in shivers or in ice on the skin. It is a bone-deep cold, that turns all joints to stone and makes every toe and every hair ache with the weight of ages. It makes the smallest motions, even the twitching of a finger, an act of intense will, and the lifting of a feather tantamount to the lifting of stone. And today, so it seemed, it was making a special two-limbs-locked-up-for-the-price-of-one offer.

Lyle swam through the black water of the flooded lower deck of the *Pegasus*, which was illuminated a garish greeny-white by his torch of tin cans and magnesium, and hoped that this was going to prove worth his while. He didn't like dark places, especially not when they were cold, wet, dark places full of odd shadows, although his dislike of them was nothing compared to his dislike of heights. So he swam on, telling himself that it was for the greater investigative purpose, as if this were a holy mantra.

The ship creaked again. In the water, the sound was louder, deeper and seemed to make his ears hum for a long time after. He could feel the bending of the old, battered wood as shivers in the water, which was full of little drifting splinters and wisps of dirt, the origin of which he didn't dare speculate on. Lyle kept one fist closed tightly round the end of the hosepipe as he swam, but every now and again paused to hold the pipe to his mouth and take in a quick breath of air, which tasted hot and dirty and came in tiny shallow gulps.

He swam, skin whiter now than his shirt, squinting through

the cloudy water. Things had come loose from their moorings, and the lighter boxes were drifting gently through the water, bumping against each other and rolling over, while the heavy boxes sat, sliding loosely on the floor of the ship, weighed down by their contents. Something cold brushed Lyle's ankle and he jerked, torch slipping in his hand and starting to slide downwards. An eel, slim and dirty, wriggled past him and into the gloom of the ship. He took a hasty breath of air from the pipe and swam to catch the torch and hold it up again, half-blinded by the stinging water and the cold that seemed to dull colour and thought.

The circle of faint light in which he swam fell on something lying half-open in a corner. He pulled himself towards it, feet now numb from the cold, and heard again the agonized creak of the dying ship, felt the weight of water above and below, and heard ringing in his ears and the incredible weight of his own limbs dragging him down.

The thing that was half-open looked like a coffin, made entirely of stone. It was dull and crude and slab-like, and looked as if it was designed to contain a figure slightly larger than Lyle, in both height and width. But instead of tapering towards the toes it was square. On the lid was a very large, slightly crooked cross. Lyle ran his fingers over one side of it, but his white fingertips, tainted pale blue, couldn't feel anything. He swung round gracelessly, clinging on to the edge of the coffin, and dragged himself bodily down until his nose almost touched the sarcophagus. He saw what his fingers were too numb to feel – the small marks around the centre and edges, where a crowbar had been inserted – and felt almost relieved to see a sign of foul play. Heavy on the floor lay half of a broken stone seal. He half-swam, half-bent down and picked it up, turning it this way and that to see again the crooked cross, shattered in two. He dropped the seal, brought the torch closer until he imagined he could feel its warmth on his cheek, and peered at the coffin lid. Inside the lid, underneath the giant cross, there were hundreds of little scratches.

And there it was. The sense of dread, a deep, old suspicion, colder than the ice in his blood, began to settle over him. He ran his hands over the inside of the coffin lid, but it was a futile gesture and he knew it. Even if his fingers couldn't feel precisely, he could count the marks – five parallel lines here, five parallel lines there – and knew that hands had clawed at the inside of this lid in the past, trying to get out. Lyle suddenly felt very alone and exposed, his mind drifting into places where the rest of him didn't want to be.

About to push away, his eye caught, just in one corner, another very small mark. He moved closer and peered at it, no larger than the area inside his hooped finger and thumb. The light from the torch began to flicker erratically, the hissing flame drawing down lower. But as the white magnesium flare began to die, he saw by the dirty yellow light two cogs, one set inside the other, counting down the minutes to midnight, or noon, whichever one it was, and he thought of the ring he had pulled from Stanlaw's dead white hand, and shuddered through the frozen weight of his own skin.

He turned to swim away, and a pair of eyes, stone cold, angry and hateful, glared back at him. He choked on his own cry, bubbles exploding from his nose and mouth and briefly blinding him, and kicked out instinctively. His foot struck something hard and sharp, which rolled away, spinning off into the darkness, taking the hate-filled eyes with them. Something went *thump* in the dark. He hesitated, leaning back into the shadows of the alcove which held the stone coffin, his lungs suddenly burning and the ringing in his ears rising to a new and insistent pitch. He held the pipe to his mouth and breathed, until the pipe was just a thin contracted rope behind him, all the air sucked out.

The warmer air was calming, but not much. He swam, very cautiously, torch held out at arm's length, until he saw the eyes again, this time glaring up at the ceiling. They belonged to a small stone gargoyle: huge eyes in a small face, a chin so sharp it could have cut diamond, and eight razor-sharp stone claws at the end of stick-like arms, ready to scratch and tear. The little stone monstrosity was scarred and scratched from its journey, especially around the hands, but now lay on the bottom of the deck staring at nothing with a furious expression, as if about to demand a refund and ticket to a better destination, or else.

There was a sound in the hold that was louder here. It was the sound of ice gently bumping against the walls of the deck, and the whisper of water rushing in and out, like a whale breathing. Lyle followed the drag and push of the water until his hand bumped up against the wall of the ship. He let himself hang in front of the black tear in the ship's side, running the light round the edges of the torn and shattered wood. It wasn't a very large hole, but it had clearly been enough to seal the fate of the *Pegasus* for ever. He levered himself down and turned his head this way and that, trying to see clearly the cuts that had broken the wood. He was beginning to feel warm now, a pink warmness all over that he knew was a bad sign. The light was almost out, and giving off a dirty yellow vapour that made the greenish water seem even dirtier and more sickly. In its last glow he reached out and touched the marks around the wood. They were small but deep, and clearly had been administered with some considerable strength to have torn the planks apart.

In the dying light, Mister Horatio Lyle saw, quite clearly against one of the planks, eight tiny claw marks, like the hands of the glaring gargoyle, and in his heart of hearts, he *knew* it was a clue. The thought terrified him. He spun in the water, less aware of his own weight now as nerves started to shut down in the cold; and, as if it wanted to provide an appropriate comment on this discovery, and to make its participation in the affair noticed and appreciated, the torch gave one last hiss, and went out, plunging him into darkness.

For a second, fear was colder than the ice in Lyle's blood. He had the feeling of being watched, of something else outside peering in, of a consciousness down there apart from the fish and shimmering eels that had crawled through the shattered wood. He felt along the length of the hosepipe, using it to pull himself forward, back towards a distant patch of slightly patchier dark-ness where the water lapped up from the hold, and though he knew not to fear, there it was, the drumming in his ears, the ham-mering in his chest, the heavy pulse of the blood under his skin, beating out a tiny rhythm, catching at the senses like a half-heard *Hark, hark* . . .

He felt something move in the water, and knew he hadn't imagined it, and thought that he should have. He thought of fish nibbling at bare toes and eels rubbing against frozen skin and the terror was there, bubbling just below the iron vault of his scientific objectivity, and he tugged at the hosepipe now, using it more as a rope than a supply of air, and the pressure was there in the water again, a ripple of displacement behind him where there should have been none and *something closed around his ankle* – oh God, something hard and colder even than he was, clutching at his skin, digging into it, dragging him back with a strength and a grip that amazed him.

He flailed uselessly in the water against it, but it didn't let go, dragging him down like a stone, pulling his hands free of the hosepipe and its precious air, so that it twisted and bubbled wildly around his face, stinging his eyes as he was pulled back down. He kicked at the invisible, unseen thing, but it didn't seem to care. The dead torch fell from his fingers, and he felt sorry that Tess wouldn't be able to keep it as a souvenir, and wondered that he should think of a thing like that at a time like this, with the air burning hotter in his lungs, bubbling out of his lips in its desperation to get out and be replaced, a heavy constriction in his throat, a drying shrinking at the back of his neck, a dull weight in his chest, until his eyes started to burn with it. He twisted, reaching down to his own ankle and prising at the stone-hard things that seemed to have caught at his foot, wrenching at them with all his might, pulling with an instinctive, terrified strength that only emerged when the brain was too busy suffocating to question the acts of the body. He felt something snap, something made brittle and hard by the cold, until with a kick, the heavy thing at his ankle fell away, scratching and tearing thin lines across his flesh, bringing hot blood back to numb skin. Lyle kicked for the surface, trusting entirely to instinct, and his head bumped against the wooden top and for a moment he hammered against it, trying to find a way out in the pitch darkness, trying to find the rope, a stair, a ladder, anything to guide him out of this airless wet tomb, driving his palms against the wood until his ears burned and even the instincts started to fade into dull pink numbness.

For a moment – just a moment – Lyle drifted in the place between entrapment and escape, where thoughts were thought without words, and blood circulated on momentum only. He thought he heard . . . he *heard* . . .

Hark, hark . . .

And he heard . . .

Blacks and bays,
Dapples and greys . . .

And just a few feet away, the wood above his head shattered, splintering inwards and downwards, an explosion of sound and sensation and *air* into that airless blackness, tearing the water into a thousand drops with light and motion, as Thomas, face beet-root red from the effort, threw his axe aside and pulled Lyle up from the waters of the lower deck.

CHAPTER 5

Housekeeping

It took two blankets, a shot of whisky, a large mug of hot pea soup and half an hour by the fireside of the Hanged Sailor – a dockside tavern which had a reputation for frequently storing more bodies in the cellar than barrels, such was the local clientele – before Lyle turned from blue to merely bleached white and the sound of his teeth chattering was no longer loud enough to disturb drunks sinking into oblivion on the other side of the room. It took another half hour, sitting staring into the fire with an expression of determination, before a little colour returned to his cheeks and he announced in the first normal voice of the hour's wait, 'I think, perhaps, it might be time to risk a pair of shoes.'

Only when Tess had gone in search of dry socks and Thomas was staring in horrified fascination at the other inhabitants of the tavern did Lyle carefully examine his ankle, red and sore from the thing that had gripped it in the hold of the *Pegasus*, and notice without word or expression the tiny claw-like marks where the same thing had finally let go, like the shallow scratching of a cat, or of fine needles, or even, if he were given over to such imaginative fancies, the claws of a very small gargoyle.

By the time they left the tavern, the streets outside had changed. No longer was the day blue-grey from the thick fog, but had deepened to an almost impenetrable deep bruised black that made light from any doorway into a fuzzy-edged square and framed every window with an uncertain wobble of darkness. The church bells, however, announced it to be no later than three in the afternoon. Already the lamplighters were beginning to drag out their ladders, and the bobbies walked with their shuttered lanterns lit. What light didn't come from the yellow glow of fires and candles was weak and grey, more like the light of the moon than the sun. Fresh snow piled up against every doorway and down every street, and still it fell, until many of the weaker roofs creaked. In darker corners of the darker houses, icicles formed *inside* the walls. Everything except the blurred light seemed drained of colour, so that the shadows of people moved in a black-and-white world, the sounds of which were muffled by the snow and fog.

The four walked through the streets in silence. Where Thomas stood, to the left of Mister Lyle, he couldn't clearly see Tess's face to the right of Mister Lyle, so thick and quiet fell the snow. Tate was just a vague shadow at Lyle's feet.

'Mister Lyle?'

Lyle didn't take his eyes off the road in front of him, as if trying to judge their position by each cobble. 'Yes, Thomas?'

'Where are we going?'

Lyle's hand opened. He was holding a scrap of paper. Thomas recognized it from the boat.

'To see Captain Fabrio's housekeeper.'

'Shouldn't that paper be with the police and the rest of . . .' Thomas realized what he was saying, and closed his mouth.

Tess leant round behind Lyle and said, in a tone of awe, 'The way how you ain't said what you was about to 'ave said were the smartest thing I ever seen you do, bigwig.'

'Oh. Thank you, Miss Teresa,' mumbled Thomas, simultaneously attempting to translate Tess's words into a language he could understand.

Navigating through the snow and fog was a challenge that made even Tess hesitate and frown at every half-familiar street corner. Thomas grew uneasy, and jumped whenever a shadow overtook them, drifting silently out and back into the fog. Time too seemed to become lost until he found it hard to judge how long his legs, unaccustomed to walking such a distance, had been aching.

When Lyle stopped, it was so sudden that Tess walked straight into him. Tate sniffed the short, narrow door they were standing before, a little beam of wishy-washy yellow light etched round its edges. Lyle knocked, and even that sound was dead in the fog. When no one answered, he slipped the catch and half-opened the door. A single candle burned on a desk, the wax dribbled down around it. A narrow flight of flimsy steps ran upwards. Lyle paused, then started climbing. As they rose, their hands pressed into the walls for support and the stairs bending slightly under their weight, each in turn became aware of a gentle *creakcreakcreakcreak* coming regularly from upstairs. Lyle hesitated, head slightly on one side, by the door from behind which the noise seemed to be coming. The faintest of lights showed from underneath it. He knocked. The *creaking* noise stopped abruptly. A voice said with a strong accent that Lyle couldn't place, but which certainly hadn't come from the city, 'Who's there?'

'My name's Lyle,' he said in a clear, reassuring voice. 'May I come in?'

The tortured creaking noise started again. 'Yes. But leave that dog and the children outside.'

Lyle glanced down at the children. Then smiled, pushed the door open and slipped inside, closing it behind him.

The room was small, the ceiling slightly too low for Lyle's height, though he was hardly a tall man, so that he had to shuffle along with his head uncomfortably bowed. There was the smallest of all possible fires burning in the grate: just a few hot coals that gave out the minimum of heat. A rocking chair sat in front of it, old and flimsy, *creakcreakcreak*, the lady in it with her back turned to the door. Lyle moved closer, but the lady, without turning, said, 'Please sit in front of me, Mister Lyle, and put another coal on the fire.'

Lyle edged round uneasily in front of the woman and sat down on the single, three-legged stool in front of the chair. Next to the fireplace was a grand total of five coals. He placed one carefully on to the fire. It landed with a dull fizz, and didn't seem to do anything else. Lyle felt cold just looking at it.

The lady in the rocking chair smiled. She was old, dressed in a patchwork of ancient woollens sewn together with an expert touch, but she wore so many layers that she seemed to bulge out into almost spherical proportions, though her wrists and cheeks were sunk down to the bone. She was, Lyle realized, almost entirely blind.

Quietly, she said, 'Ask, Mister Lyle.'

'I can't place your accent.'

'My father was English, my mother Italian, and I spent the first ten years of my life following the army and my father across much of the Empire. Is that a good enough answer?'

'Are you Mrs Milner?'

'I am.'

'Is Captain Fabrio one of your tenants?'

'He is. But what does your tone imply, Mister Lyle?'

'Ma'am, I suspect you are the kind of lady who can surmise already what my tone implies.'

'That he is either in trouble, injured or dead, Mister Lyle.' A faint smile. 'You are surprised at my bluntness? You must forgive me – I have spent three years with my own company. My social skills have deteriorated.'

'Ma'am, you do not do yourself justice.'

'Do not toy, Mister Lyle. Is the good Captain injured?'

Lyle took a deep breath, and Mrs Milner's head moved sharply at the sound. 'Ah,' she murmured, cutting him off. 'He is dead, then. How?'

'He was killed last night. I'm trying to find out who killed him.'

'You do not have the walk of a copper.'

'I'm not just a copper.'

'Of course. You are . . . what shall I call it? An expert? In murder?'

'No, ma'am, that would be a murderer; I'm an amateur if anything. When did you last see the Captain?'

'Last night.'

'What time?'

'The *Pegasus* arrived in port yesterday morning, almost first thing. I sent to him to know on his arrival if he wanted his old rooms. In the afternoon he came in person and said he would be honoured to have them back; a charming man, Captain Fabrio. In the evening he arrived here, then was joined by another man at about eleven; a tall man by his footsteps, who banged his head against the ceiling repeatedly and wasn't comfortable in this place. A well-bred voice, but utterly cold. They quarrelled. The Captain wasn't expecting him; I heard raised voices.'

'Did the Captain know him?'

'I do not believe so. I suspect that the Captain was rather afraid of him, though. I certainly was. When he entered the room I felt a chill right through my bones, and I don't really feel the cold. A powerful man, I think. He almost knocked my door off the hinges with banging.'

'Did he have a name?'

'Stanlaw. I do not know if that is of any use to you.'

Lyle had frozen. Mrs Milner put her head on one side, listening to his sudden silence. Finally she said, 'Mister Lyle, is there something else you wish to tell me?'

'Stanlaw was also found murdered at the scene of the crime.'

Very, very quietly. 'I see.'

Silence while Lyle assembled his thoughts. 'Did they leave together?'

'No. Mr Stanlaw left at around eleven thirty. The Captain left half an hour later. He seemed quieter, subdued – something he never was. The Captain was, I might say, one of those swash-buckling types that we warn our children to keep away from. But charming.'

'Was he religious?'

'Yes, indeed; but I do not know if you would approve of his religion.'

'Ma'am,' said Lyle with firm politeness, 'there are slabs of granite yet uncut which have more interest in theology than I do.'

'An atheist?'

'Worse. A scientist.'

'I hope you recover. It won't offend you, then, to hear that the Captain was a devout follower of the Roman Catholic faith.'

'Did he take employment from a priest?'

'I don't know.'

'Did he give any indication of . . . a recent change in his fortune?'

She put her head slightly on one side. 'Recently? He said no matter what happened, he would always board here out of "fondness".'

'What did you take that to mean?'

'That he didn't need to board with me, but would.'

'Was he wealthy?'

'No, not at all. Do you think anyone would board with me if they had a choice?'

'There are worse places. Did he speak of a place called Isalia, ever?'

'The Captain rarely conducted business in this place. It wouldn't have suited a man of his character.'

'You don't seem very upset by his death.'

'Do not think I am heartless, Mister Lyle. I am practical. I will save my grief for the time when I am alone, and when it will not cause inconvenience to others. I am by myself enough to have that opportunity. Do you have any more questions?'

Lyle was silent again, but this time his eyes were fixed on her face. She smiled faintly. 'You are pitying me, Mister Lyle. Please; I have no desire for pity.'

'Ma'am, it is not pity, it is concern. Pity implies something directed at another person with a hint of your own superiority. Concern, however, is just a perfectly natural reaction at seeing another human in distress. It implies a desire to change something. Pity is passive. Can I look at the Captain's room?'

'You may.' The faintest of smiles on the old lady's face, pleased.

'And may I send my companions in search of more coals for the fire?'

The smallest hesitation; then the smile again. 'You may.'

'Thank you, ma'am.'

'Thank you, Mister Lyle.'

The sun is setting, slightly sheepish, knowing it hasn't made much of an impact on the day, and hoping people won't mind.

Gradually, spreading from sunset to seashore, the Thames is turning hard as stone.

The ice begins under the bridges and under the wharves, where the meagre light hasn't dared penetrate. It begins furthest away from the ships, mud banks and salt of the Thames estuary, creeping east from Hampton Court Palace where thin glass on water grows pale and white and the freezing wading birds coming in to land find their legs suddenly skidding out from under them. It crawls past the village of Richmond where the fishermen and eel-catchers burn holes in it to let their prey breathe a deadly last breath; clings to the mud and reeds of Hammersmith; settles under Westminster Bridge; and bumps against the side of the barges sleeping in the river.

Although, as Mister Lyle would have pointed out, if he had bothered to check his thermometer and make a few simple calculations, it's not yet quite cold enough.

But he hasn't. So he won't find out until after it's all over.

And finally, the sun sets. Its departure is hardly noticed – it is just a deepening of the dark, rather than a fading of the light.

And somewhere in the deep dark, eyes open.

And a voice like warm marble says, 'Is all well?'

'His grace is here, just as the father promised, m'lady.'

'Good. And the holy father?'

'Is in the garden.'

'Excellent.' A swish of silk on a polished stone floor.

'M'lady?'

'Yes, Henton?'

'The father . . . has left a number of loose ends.'

The swishing sound stops abruptly. 'Which loose ends?'

'A couple of individuals who may threaten us.'

'You believe that the police may be capable of tracing us by them?'

'It is not the police that concern me, m'lady. You spoke of the storm at St Paul's . . .'

'Lyle?'

'Yes, m'lady.'

'They said Lincoln might send him. You were wise to inform me.'

'Thank you, m'lady.'

Marble eyes burning in a cold darkness. Marble voice edged with fire. '*I* will deal with the situation.'

And in the gloom and the fog, footsteps clatter through the docks, and a voice mutters rebelliously, '"Get this, get that, find coals, find *sulphur*." 'Ave you ever gone an' looked for sulphur in this parta town, bigwig?'

'Well, I can't say that the situation has ever —'

'An' if he wants coals for the lady why don't *he* go an' find coals an' let me rest my feet?'

'If you want I could go on by myself . . .'

'An' then Mister Lyle 'd kill me for lettin' you get all killed! You just do what I say, right, an' it'll be all right when it's done.'

'Well, as the older party, not to mention the gentleman of this expedition, I feel it is in every way my duty to ensure that . . . *ow*!'

'Sorry. Was that your foot?'

In the darkness of the settling night, Horatio Lyle struck a match in a small, dingy room and lit a small, dingy lamp hanging from a small, dingy hook nailed into a low, leaking ceiling.

There was a bed in this room and a wooden crucifix. Nothing else gave it even the suggestion of being inhabited. It smelt of mould, dust, dirt and the faint aroma of tobacco; and from outside the window, the stink of the refuse pile in the courtyard of shed-like tenements rose up until it seemed to seep through the walls, despite the covering of snow and ice trying to shutter down the smell. Lyle looked round, feeling more depressed as each sense reported its dismal findings.

Only one thing in the room caught his eye, and even then he almost missed it. He knelt down and reached cautiously under the bed, imagining – or maybe not – the scuttling of ratty claws as he did.

Lyle unscrunched the note, and read it.

And it too terrified him, though he would never have admitted it. He already knew there was too much at stake.

In the darkness and the night, a man wrapped in a burgundy scarf looked up at the dim light of the room that had once housed Captain Fabrio, and saw the shadow of Horatio Lyle against it, head bowed, clearly reading something. And the man smiled, and thought, *Don't be afraid yet, my friend. I will see that everything is all right.*

As if to seal this silent bargain, he held up in salute to the shadow a hand that had something clasped in it and, with the reverence of a priest taking a sacrament, he carefully ate the ginger biscuit.

Voices rose out of the fog, and the man retreated into the darkness of a doorway.

'Wait, Miss Teresa!' A breathless voice.

Behind the burgundy scarf, the man smiled, with a strange fondness.

'Yes, bigwig?'

'I just need . . . to catch . . . my breath . . .'

'You make it sound like you're carryin' too much!'

'It's just . . . I don't usually carry coals myself.'

'Oh, that's typi . . . typic . . . that's just like you bigwigs what all 'ave people what do your carryin' for you. You oughta carry things, now that I'm a lady an' it's your *duty*,' the malevolent grin was almost visible in the darkness, 'it's your *duty* to do the carryin'.'

Whatever answer there might have been was lost in a breathless wheeze. The voices drifted on into the fog. Something, however, lingered. Tate, ears trailing in the snow, slowed, turned, sniffed the air, sniffed the ground, nose wrinkling up in dismay. Two immensely large, deep brown eyes turned slowly on a black doorway. The tail twitched. Tate started to whine.

A gloved hand emerged out of the darkness, holding half a ginger biscuit. Tate sniffed the hand, sniffed the biscuit, then ate the biscuit, tail wagging happily. The hand scratched Tate behind the ears, and faded back into shadow.

Tate trotted on, knowing full well that since everything would probably sort itself out, none of this was worth his worrying about.

CHAPTER 6

Dusk

'Is everything satisfactory, your grace?' A voice like maple syrup. 'Her ladyship has assisted most generously in gathering together everything possible. Sandstone, Portland stone, marble, granite, flint, slate, Caen stone, limestone, sarcen, serpentine, Bedfordshire, Staffordshire and Suffolk clays; and of course, the all-important London clay. This is what the city is made of, your grace. Every street, every house contains some of these. It is said that the very cobbles themselves remember the land they were once torn from; so many parts to make up a whole, so many disparate characters coming together. Remarkable, don't you think, your grace? This city is made up of so much melding into one, ancient personality. Now degraded, of course.'

Silence. Then a clink, as of stone rubbing against stone. A faint breath.

'The city is sick, your grace. Sick in its soul. The people are not people any more. They live like animals, think like animals, and it is this city, this ancient monster squatting on the bones of its own past, which has made them this way. Together, your grace, we can change it. Everything that made the city is here for you to see, to master, according to our bargain.'

The silence of consideration.

'Your grace? We have found everything.'

Somewhere in the distance, a carriage rattles, a long way off. Glass tinkles on glass. Someone laughs, giggles, the sound carried by the wind crawling through the fog. There is the dead quiet of snow falling on stone.

'Your grace?'

The voice that answers is a roar, shattering the fog and the night, although neither moves for the breath that utters it.

'Where is Selene? Where is the blade? Power is nothing without the black blade!'

The echoes bounce from stone to stone, wall to wall, humming with a sympathetic power; ripple through the fog, tearing at it, as if it weren't there, and fade gently into shadow.

A few miles away, Lyle jerks out of his contemplations. At his feet Tate whimpers, as if having a bad dream. The hansom cab rattles on, across the sleeping cobbles of London.

Mister Lyle's house, which had in recent months undergone extensive restoration following an embarrassing incident involving a small mob and an exploding furnace, was a thing far too large for him, and far too small for both him and Tess. Arguably, it could have accommodated several large families. But no number of compressed people could possibly have made the same amount of noise Tess did when faced with such horrors as, say, a bath. Or indeed that Lyle did when faced with, say, a positive current through an electrolyte solution, and a consequent rapid and unexpected, if not downright messy, ionisation induced by the potential difference between two terminals, which in itself was of such an embarrassingly exothermic nature as to cause rapid combustion of all local products and the subsequent but essential purchase of a new pair of trousers.

Thomas hesitated on the step as Tess bounded indoors, Tate plodding at her side. Though he had on many occasions stayed at Mister Lyle's house, usually informing his parents that he was hunting with 'new money', and hoping that his father's pragmatism would overwhelm his social indifference, Thomas always felt just a bit . . . outside. Lyle and Tess, even Tate, had, in their own bickering way, formed an attachment that still amazed him. Somehow, they didn't just get on, they cared, though neither party would admit it. It was a warmth and mutual understanding that Thomas had never experienced in his own life.

In the doorway Lyle, as if sensing Thomas's reluctance, looked back at him. 'Lad?'

'I ought to be looking for my boatman, Mister Lyle; it's a long way back to —'

'Stay here tonight.'

'Oh, but I don't want to intrude, and my family —'

'Where are your parents?'

Thomas hesitated. Lyle raised his eyebrows, a polite but firm expression settling over his face – one of *those* faces that Thomas had never dared defy.

He hung his head, and said, 'Somerset.'

'Why aren't you in Somerset?'

'I'm to remain in London and study.'

'Then come in and learn a little.'

'Sir, my father expressly said that the study of Latin and Greek would be more beneficial to me than –'

'And what do you think?'

'I . . .' He looked up at Lyle's face. In the hall behind him, Tess had struck a light and was looking back, the orange light casting odd shadows across her face. Tate sneezed.

'I'd be delighted to stay, sir.'

Lyle patted him on the shoulder as he walked across the threshold. 'Well done, lad.'

Only when Thomas was inside did Lyle look back into the fog, studying the shadows. When he saw nothing, he looked away, although he knew in his heart that seeing nothing didn't necessarily mean that nothing was there.

Supper was like most things Lyle cooked: made with an exceptional understanding of the chemical processes involved, but no sense of taste. Tess had long ago discovered that the only meal Mister Lyle was really *good* at cooking was breakfast. Consequently she tried to time things every morning so that she could be up too early for lunch but too late for breakfast. That way Lyle would tut and say, 'Well, you'd better just have a very *large* breakfast, to see you through to supper.'

At pudding (uninteresting egg custard), Tess was the one who asked the question that Thomas had been dying to ask from the first minute, through her spoon. 'Mnnm mnnm mn?'

'Well, that's something I've been wondering too,' replied Lyle, not glancing up from a deep contemplation of his pudding cup.

'Forgive me, Miss Teresa, but I didn't quite catch –' began Thomas.

Tess removed the spoon from her mouth and waved it imperiously, like a conductor's baton. 'What in all hells is goin' on?'

'Oh, Miss Teresa, I thought such language was –'

'I think it's quite clear *what's* going on,' continued Lyle, still distracted, 'but I'm not sure *why* it's going on. Or if it's going to turn out well.'

'Oh.' Tess frowned, thought about it, shrugged, and went back to the more interesting pastime of cleaning out her cup.

It took Thomas three minutes to blurt the question. 'But what is . . . going on?'

In those minutes Lyle had drifted to yet another place. He came back with a jerk. 'Pardon?'

'What's going on, sir? Who killed Captain Fabrio and Mr Stanlaw? Where are they now? What was happening on the *Pegasus*?'

Lyle smiled at him, in a way that made Thomas almost proud that he'd asked such questions and received such a look in return. 'Those, lad, are very good questions. Let's go upstairs and have a hot drink by the fire, shall we?'

Tess snoozed in the giant armchair, wrapped in Lyle's giant coat. Tate lay by his master's feet, paws idly sticking up, while Lyle talked.

'The first thing you have to ask yourself is about the victims: Captain Fabrio and Mr Stanlaw. Mr Stanlaw seems in many ways the easier case to discuss: an employee of Lord Lincoln, you can assume that he was sent to the docks by Lord Lincoln to meet Captain Fabrio. *Why*, we don't know. It's the "why"s in this case, lad, that are not easy. Stanlaw was a tough man, large, well built, well fed, and difficult, I would imagine, to catch off guard. Mrs Milner made it clear that the Captain was, at the very least, afraid of Mr Stanlaw. More importantly, the Captain hadn't been expecting him on the night they both died, but they left separately.'

'How is that important?'

'It's important when you consider the chronology of what happened on the boat.'

Thomas waited impatiently. Lyle continued, 'Edgar said he heard voices on the boat at one in the morning. That leaves a whole hour and a half between Stanlaw leaving the Captain and Mrs Milner's, and his murder on the boat. In that time I believe someone else arrived on board, went down to the cargo hold, and . . .'

'Yes, Mister Lyle?'

'Lad, I don't want you telling Teresa this. She's a good lass, but still young. I found a coffin in the hold. A large stone coffin. Someone had recently broken it open. There were fingernail marks on the inside.'

'Sir?'

'It's just possible someone was being transported in that ship, sealed alive in their own coffin. The coffin carried the same mark as the letter in Latin to the Captain, warning of a dangerous passenger: the cross from Isalia. It is possible that the dangerous passenger was picked up from Isalia and sealed alive in that coffin. With enough space to breathe and essential supplies already in the coffin for the journey, it would be possible to keep a passenger trapped down there.'

'Alive? In a coffin?'

'Yes.'

'But why . . .'

'Think about the letter. It said that the inhabitant was very dangerous. Now, I looked at the footprints which came up from the hold; the footprints which wore no shoes and which hadn't boarded the ship, like the others had. The stride and the depth of the marks gave the indication of a man weighing no less than sixteen stone and no smaller than six foot three inches. Lad, the coffin was the right proportion for a man of exactly that description.'

'You mean . . .' Thomas's voice was a whisper, 'they carried someone trapped and alive for days, and then he got out in the night and *killed* them?'

'Not got out. Was let out. There was a fourth set of footprints, belonging to neither Stanlaw nor the Captain. Its owner boarded the ship before the others, went down to the cargo hold, broke the seal on the coffin . . .'

'The one that the letter mentioned?'

'That's the one. This fourth person broke the seal, and released the coffin's inhabitant. Stanlaw and the Captain arrive just in time to meet this person, who kills them and then departs with the owner of the fourth set of footprints.'

'Are you . . . do you think that's what happened?'

'I have no idea; it's pure speculation.'

'But then that makes the fourth person bad! It means that they must have broken in and –'

'Don't leap there yet, lad. There's more. The letter from the Abbot of Isalia told the Captain about having a "holy father" present if he broke the seal on the coffin. Now, think back to the Captain's cabin. What stood out?'

Thomas thought. 'The cross? The golden cross?'

'*Exactly*. The *Pegasus* is a ramshackle old ship; the Captain lived in the poorest rooms he could find. But he suddenly has this rich gift in his cabin and is hinting at Mrs Milner that his fortunes have taken a change for the better – so, what can we conclude?'

'That he was very well paid?'

'Think, lad, think! Who pays a sea captain with a golden cross, something emblazoned only for the highest cardinal or the most powerful abbot?'

'A . . . uh . . .'

'Think about it . . . cardinals, from Italy . . .'

Thomas's mouth moved soundlessly while he tried to work it out. Then his eyes lit up. 'The fourth man is a priest! He must have paid the Captain to sail to Isalia to pick up the coffin – that's why the abbot knew about him, wrote about the "holy father" in his letter, because he *knew* the Captain had been sent by the priest to collect the coffin and then the Captain, having been so well paid, transported the coffin back to London where the priest went on board and freed its trapped inhabitant.'

'I'm thinking,' continued Lyle in a low, calm voice, 'that the priest was expecting just to pick up his cargo without a fuss – after all, he had paid a fortune. I'm thinking something happened that made him change his plans and release the coffin's inhabitant. I'm thinking he deliberately holed the ship to try and cover up this crime.'

'Mr Stanlaw met the Captain?'

'That's right. Lord Lincoln sent one of his agents to see Captain Fabrio. The Captain wasn't expecting him, was afraid of him, even. Isn't it just possible that if the Captain was surprised, our mysterious priest would also have been surprised, and might have reacted in the only way that seemed sensible at the time?'

'So the priest released whoever was in the coffin to *murder* them?'

'It's possible. After all, only the fourth set of footprints, and the killer's, left the ship. A priest pays a captain to sail to an isolated monastic island, collect a coffin containing a living man, and sail back to London; then uses the trapped and presumably very, very angry prisoner to kill both the captain and an agent of the government in order to keep his secret. The two leave together. Wherever the priest is, there too is the murderer.'

Thomas almost bounced in his seat. 'Edgar said he heard a foreign voice: an American!'

'So our priest might be an American. And clearly, despite his holy vows, one with access to money, if he can so liberally pay for the Captain's passage with such a valuable item.'

'But can we be sure of any of this?'

Lyle smiled, eyes crinkling up with a happy secret. 'Oh, yes, I suspect so.'

'Who is he? Who is the priest?'

Lyle leant back in his chair, radiating satisfaction. 'I'd say he is about five foot nine, weighs fourteen stone, wears expensive leather shoes, has an American accent, a slight limp in the left foot, wears a very long black coat that trails in the snow, has a two-horse, four-wheeled carriage at his disposal and is called Ignatius.'

Thomas gaped. '*Ignatius?* But . . . but how could you possibly . . .'

Lyle held up a crumpled note between thumb and forefinger. 'I knew all along. I just felt like a conversation.'

The deepest dark settles over the streets of London. It isn't dark that just excludes light, it is the dark that absorbs it, gobbles it up like a whale swimming through plankton. It is a dark that crushes everything: smell, sight, sound; creeps into every corner and under every door, pushing back even the warmth of the fire to a small circle around the heart of the flame.

The ice spreads across the river, and thickens still. Even the rats are too cold to fight, and huddle together in the sewers for any warmth they can find.

A footstep on a stair. Heavy, slow, but followed in smooth succession by another, and another, so that the normal process of knee joints bending doesn't seem to be happening, and the sound is that of a continuous but heavy glide; a mêlée of contradictions.

'I can hear you, miss. But I don't know your tread.'

'Mrs Milner.' A voice like warm marble.

'Who are you?'

'I see you have just put on some more coals – visitors? I'm told that Captain Fabrio boarded with you here.'

'That is so.'

'You must have heard things. With your very good ears.'

'I don't intrude on other people's concerns.'

'Have you heard a man with an American accent speaking here in the night?'

'American . . . odd accent? Can't say I remember, miss.'

'Did you let Lyle into the Captain's room?' Silence. 'Did you tell him things? Was it he who put coals on your fire?' Silence. 'Oh, Mrs Milner. I had hoped you were just a foolish interfering blind woman whom no one would believe and who would be too mad to know a pigeon from a paperweight.'

'I'm sorry to disappoint you, miss. You sound as if you are used to getting your own way.'

'I am. Now you're going to have to be something else.'

'What would that be, miss?'

Shadow across the fire, drawing itself up. Darkness at the window, crawling under the door, whispering in for the spectacle. Bells ringing the hour in the distance, a perpetual hourly alarm trying to wake the sleeping city, calling out the new warning of the new hour, *Hark, hark, the dogs do bark,* sleep and empty wretched stillness pressed into every eye from every corner and . . .

And a hand like marble, crushing old, thin paper. And a voice like warm marble. 'An epitaph, Mrs Milner.'

The dark crushes the light from the lamplighter's taper, suffocates the light from the window of the tavern, sweeps dirty, unswept streets and pushes at each chimney stack, meets for secret, cruel, crowded meetings in every winding alley and whispers with the fog through every exposed cellar of every rookery, and races on, chasing the sunlight away into the west.

The note was short, written in English, in a neat hand, and read:

My dear Sir,

*My blessings on you, and thanks for your safe delivery
back to port. I will be arriving tonight to collect my cargo; do
not attempt to move the coffin until I am present. I am sure
the holy father on Isalia has warned you of the dangers of
disturbing the seal, but I wish to reassert the necessity of
caution. As always, do not speak to anyone of what your
mission has been, not even to Father Fornaio. I will arrive
shortly.*

Your most humble servant,
Father Ignatius Caryway

'Sir?'

'Yes?'

'Where did – I mean, how did . . .'

'It was in Captain Fabrio's room, with Mrs Milner. Clearly this Father Caryway was expecting to take delivery of the coffin – and its inhabitant – but Stanlaw interrupted things.'

'Who's Father Ignatius Caryway?'

'I have no idea.'

'Oh.' After all that drama, Thomas felt this was a bit of a let-down.

'But I think I know where we can start looking.'

Tate sleeps by the fire and dreams of ginger biscuits and a soft silent step in the night, and scratches an ear contentedly, and wonders how long until the others work it out.

Lyle carries Tess silently up to her room, pulls the blanket up to her chin and blows the candle out, closing the door and creeping away to leave her dreaming of a light burning in the darkness and little ideas forming together into something that might almost be called knowledge, or might almost be called hope. A rhyme tickles through her mind and sings,

> *'When will you pay me?' say the bells of Old Bailey.*
> *'When I grow rich,' say the bells of Shoreditch.*

Thomas lies on his side and dreams of flying away from it all, of making the sky his world, the clouds his cushions, a kingdom far below to call his own, a home in the winds and above the lights, of escaping to another and a better place, of watching the land drop away and seeing possibility spread, inviting, all around; and he smiles, and rolls over in his sleep to dream again.

And Horatio Lyle lies in his bed and stares at the sky, and does not sleep, and does not dream, but instead feels the cold terror of uncertainty in his heart, and knows with the crudity of instinct and surmise that something is wrong, something that cannot be explained away with logic or science, something terribly irrational, cruel and real. And though he tells himself that there is no proof to give credence to his fears, nothing on which to base the instinct which says that everything about this is wrong, from the merest fact that Lord Lincoln was involved, to the stone coffin that contained a living being which scratched at the stone with sharp nails and *had no air holes* – though he tells himself all this, Horatio Lyle lies awake, and is afraid of what the morning may bring.

And somewhere, where the windows are high and the walls are thick, and nothing but stone and iron decorates the plain walls,

Lord Lincoln turns from his contemplation of the city, puts his hands, fists down, on a large, round iron table and says quietly, 'Where is he?'

'We are still investigating.'

'*You* are investigating, *xiansheng*. *You* are investigating, father. The whole police force is investigating, my agents are investigating, Lyle is investigating. So I ask myself, with such powers at our disposal, where is he? Why haven't we found his grace yet?'

There is an embarrassed silence.

A nervous voice chirrups, 'It's possible that *they* are helping to hide –'

'They are weak. Their power in this city was damaged when they were defeated at St Paul's. I do not fear the Tseiqin's involvement at this time and, besides, his grace threatens their welfare just as much as ours. If he finds Selene, and if he finds the blade, his power will extend beyond all measure. They would not risk freeing his grace from Isalia. It is a madman's ploy. Why have we not found a madman yet, gentlemen?'

'Lord Lincoln,' says a voice heavy with a foreign accent that isn't happy with English sounds, 'we know that it would take a priest to have authority to free his grace from Isalia. And priests are easy to find.'

'We have already investigated that possibility, Mr Lingdao. If a priest has indeed so broken with his masters and his covenant to free his grace, he must have a powerful friend to hide him from our eyes.'

'My lord, I fail to see –' the weak voice, the kind of voice that always meant to take exercise, but kept on losing its socks on the way out '– why this is such a threat. Perhaps he can control part of the city; but without the blade the ultimate power remains beyond his grasp. As we still have . . .'

A sharp interruption from Lord Lincoln – the anger of an intelligent man impatient with a fool. 'He can destroy the city without the blade, father. You made the stone coffin that held him, you should know his power and *why* we have always dreaded the day he was set free. London is the heart of Empire. If this city falls, it will be as though the Empire falls, and everything we have been working towards will be as if for nothing.'

'Wars encourage progress, my lord, and this Empire is old –'

'It is also the future, father. A future your people have been reluctant to embrace.'

'Forgive me, my lord. I spoke out of turn.'

Lord Lincoln turns his attention elsewhere, with an almost audible snort of displeasure. 'Mr Lingdao?'

'Lord Lincoln.' The foreign voice of a purring tiger.

'What is your agent doing?'

'Trailing Lyle.'

'Why?'

'Lyle finds things. But he does not necessarily report his findings. I know he was useful in opposing *them* when they tried to take control at St Paul's. But I have often stressed how unreliable he is, how unpredictable, and I feel that –'

'You have a better suggestion, *xiansheng*?'

'There are other options. Havelock, I believe, is willing to –'

'Havelock is a useful associate, but lacks Lyle's professional flair. We take a risk on Lyle, and hope that Lyle finds his grace before his grace finds us or the blade.'

'My lord.'

'I have nothing more to say to you. Find his grace. Find the Marquis. When you do, spare no effort in his destruction.' Lord Lincoln's voice is edged with ice. 'I will *not* have all that we have worked for threatened by this man. Not any more.'

And last, in the side of a large house, shrouded in the darkness of night and cold and fog, a small door opens and a woman sidles out, breathing deeply the cool night air. By her clothes she is a cook, and she is accompanied through the kitchen door by a blast of hot air that disappears at once in the freezing night. She leans against the icy wall of the house for a long minute, breathing deeply of the night air, and sighs. Inside, someone calls out, 'Ellen? Damn it, where is Ellen?'

The cook rolls her eyes and slips away from the door, sliding like a thief into the darkness. She walks idly through the night, picks up a handful of snow, rolls it into a ball and throws it against the wall with a sense of childish glee, enjoying the security that the dark offers. Turning to pick up another handful of snow, she stumbles against something, unseen in the dark, stubbing her toe. With a hiss of pain, hopping clumsily, she sits down heavily on the unseen something, which is hard and slightly warm under her; unlikely in the cold. She runs her hand over it, feels stone under her fingers. Frowning, she feels around her, fumbling in the dark. Her hands brush dusty sandstone, hard, smooth marble, worn Portland stone, sticky clay, dusty clay, rough granite, cracked limestone. Her fingers pause, running over the edge of the stone. Each one is carrying an impression, roughly the same in each material. She feels each mark with the pads of her fingers, the cold suddenly starting to bite down to her bones. She runs her fingers along it, then down, brushing every indentation. She starts to shake. From the distant doorway, a voice rolls out. 'Ellen? Ellen, where are you?'

She kneels down in front of the nearest stone and tries to see in the dark, squinting at the shadows. She tells herself that it's clearly the work of some deranged carver, that her imagination is getting the better of her.

'Ellen? Ellen, when I find you, you are in so much trouble!'

She stands up, turns and runs back towards the house, suddenly pale and shaken. Behind her, the stones sit as they had sat before, piled up loosely against the wall, the regular teeth marks in each one all but invisible to the naked eye, unless it already knew that they were there.

Below, but not that far below Ellen's feet, a man who weighs sixteen stone if you can trust the depth of impressions a bare foot leaves in snow, is at least six foot three by the length of his stride and may just be almost unnaturally strong, considers the taste of stone in his mouth, and closes his eyes, and tries to hear a sound that only he can hear, something ancient, just on the edge of perception. He tilts his head like a man with water in his ear and hears it, for a moment, strains to catch the sound again, remembers the taste of the city, the press of the city in his mind, the smell of it, the sound of it, all the old songs of the city, and for an instant is aware of every footfall tapping against stone, every skulking barefoot child and every nail-heeled collier, every iron-shoed horse and every clattering wooden cart, and maybe, just maybe, a humming that might have run, *London's burning, London's burning, Fetch the engines, fetch the engines,* before the feeling is lost.

He sits, and doesn't care. It will get stronger soon; he knows this from experience. Until it does, he will sit and listen and wait. He is very good at waiting.

CHAPTER 7

Witnesses

The knock on the door was short and quick. The open door revealed Constable Charles, red-faced and breathless, standing in three inches of fresh snow. 'Horatio,' he gasped between wheezes, 'what's the worst thing you could imagine?'

'I wish you wouldn't begin a greeting like that, Charles. It fills my mind with thoughts of falling from great heights on to hard surfaces, and things that go bang in the night. Why don't you offer a suggestion, and I'll tell you whether I could have imagined it?'

'Have you seen the morning papers?'

'No, I was woken up instead by someone knocking on the door.'

'Someone talked to *The Times* about the case. The papers are carrying every detail, from time of death to possible witnesses.'

'Have you stationed constables at the scene?'

'It's already too late for that.'

Lyle saw the look in Charles's face, then turned white. 'How were they killed?'

'She was. Neck broken. We're still looking for Edgar. No witnesses. No footprints – the snow was falling too heavily. Single blow to the neck.'

'I want to see the body. Now.'

'Thomas?'

'Mmm?'

'Thomas, come on, wake up.'

Thomas blearily opened his eyes. 'Father?' He opened his eyes a little bit further. 'Mister Lyle?' He opened his eyes all the way. 'Why are you in your coat? Is something the matter?'

'I'm just nipping out for a bit. No – don't get up. I want you to look after Teresa and Tate while I'm gone. You know where the breakfast things are. Will you be all right?'

'Where are you going?'

'It's not important.' Then, slightly more uncertainly, '*Will* you be all right?'

'Yes, Mister Lyle.'

'Good. Now go back to sleep.'

'Yes, sir.'

It took almost half an hour to reach the morgue. Three bodies were lined up next to each other in the ice-cold basement, which smelt of formaldehyde, soap and something horrible and sharp which Lyle didn't want to speculate about. He walked past Captain Fabrio, Stanlaw and Mrs Milner, and said not a word on his processional. Charles, hovering in the background, opened his mouth several times to speak, then saw Lyle's frown of pained concentration. Outside, a large and rather out of place grandfather clock ticked on through the hour. Lyle leant in until his face was inches from the white mask of Mrs Milner, studying it, hands tightening up into fists at his side, the only sign of anger that managed to escape him. He looked at her wrists, her hands, her fingers, then finally, under her nails. He dug into his pocket and came out with a thin metal file. He ran it under a nail and peered at the substance that came with it. 'Clay,' he murmured to himself absently. 'White clay.' A frown began on his face, a little thought trying to be heard.

Footsteps were heard outside. The grandfather clock ticked on. The door opened. Inspector Vellum stood in the doorway. 'Mister Lyle.'

Lyle straightened up, but didn't turn to look at the Inspector. Something hard and tight settled over his face. 'Inspector Vellum.'

'I see you're still playing detective, Mister Lyle.'

'This,' snapped Lyle, indicating the bodies, 'is a stupid, pointless, humiliating travesty.'

'I concur.'

'Since when, Inspector, was it the policy of the Metropolitan Police to reveal to *anyone* what witnesses there were to a crime?'

'Come now, Mister Lyle, it hardly seems a matter of great difficulty; the Captain's housekeeper was well known. The murderer clearly waited at the scene and observed who the police talked to, and who *you* talked to, Mister Lyle, and when they were alone, killed Mrs Milner in the night.'

'And whom did you talk to, Inspector?'

'Mister Lyle, I'm a –'

'*I've seen the papers, Inspector Vellum; don't take me for a fool!*'

The vehemence that leapt out of Lyle's voice and lashed across the room took the Inspector by surprise. He leant back, paling. Lyle bore down on him, a finger stabbing accusingly across the room. 'You couldn't resist it, could you, the chance to show what a wonderful detective you were, how you were the essence of mature, incisive investigation? You just had to talk to the press and let them see how good you were at your job, didn't you? And now someone else has found out and the witness is dead, for *nothing*, a stupid, pointless act to prevent people telling us everything, every dirty little secret that might hint this way or that!'

Vellum's lips trembled as he tried to answer in his steadiest nasal voice, 'On the contrary, I have reasons to believe that no one told the police every –'

'They didn't tell *you* because *you* are a pompous little wart, a fungal eruption on the hayfever-ridden nose of a deranged anteater bitten once too often by its supper, and for knowing anything and being able to say anything they are now dead and . . . *and* . . .' Lyle grabbed the Inspector by the scruff of the shirt, trembling with fury, and a little yelp escaped the Inspector, who screwed up his eyes tightly. Lyle hesitated. For a second he teetered on the edge, then let out a long breath and let go, stepping away and turning his back on the Inspector who, breathless and pale, slumped with relief.

Lyle stared morosely at the three bodies, hands buried in his pockets, head bowed.

Finally the Inspector said, in his more normal, grating voice, 'You were in a passion, Mister Lyle. I am very understanding of weak men.'

Lyle didn't move.

'There is, I believe as you might say, a silver lining to this situation.'

The only answer was a sour grunt.

Vellum's voice rang out with more confidence. He was aware of making almost a formal address to an audience, and was proud of his insight. 'The murderer has felt forced to show his hand again. I believe that we can deduce much from this new occurrence, and continue with renewed vigour to pursue this perpetrator of no less than three confirmed . . .'

'Two.'

Vellum floundered, not used to being interrupted. 'Mister Lyle, you can count?'

'Two murders. The murderer who came up from inside the *Pegasus* and breaks necks with a single blow has killed two people for certain. Not three.'

'Mister Lyle, are you quite well? Or is this a misconceived attempt at humour?'

Lyle sighed and said in an unnaturally calm voice, 'Look at the way their necks have been broken, Inspector, and do try to draw a few conclusive insights of your own. The murderer of Fabrio and Stanlaw on the *Pegasus* was right-handed and broke their necks with a single blow of incredible strength. The murderer of Mrs Milner has also broken her neck with a single blow of incredible strength, but from the opposite side. Look at the bruising – Mrs Milner has broken skin on her neck where nails have dug in, unlike Fabrio and Stanlaw. And whoever killed her was left-handed, Inspector Vellum. Left-handed, *not* right-handed. You're looking for two killers now, not one. And if you don't find Edgar soon, you'll probably have another corpse to prove that the lining really is silver. Good morning to you.'

And Lyle turned, not looking once at Vellum's face, and swept out in silence.

'Mister Lyle, where you been?'

'Nowhere, Teresa. Erm . . . what exactly has been happening here?'

'Well, the bigwig here said how he was goin' to make breakfast 'cos of how he was in charge, an' *I* said . . .'

'For goodness' sake, open a window!'

'That'd be how he went and *burnt* . . .'

Thomas's indignant voice. 'It's crispy!'

'. . . burnt the bacon an' then . . .'

An outraged squeak from Lyle. 'Why is there *flour* everywhere?'

'I was comin' to that . . .'

'Sir, I can explain everything . . .'

'And what the *hell* is that?'

'Eggs, sir.'

'Eggs? *Eggs?* Is it chemically possible or even probable that something that cruel, unnatural and unlikely could possibly have befallen an egg in this modern age of Newtonian science?'

'Sir, I can explain about them too . . .'

'I mean, what can you conceivably have done to an egg with the equipment available to create something so . . . so . . . *biological*?'

'. . . an', an', an' then he tried addin' flour an' he slipped 'cos it were high on the shelf, Mister Lyle, an', *I wanna have breakfast* an' it went everywhere an' then Tate slipped on it and tripped over his own ear an' . . .'

'How do you even begin to dispose of eggs like that? I'm not sure if ordinary processes of decay even apply to something quite so . . .'

'So I says how about a bit of bread 'cos I'm thinkin' by now maybe I don't want to be pushin' my luck with breakfast this morning an' *I wanna have breakfast* an', then he says do I want to have it all hot an' –'

'Perhaps we could develop the eggs into a potential biomass energy generator? A few electrodes and a suitably deep pit somewhere where no noses dare sniff, or sell to crackpot alchemists as the missing link in Darwin's evolutionary chain . . .'

And a cry rends the air, full of pain and desperation. '*I don't know how to cook! No one ever told me how!*'

Silence, as the flour settles. 'Well, lad,' says Lyle kindly, 'why didn't you just say so?'

There were people walking on the Thames. Snow had fallen on the thick ice that covered the river, the only really white snow of the city, everything else already made mucky by the passage of too many carts, boots and horses. Children played around boats that were trapped in the middle of the river like statues frozen in the ground: a maze of barges and yachts and even a few small frigates that had crawled upriver as far as London Bridge. Some enthusiastic soul had already begun sweeping away the snow below Westminster Bridge to create a small ice rink between the boats where braver souls skated on bone, and very occasionally iron, skates.

Lyle, Tess, Thomas and Tate stood together, elbows on the Embankment walls or, in the case of Tate, nose on Lyle's shoe, and ate greasy pies in contemplative silence.

'I ain't never seen it freeze like that before,' said Tess. 'It looks all pretty.'

'What are we going to do now, sir?' asked Thomas.

Lyle pulled out the crumpled note from his pocket. 'Find Father Ignatius Caryway, I'd say. The man who hired Captain Fabrio to bring in our mysterious passenger.'

'The mysterious passenger what was the killer?'

'So we suspect.'

'How will we find him?'

'At the moment, I'm not entirely certain. But there was someone else mentioned in the letter. And I think I know where we can find *him*.'

CHAPTER 8

Church

In the plush suburb of St John's Wood, the Church of Our Blessed Lady stood far enough out of town to keep the smoke of the city's factories off its new, especially pointy, especially knobbly spire, while close enough to Regent's Park to attract a certain kind of gentry: the kind who understood that Church was a social as well as a religious experience.

To an artist of certain taste, the church was a monstrosity. The stone arches along the centre aisle were well enough, and it was doubtful if fault could be found with the simple wood benches. However, the gargoyles that clung with pointed talons to every corner and stuck out their long, thin tongues in a perpetual leer, and the cherubs who smiled angelically from every wall, with bloated cheeks and huge popping eyes, had an unhealthy disproportion about them, not to mention, as Lyle would have pointed out, a certain aerodynamic unsoundness. The stained-glass windows, showing this saint dying horribly or that angel blessing this bishop, or this virtue overcoming that sin, or this sinner burning for all eternity, or that demon doing something unhygienic with a particularly pointy poker, were at best tackily graphic.

Into this church on the edge of the city and the edge of the country, a boundary defined by prim houses and manners, walked Horatio Lyle and Friends at eleven a.m. on a cold, snow-covered morning.

'Father Fornaio?' Lyle's breath was visible in the chill of the nave. The light crawling through the windows was meagre, and most illumination came from giant candles.

Father Fornaio, still in the robes of his morning's duty, examined the visitors from where he'd been restoring the altar to its original pristine glory. Lyle approached down the aisle, followed by the children at a cautious pace. Tess's eyes darted off every gold chalice and candlestick with a hungry gleam, and Thomas shuffled along with the suspicious glare of a religious critic.

'Can I help you?' The priest's voice took Thomas by surprise. Father Fornaio, a short, neat man, oddly proportioned in his voluminous robes, had an East End accent, close to Tess's but twisted by an educated refinement that gave Thomas the feeling of being trapped in a schoolroom. The priest smiled politely as they drew nearer, until Lyle stopped, just below the altar, looking up at him.

'Are you Father Fornaio?'

'I am.'

'Confessor to Captain Fabrio?'

The smile remained, though a frown flickered across the priest's features. 'I know the Captain.'

'Sir,' said Lyle in a restrained voice, 'I am with the police. May we talk?'

In the vestry and without his robes, Father Fornaio looked, to Thomas, a lot less intimidating.

'You are an interesting policeman, who brings two children and a pet . . .' Tate growled '. . . on your investigations.'

'Yes, well, it wasn't safe to leave them in the kitchen,' said Lyle meekly.

'I hope you understand, even if the Captain had told me anything, I would not break the confidences of the confessional.'

'Did he tell you anything?'

'No. I haven't seen the good Captain for nearly two months.'

'Did he come to this church often when in England?'

'Very rarely. I used to see him more frequently down in the docks. He was not a wealthy man.' Thomas glanced at Lyle, who shook his head very slightly. Thomas looked away again, and wished he knew how much money a giant gold cross was worth, and how much a loaf of bread would cost in comparison.

'What were you doing in the docks?'

'I serve the Italian immigrant community in that area, as well as any other souls who can't find a guide of the appropriate denomination. The city has grown so rapidly in that direction that I fear the Roman Catholic Church has been too slow in catching up with the needs of the people. I sometimes fear, Mister Lyle, there is more than enough danger and dirt and darkness in that maze for religion to cure. It is sometimes enough to make a man doubt his faith.'

Lyle hesitated, then said in a less brisk voice, 'Are you Italian? You don't sound very –'

'My parents were Italian, but I was raised from birth in this city.'

'Did Fabrio trust you as a fellow Italian, or as a fellow Catholic?'

'Both, I hope. He was a friend as well as a member of the flock.'

'Do you know where he went on his last voyage?'

'I believe it was back to Italy. On the Church's business, so he claimed, although I never entirely believed him – the Captain was a good soul, but . . .'

'Flamboyant?' suggested Lyle politely.

'That is one way of seeing the matter.'

'Have you heard of an island called Isalia?'

Surprise passed across Fornaio's face, followed by an answer that was just a bit too sharp. 'Why do you ask?'

'It was where Captain Fabrio last sailed. We believe he was paid to go to Isalia, collect something from the island and return it to London. You know of Isalia?'

'There is a monastery there. Nothing more.'

'Father Fornaio,' said Lyle, smiling a little, pained smile, 'forgive me for saying this, but it hardly seems like nothing more.'

'What gives you that impression?' Even Thomas heard it – the priest's reply was too fast. At his feet, Tate began to growl.

'The way your hand went to the cross around your neck the instant I mentioned it, sir.'

A heavy silence. 'Are you trustworthy, Mister Lyle? Are these children secretive, will they do what you say?'

'I don't do *nothin'* unless I want'a,' said Tess firmly. Lyle glared at her. She shrank back into her usual slouch and mumbled, 'An' today I want'a be all secret.'

'Sir, it would be my honour and privilege to guard any secret until my death, whenever that may be, and give you my word as a gentleman that, no matter what may –'

'The lad can keep a secret,' Lyle said quickly.

Fornaio sat down, laying his hands flat on the vestry table and looking at each pair of eyes in turn. Finally he said, 'There are only rumours, but Isalia is . . . sometimes whispered of. The monks there keep things that the Vatican doesn't want in the world. It is a place of protection – protecting us from *them*.'

'Who's *them*?'

'I don't know. You sometimes hear stories of . . . things leaving Isalia. Strange men or creatures, dogs grown to the size of a man or men shrivelled to the size of dogs. Stories of men and women with bright green eyes who talk the sweetest, most seductive words –'

'Green eyes?' Lyle's head snapped up. 'Tall, thin people, pale skin, emerald green eyes? Certain allergy for iron and magnetic fields?'

'I don't know.' A shard of fear was visible behind the priest's eyes. 'You haven't had contact with . . . I mean to say, you aren't . . .'

'Does the word "Tseiqin" mean anything to you?'

'No. Who are they?'

'They are usually *them*,' said Lyle darkly.

Tess's head rose from its usual slouch and she sat upright, eyes wide. '*Them?* There's *them* again? But they were all dead, we beat 'em good an' —'

'Enough, Teresa.'

'But Mister Lyle, he said how that they —'

'Teresa! Enough!' Tess met Lyle's eyes. Just for a second she saw the fear that had been stewing deep, deep down inside, the fear of a rational man confronted with something inexplicable by any normal laws of logic or reasoning, and remembered bright green eyes and the thunderstorm when Lyle had fallen too long and too far, and hastily closed her mouth.

Lyle coughed and said quietly, 'Forgive me. Let's talk about something else. Does the name Father Ignatius Caryway mean anything to you?'

Fornaio shook his head.

'We think he's a Roman Catholic priest, possibly the one who arranged for the Captain to go to Isalia. Possibly American, about . . .'

'American?'

'You know him?'

'Not by name, but I met an American with the Captain, once. He did not tell me his name, but he shook my hand most warmly and commended me on my sermon.'

'This was here?'

'Yes, at evening Mass. With a lady who sometimes comes in the evenings.'

'What did he look like?'

'Shorter than you, with auburn eyes and a very intense gaze. Auburn hair too, good skin, worn hands, strong grip.'

'When was this?'

'Just before the Captain sailed, I think – yes, I remember the weather had just started to turn bad.'

'Who was the lady?'

'That I do know. Lady Diane Lumire. She comes quite a lot – but only in the evening.'

'Does Lady Diane live near here?'

'I never asked. We get people from many places.'

Lyle was already on his feet. 'Thank you, father, you've been most helpful and generous.'

Thomas was ahead of him at the door, Tess not much further behind. Her face was lit up with the sweet, tantalizing prospect of that most magical of wonders, *a clue*. Tate darted between their legs, racing out into the nave of the church. Lyle turned to follow and . . .

'Mister Lyle?'

'Yes?'

'Mister Lyle, you must understand, there are things in men's lives beyond our control. Call it magic, call it God, call it luck, call it fate; we cannot control it, we do not even know what it is. You are already afraid of secrets that you know, the things that you cannot explain or control, the things that come out at you from nowhere and which you have to fight though you cannot explain them or say why you have been chosen. Please understand.'

Lyle hesitated, then nodded. 'Thank you, father. We'll take no more of your time.'

CHAPTER 9

Houses

In a room plush with decadence, a man with auburn eyes, a voice like rich maple syrup and an accent distinctly American, a man who may or may not travel by the name of Ignatius Caryway and may or may not wear a small golden cross on a chain underneath his black shirt, slammed a newspaper down on a nearby table and snapped in a voice slightly louder than usual, 'Henton!'

'Yes, sir?'

'I read that there was another murder in the docks last night.'

'Yes, sir.'

'Of a potential witness?'

'So I hear, sir.'

'I thought you said you were with his grace all last night.'

'I was, sir. Perhaps her ladyship . . .'

'Her ladyship is a child of nature, Henton! She would not understand the sacrifices demanded by the cause.' His voice darkened. '*How* did his grace do it? I saw him kill the captain and the spy . . . but how did he leave in the night and kill that witness? Unless he . . .' The voice trailed away. The auburn eyes widened. 'Where is his grace?'

'In the cellar, father. Hiding from the light.'

'And her ladyship?'

'In her room.'

'Good. Inform me if she leaves it.'

And the man with the eyes that burn with a bright, auburn fervour and who walks with a determined step, stood up, and strode from the room into a long, gloomy corridor, dully illuminated by the occasional candle. His face was set in a cold expression, and his feet clicked on bare stone as he trotted down a flight of stairs, then padded across deep burgundy carpet. As he descended, the air got thicker and colder; his breath steamed. Down he went to the darkest part of the house, where he picked up a lantern glowing feebly by a heavy wooden door, inserted a slim metal key in the lock and turned it. Light crawled weakly from a single high window, forming a small rectangle on the floor. Behind it, in total darkness, a shape, long and wide and powerful, sat utterly still.

'Your grace.'

The shape didn't move.

'Your grace, I trust you are well.'

Something gently raised itself up from its hunched position. Eyes gleamed for a second in the darkness, catching the orange lantern light. 'I was re-examining this city. There are some things you have neglected to say, Father Caryway.' In the tight, claustrophobic darkness, the sound was almost overwhelming.

'Such as?'

'There is a church nearby.'

Did Father Ignatius Caryway feel, just for a second, a moment of fear, or a moment of guilt about the inevitable? Perhaps, but he hid it well behind the lamplight. 'Your grace, I would like to ask you a few questions.' Silence. 'I am looking for the blade.' Silence. 'I found a reference to Selene. The most beautiful woman of her age, they said. Emerald green eyes and a voice like warm marble, cold and passionate all at once. They said she never grew old. There was no mention of the blade.'

'The blade is made of hyresium, the first element formed on this planet. Once, people known as Tseiqin knew how to manipulate it. The knowledge died.'

Ignatius cleared his throat, telling himself he wasn't nervous, though sweat was beginning to gleam on his face. 'You say you have been exploring the city? How, your grace, have you been doing that?'

'The stones are speaking, whispering, frightened. Are you frightened, priest?'

'What are the stones saying?'

No answer. Then a tap, loud and hard, fingers tapping against a rough stone wall. *Tap, tap, tap-a-tap, tap, tap.* 'You wouldn't understand.'

'There was a witness, to when you arrived, and there are people looking . . .'

'I can kill anyone who walks these streets, priest. It is but a thought. I merely choose to wait. The daylight . . . is painful to me. It turns my skin to stone, no one cannot see me for what I am . . . I prefer the night.'

Tap, tap-a-tap, tap, tap-a-tap, tap, tap.

The sound put Ignatius in mind of a rhyme he'd once heard, or possibly a chant, but when he tried to remember it, it seemed to dart out of reach, laughing a child's laugh, and hide in the fog of memory. *Hark, hark* . . .

'You are . . . stronger? I have found more stones, you said that you need stones to control and . . .' Ignatius's voice trailed away.

'I do.' Ignatius swallowed, then immediately wondered why. 'Priest.' The shadow had unfolded itself, risen to its full height. It moved forward. He saw brown eyes, dark skin, dark hair, fine silks cut in an oddly old-fashioned style, to a point where they were almost dramatic costume rather than clothes any more; he felt the shadow fall over him. 'Your grace?' He kept his face straight, his voice steady.

The figure moved towards him, but he held his ground, holding the lantern up at shoulder height. As it neared him, the figure passed through the tiny square of light from the window. Ignatius watched it travel up across his foot, his shin, his knee, and as it moved, the colours of the silk and the tiny hint of skin between trouser and shoe changed, dulled, turned old and hard and grey, and the bend of the joint as the light passed over the knee suddenly seemed old and crooked and stiff, instead of the fluid, powerful movement which had preceded it. The figure stopped, right in front of Ignatius, towering over him. The light fell on half his face, where smooth dark skin shimmered, dulled, drained of colour until it was grey and hard, worn rough with centuries of erosion. His features were frozen, his eye a dull grey fixed point, with just a tiny spot of blackness in the centre. He spoke through one side of his mouth only, the other unable to move, but now his whole shape seemed to vibrate with the sound, ringing out. 'I have eaten the stones of the city, and hear its song. Do not think for a moment, priest, that you have tamed me. You serve me, priest, my purpose and my revenge. I am immortal, I am stone, I am unstoppable and indestructible, *and I cannot be tamed!'*

Now, only now, when it was arguably too late, did Father Ignatius Caryway feel fear.

A hansom cab, rattling through the streets of London.

'Mister Lyle?'

'Yes, Teresa?'

'You gone all quiet, Mister Lyle.'

'Yes, Teresa.'

'You thinkin' bad thoughts, Mister Lyle?'

'Not now, Teresa.'

Tess sighed and turned her head to look out of the window as they passed Regent's Park. 'I got a bad feelin',' she muttered, idly tickling Tate behind the ears. 'It's all goin' to be bad. An' I'm hungry.'

'Miss Teresa,' said Thomas half-laughingly, 'you have a remarkable appetite.'

Tess glared. 'Don't you be rude!' As Thomas recoiled, she turned her glare on Lyle. 'Can we 'ave food now, Mister Lyle?'

'Yes, Teresa,' murmured Lyle absently.

'Lots of food?'

'Yes, Teresa.'

'An' then . . . an' *then* can we go on holiday? Somewhere really far from this place 'cos I got a bad feelin', Mister Lyle, it's all goin' to go really bad.'

'Not now, Teresa.'

She hissed in frustration, put her chin in her hand and stared moodily out of the window again. The cab rattled on in silence. To Thomas, the silence weighed down oppressively, he heard each breath his companions made, each shuffle of Tate's, smelt overwhelmingly the sweaty, dirty, coal-stained stench of the city, the rotting feet and the rotting teeth, heard the cry of the street-sellers and street-walkers and bobbies and thieves and horses and cabbies and felt as if the silence was going to suffocate him.

When Tess spoke again, it was quietly.

'We're bein' followed.'

'Yes, Teresa.' Lyle's voice could have announced a funeral.

'I think we was followed yesterday too. Man in a red scarf. Saw 'im at the docks.'

'Yes, Teresa.'

'He's a good 'un, sly an' all. Thought I saw 'im when I was gettin' coals, even though it ain't no job for no lady . . .'

'In fairness, Miss Teresa, I did the carrying.'

'. . . especially no lady what has to deal with people complai . . . makin' a fuss all the time. Anyhow, I thought he was there then. Tate's been all nervous. Been barkin' lots, like he was upset. Yes you 'ave, 'aven't you, little Tatey-watey, little doggy-woggy, coo-coo . . .'

'Yes, Teresa.'

She glared at Lyle. 'You ain't listenin' to a word I been sayin', 'ave you, Mister Lyle?'

'Whoever's been following us, Teresa, gave Tate a biscuit to stop him barking.'

'He what?' Tess looked outraged. 'Biscuits ain't good for Tate!'

Lyle stared absently into the distance, his voice a monotone. 'There were a few crumbs in Tate's coat – the man clearly broke off a bit of biscuit to give it to Tate, and that left crumbs everywhere. Ginger biscuit, to be exact.'

Contemplative silence. 'Mister Lyle?'

'Yes, Teresa?'

'We don't mind how this biscuit person is followin' us, do we?'

'No.'

'Why not?'

'Because he's probably just one of Lord Lincoln's spies sent to ensure that we're doing our job. And if he's not, then he might be useful in an emergency.'

'How's that?'

'He might know things we don't.'

'An' that's a good thing?'

'It is if we can catch him.'

'Oh.' Tess thought about this. 'So can we eat now, Mister Lyle?'

An almost inaudible sigh. 'Not now, Teresa.'

And just a little bit later: 'Mister Lyle?'

'Yes, Teresa?'

'Why you grinnin' like that?'

'I think I have an idea.'

'Is it a good idea?'

'It needs a few things. Thomas, do you wear anything in particular when you visit relatives?'

'Well, naturally it is necessary to put on a certain polite aspect that I might not otherwise indulge in when –'

'Good. We'll get you something formal to wear, and I'll get my gloves and coat, and Teresa . . .'

'I ain't likin' your grin, Mister Lyle. Please stop.'

'Teresa, we're getting you a *dress*.' The evil relish with which Lyle made this announcement was matched only by Tess's cry of dismay.

The hansom cab stopped in front of Lyle's house. At the door Lyle reached into his pocket, pulled out a key, slipped it into the lock – and stopped. He leant in towards the door, squinting at the frame, and the wood around the keyhole. Then sighed ever so slightly, unlocked the door and stepped cautiously inside.

A man was hanging, suspended upside-down by his ankles in the hallway, face bright red. Lyle peered up at his features and said brightly, 'Good morning, sir. May I be of assistance?'

The man gulped. 'Jolly decent of you.'

'Now, it seems to me that you've been caught in a thoroughly traditional fowl trap of the kind laid down by people who don't like their homes being broken into . . .' His face fell, and his voice became laced with a theatrical sadness. 'Oh *dear*. You didn't . . . I mean, surely a decent man like yourself wouldn't try to break into this house, would you? I'm sure there's been a terrible misunderstanding. I mean, you could have been killed by

126

the acid in the lock or the bear trap in the cupboard or the steps that fold up beneath you if you haven't reset the gears, or the deadly falling spikes that I've always considered installing in order to test the relationship between downward velocity, changing force over time, a very little time, and pressure on a point. Tell me,' Lyle's face radiated concern, 'how do you feel about *voltage*?'

Below, a long way below, Tess bounced up and down excitedly. 'Poke him with a stick, Mister Lyle, poke him with a stick!'

'Shall I inform the police?' hazarded Thomas.

'That,' said an icy, calm voice, 'will not be necessary.'

Lord Lincoln detached himself from the shadows. Lyle's face slipped almost unnoticeably into an uninterested expression, and his voice became dead and cold as, without taking his eyes off Lord Lincoln, he murmured, 'Teresa, take a couple of shillings, take Thomas, and go and find something to eat. Thomas, make sure it's something reasonably healthy. We could be here a while.'

CHAPTER 10

Honesty

Lord Lincoln deposited himself in Lyle's armchair by the fire without saying a word or glancing at Lyle. He set his hat on top of a pile of books, put his feet up on a table laden with springs and cogs, leaned his head back and stared thoughtfully at the ceiling. Lyle stood in front of him and tried not to let his anger show.

'You broke into my house,' he said finally.

'You were out. I had hoped to find you earlier, but there have been incidents.'

'What sort of incidents?'

'A stonemason has been murdered, a quantity of stone stolen.'

'This is an incident to *you*?'

'Is it not to you?'

'Of course it is! But I . . .'

'You what, Mister Lyle? You have sentiments regarding murder that I do not, perhaps? Or you know things that I should? Or some other thing that separates who you are from who I am, maybe?'

Lyle scowled and said nothing. The room seemed like a place that was very much lived in and possibly loved, not as an ordinary room fit for dinner or receiving guests, but as somewhere to find another book, or to put another design that went wrong, and tinker with it late at night by the fireside. Much of Lyle's house had that feel. But the firelight did nothing to warm the look in Lincoln's eye.

The two men waited in silence, each daring the other to speak first. Sounds outside grew louder. The grandfather clock ticking in the hall. A cab rattling far off. Snow sliding down the roof where a pigeon stirred. The clop of horses' hooves. The *click, click* of iron heavy with icicles, trying to work out whether it wants to contract in the snow and the ice and the rising fog. The rattle of the dust cart, cough of the coalman. The bark of a dog somewhere behind the houses.

For a second, Lyle was reminded of a rhythm, a chant he'd heard a long time in his youth, a little rhythm, *dum, dum, de-dum, dum, dum.*

'Mister Lyle.'

He hardly heard Lincoln speak. *Hark, hark, the dogs do bark . . .*

'Lyle!'

His attention snapped back. 'Yes? . . . My lord?' he added through gritted teeth.

'I await your report on the progress of the investigation.'

'Do you want the hard facts or the blind assumptions?'

'I know the facts, Mister Lyle. Even the police know the facts; those are hardly what concern me. What have you deduced?'

'That Fabrio and Stanlaw were murdered by a man kept imprisoned in a stone coffin, the same man Fabrio was paid by a Roman Catholic priest to collect from an Italian monastery, a giant man. And that someone associated with this man, this passenger, this murderer, has now killed a potential witness.'

'Not the same person?'

'No. The murderer whom Fabrio was transporting was right-handed. The person who killed Mrs Milner was left-handed.'

'And the other witness? Where is he?'

'I don't know.'

'Perhaps you should find out? Could this be a clever way of misdirecting our attentions?'

'I doubt it. Why are you so hopeful that it is?'

The brief flash on Lincoln's face disappeared. 'Merely hypothesizing. I'm surprised that you have to enquire.'

Lyle scowled. 'Listen, I'm going to say this just once, because I might not be angry enough to say it again, so I don't want to miss the opportunity. You are a scheming, manipulative liar, who recklessly uses lives for a cause you won't reveal and that you may have killed for. Now people are dying and I don't trust you far enough to want to set a foot out of this house until I know whatever it is you're not telling me, *now*. Because last time I trusted you, people died, *I* nearly died, the *children* were put through things that no child should ever have to experience, so if you don't tell me this instant what you're hiding, I swear I will never help you again. And I will do everything in my power to see you exposed as the bucket of effluence that you are.'

Lord Lincoln thought about it, staring up at the ceiling. 'Yes,' he said finally.

'And don't try to threaten me,' added Lyle, 'because – what?'

'I said, yes.'

Astonishment blazed on Lyle's face. 'Really?'

'I have been unwise in keeping you from the truth of the matter.'

Lyle thought about this, then, just to make sure he heard right, '*Really?*'

'Absolutely.'

'Then . . . ?'

'The truth,' said Lincoln, stretching easily, 'is that I was informed that a dangerous murderer had been freed from a prison in Italy and was on the way to London, under lock and key in the hold of the *Pegasus*, with the intention of wreaking havoc in the city. I did not know how he had been freed, but I assume an inside source must have helped him for their own malign purpose, and I had no intention of letting him loose on this city. Sadly, my agent, Stanlaw, was murdered before he could prevent the killer's release.'

Lyle sat down heavily. In a suspicious voice he said, 'Did I . . . just call you a bucket of effluence, my lord?'

'I believe that was the phrase.'

'Oh.' Lyle thought about it. 'Are you sure?'

'About what?'

'Truth, honesty, effluence, full and frank disclosure, that kind of thing?' Lord Lincoln's glare could have frozen salt water. Lyle shifted uncomfortably. 'Tell me about Isalia.'

Lincoln sat forward, smiling so widely that Lyle almost jumped out of his seat again. 'How much do you know?'

'Oh nonononono! We're not playing the game where I tell you the extent of my ignorance so that you can give me as little information as possible! Let's assume I know everything there is possibly to know, and this is merely a test of your new-found openness.'

To his surprise, Lord Lincoln smiled. It was like having a skeletal hand dance across Lyle's spine. 'Isalia was, I believe, where the Pope used to hold his most sacred Masses, so that no one could steal their divine music, in the days when the Church felt strongly about such things. A place of arts and culture. Since then, of course, it has declined with the times. We are no longer a world of hidden Masses, we are a world of thick smoke hiding the future, of a past shrunk by the sheer volume of events of today. In the past, kings going to war would have to wait three months for the messenger to cross the mountains before they could raise their army, then more months to march the troops across continents, then more months again for the next assignment of arrows and then more months for the engineers to find a way to break the city walls, and only then would they realize that the shot didn't fit the cannon . . . and so on. Today, the world is a busy place – even for someone like you, I imagine. Isalia is a place of the past. Where the past is locked up and kept from the sight of people, in case they remember it.'

'As cryptic as it is unhelpful.'

'Simply? It's where the things are stored which some people

call legend and which we want eventually to become nothing more than a myth, so that their reality cannot taint the future. It's where the murderer was kept. He was too dangerous to be held anywhere else. And now he is out.'

'Why is he so dangerous?'

'You have seen his passage already.'

'I've seen signs of a strong, large man who kills without qualm; not a world-shattering threat to peace and prosperity, just another waste.'

Lincoln shook his head, smiling ever so slightly. 'Lyle, you have seen the coffin that held him. And I see from your face that you observed the most obvious feature.'

Lyle nodded, the colour draining from his face. 'There were nail marks inside, new, not oxidized; someone had been trapped in there during the journey. And . . .' He didn't finish the sentence. He looked away from Lincoln's bright, cold eyes. *And there weren't any air holes.*

'Who is he?' Lyle's voice was low and tight.

'He is a marquis, although he wasn't always. His name is Lucan Sasso. He used to roam Europe in search of drink, gambling and women. He has left illegitimate heirs across the continent. Rumour, though usually not trustworthy, has it that he fell in love one day with a woman he could not have; a lady called Selene. We don't know anything more about her. She taught him blood lust and vengeance. She encouraged him, and then on a winter's night in London, rejected him and disappeared for ever. In his anger, he swore revenge, went on a casual killing spree, and finally stabbed himself by the river with the first thing she'd gifted to him: a peculiar stone blade of unknown origin.'

'He stabbed himself?'

'Yes.'

'I take it he recovered.'

'In a manner. The Church took him in, and has kept him ever since. Consequently, he hates it, and he hates this city, and has sworn revenge on it and on its people.'

'And Selene?'

'Disappeared.'

'I see.' Lyle shifted uncomfortably. 'Stone blades of unknown origin . . . it'd be too much to hope that this was one of those stone blades that did nothing of any interest whatsoever, wouldn't it?'

'Quite possibly.'

'And this lady . . . Selene . . . she's not . . .' Lyle flapped his hands uselessly around his head. 'You know . . . one of . . . of *them*, is she?'

'Them?'

'You know. Them. They. Them with the Plan. Them who do things that only they could do with . . . things.'

'I honestly don't know.'

'Oh.' Lyle found himself feeling embarrassed, and looked away. 'Right.'

Lord Lincoln cleared his throat meaningfully. 'Now . . . the fruits of your investigation?'

Lyle sighed, and answered in a matter-of-fact voice: 'Ignatius Caryway. Catholic priest, American, which seems somehow inevitable really, got Sasso off Isalia in the ship of Captain Fabrio.'

'That makes sense. The abbot wouldn't have suspected one of his own. What more?'

'This Ignatius had paid Fabrio richly to accompany the Marquis from Isalia, and transport him safely. On arrival, Ignatius was supposed to collect the coffin unopened from Fabrio, but on seeing Stanlaw with the Captain, went instead to the ship and freed the Marquis then and there. This Lucan Sasso killed the Captain and Stanlaw and left with Ignatius. At least, that's how it looks. There's not a shred of evidence that would hold up in any decent court, but thankfully,' Lyle grinned a wicked grin, 'you want neither a court nor decency, do you, Lord Lincoln?'

'What about the witnesses? Milner? The beggar?'

'Murdered by someone of the same immense strength and ruthlessness as possessed by Sasso, but left-handed, not right-handed. I don't know where Edgar is.'

'Do you have any idea where Sasso or Caryway are now?'

'First . . . tell me about this.' Lyle pulled Stanlaw's small iron ring out of his pocket. 'What's the significance of the cogs, the clock face?'

Lincoln hardly glanced at it. 'Nothing. I've never seen it before.'

Lyle grinned. 'That, my lord, was as big a lie as Napoleon's declaration in favour of republicanism.'

'Do you know where Sasso is?'

Lyle scratched his chin, rubbed his nose, tickled his forehead, then nodded. 'Yes. I think so.'

Lincoln sat back, face set in ice. 'But you are refusing to tell me.'

'Uh . . . yes.'

'Why?'

'I think the answer would be more polite from the man in the burgundy scarf who is following me.' For a second, there was a flicker on Lincoln's face, a moment of doubt. Lyle frowned, seeing something there he hadn't expected. 'Good grief,' he murmured. 'It's not you, is it?'

'I do not know to what you are referring, Mister Lyle.'

'There's . . . something . . . you're not telling me, and . . .' Lyle scowled. 'Why are you so afraid of a murderer? There are . . . parts . . . the blade, that's . . . part . . .' He frowned. His fingers had started tapping idly on the table next to him, a little sharp rhythm, that had just slipped in, as if it had been floating through the air, *Hark, hark* . . .

'You said . . . he recovered "in a manner". What does that mean?'

When Lincoln didn't answer, Lyle looked up, and found himself the object of the other man's steely, unblinking gaze.

'That, Mister Lyle, is something you must answer for yourself.'

CHAPTER 11

Diane

'Where's the evil bigwig?'

'Gone, Teresa.'

'You want cake?'

'You got *cake*? I thought I said to get something healthy . . .'

'Thomas wanted to, but when he went and looked in his pocket it seemed how he'd lost all his money . . .'

'Mister Lyle, I think that Miss Teresa actually might have *pickpock*—'

'It's got treacle in it, Mister Lyle.'

'Treacle? Really?'

'But Mister Lyle, Miss Teresa *stole* –'

'Not now, Thomas.' There was a strange slurping noise. It

was the sound made by a proud man trying to eat hot treacle cake in a dignified manner, and failing. It required a respectful silence.

When the last traces of treacle had been mopped away, Tess said, 'What we doin' now?'

'Looking for Lady Diane Lumire, companion to Ignatius Caryway and quite possibly conspirator to protect a murderer from the course of justice. At least, that's what you're doing. I'm going to find Edgar.'

'Oh. Is that good?'

'It's why you're going to wear a dress, Teresa. And . . . Teresa?'

'Yes, Mister Lyle?'

'I couldn't help notice how Thomas left some of his money on the kitchen table a few days ago.'

'But I didn't . . .' began Thomas. 'Ow!'

'Sorry, lad, was that your knee? Tess – perhaps you could go and get Thomas's money for him?'

'Yes, Mister Lyle.'

Five in the afternoon. The snow had been squashed by too many feet, and frozen as a deadly black slick across every street and between every cobble. People weren't bothering with the bridges across the river, but just walked straight across the ice, enjoying the novelty. The fog was rising again, so heavy with suspended ice that people breathed through their scarves to stop the cold searing their lungs. The lamplighters had almost considered giving up – even if they could find the lamps, it was question-able whether their light would be seen. Each man, woman and child looked for a taper or a lantern to carry through the streets, as the dark settled again, promising a long night to come.

And at one house overlooking the city, the doorbell was ringing. The man who answered it was a new employee, and though he had come from the highly respectable Norfolk Club with excellent references, he was still finding his feet. He didn't really deserve what life had in store for him.

The door opened. Mr Cartiledge looked out and saw no one. He heard an embarrassed cough at knee-height. 'Yes, miss? May I assist you?'

In the face that looked up at him, angelic light shone out from the deep brown eyes above a neat little blue dress. It somehow said, 'Here be innocent charm; love it well.'

The high-pitched voice spoke slowly, as if its owner was concentrating hard on how every syllable sounded. 'Oh good sir, I hope I ain . . . have not disturbed you but I was looking for my uncle. Is he home?'

'Forgive me, miss, but who are you?'

'Why, how dare you say something like that! Can you not recognize Lady Teresa of . . . America? Yes, that's right. Lady Teresa of America!'

The disbelieving look that Cartiledge had spent many years repressing slid back across his features. 'Of . . . North America?' hazarded the girl. Aware that she was losing the initiative she said in a louder voice, 'Anyway, I'm looking for Uncle Ignatius so I can give him this lovely bunch of flowers and tell him about Mummy.' For a second, Cartiledge thought he saw a scowl and almost heard a cynical lilt in her words. But then the almost-but-not-quite angelic smile washed back over her.

'I'm sorry, miss; who did you say your uncle was?'

'Good old Uncle Ignatius Caryway.' Her face fell. 'Please, sir, I've come such an awful long way to see him, and I'm just a poor little girl, cruelly neglected by my family, and I'm so hungry and really . . . really . . .' a tear welled in her eye '. . . miss my uncle.' At which Teresa Hatch dropped her flowers and collapsed in tears at Cartiledge's feet.

At roughly the same time that Teresa Hatch was practising good elocution and better manners, Horatio Lyle stood shivering outside a warehouse by the Amber Wharves, where the busy streets were too narrow for even the smallest of carts to squeeze through. Snow had started to fall, and a cheerful demeanour was not enough to compensate for the grating cold. As he watched the street, he sang under his breath,

London's burning, London's burning,
Fetch the engines, fetch the engines,
Fire, fire! Fire, fire!
Pour on water, pour on water!

He was aware of another figure lingering in the cold. Even though the figure kept itself well out of his line of sight, in the air he could see a regular puffing of breath from someone just around the corner, who hadn't moved for as long as Lyle himself hadn't.

He felt a little guilty at sending the children off alone to the mansions in Hampstead; but, he told himself, better there than here.

Lyle detached himself from the wall where he'd been leaning and started walking again, flapping his arms across each other like a startled chicken to get some heat back into his limbs. He rounded a corner into a crowded, slightly wider street, towered over by cranes and warehouses; boxes and bundles swung through the air overhead. A costermonger selling brown paper bagfuls of sugar pawed at Lyle's arm.

Lyle bought a bag, paid a shilling extra and said, 'I'm looking for the beggar man Edgar. Have you seen him?'

'Push off, copper.'

Lyle stood up straighter and snapped in his officious voice, 'I say, what's this then? You call that weight a pound, it looks more like an ounce to me. Let's have a feel – wouldn't be measuring crooked, would you, not a fine, upstanding, law-abiding, help-ful, I'm thinking about *helpful* here as one of several trouble-avoiding characteristics, citizen such as yourself?'

The costermonger, who was a bright lad, sucked at his teeth. 'Uh . . . Edgar . . . short cove, old, picks as many pockets with his prattle as he does with his hands, that Edgar, maybe?'

'Could be.'

'Ain't seen him all day.' The costermonger turned to go, but found his path impeded by Lyle's boot, and a heavy hand on his arm.

'But if you were Edgar, and you felt nervous, where would you go?'

Tate was snoring. It was spectacular. The snore started at the tip of his nose, which vibrated hugely like a spring in tension, then spread, rippling wave-like down his ears and back again, humming through his paws and all the way to the tip of his tail, which rose up, twitched, and relaxed again with each deep snore.

Thomas sat in the back of a hansom cab, Tate snuggled protectively beneath his outstretched feet, and worried. It was something he was good at, inherited mostly from his mother, as his father had never felt anything in his life more than mild irritation at the consternation of being. Every now and then he glanced out of the window towards Hampstead Hill, whose mansions, comfortably above the smoke line, looked down on the city; and he worried. Thomas felt that he, not Tess, should have been the one to go up to one of those grand houses to ask about Diane Lumire; he worried too because Mister Lyle was somewhere down in the docks looking for Edgar. He worried because his parents would be back from the countryside any one of these days and they'd start asking where he'd been and why he didn't know the ancient Greek for 'anthropomorphic'; he worried because he knew Mrs Milner had died, having secretly read the papers Lyle had been trying to hide just after breakfast; he realized there were Things Going On that he didn't know about; and he worried anyway because that was what Thomas did. He tried to think of Queen and Country in an attempt to calm himself down, but, unusually, it didn't work. Under his breath he tried singing a few bars of a patriotic hymn, but found the words getting jumbled. He tried to think about anything that didn't involve worry and, for a moment, imagined that he saw the world stretched out, the clouds all below him, his worries flown, snatched away by the speeding wind that held him up.

Thomas let out a sigh, and leant back into his seat. It was going to be a long night.

There was a workshop by the river, to the south of Limehouse with its workers' clubs and belching factories, with shuttered doors and nailed-up windows, waiting to be purchased and rebuilt. Once upon a time, it had produced sloops for the navy and merchantmen making the short hop across to Holland or the French ports, but in recent years it had found itself challenged by the trend in giant metal behemoths burning coal and churning giant wheels for propulsion; so after almost two hundred years of construction, its owners had put out the lights and shut down. Rot had set into the floors, now held in place only by the ice that had frozen the planks solid, so that when Lyle made his cautious entry through a broken window his feet immediately slipped out from under him and flew upwards, depositing him on his back with the acrobatic grace of a drunken elephant.

He staggered up with as much dignity as he could manage, and shuffled his way across the floor. Between the shattered floorboards, he could see dim light reflecting off thin ice over black water, while the floor groaned under his weight.

'Hello? Edgar? Edgar, it's Mister Lyle, are you in here?'

A faint sound over his head, a thud like something heavy falling a long way off. 'Edgar? It's Mister Lyle, the nice gentleman with the available money and tactful sense of compromise?'

He saw a staircase, looking as if most of it had been used for firewood, and edged towards it. 'I'm coming up!' he called, then under his breath added, 'God help us.'

At the foot of the staircase he heard a sudden outbreak of

noise, like a stone roof falling a piece at a time on to a pile of percussion instruments, and pulled himself up the staircase, clinging for support to the open top of the floor above.

The watery evening light trickled through the broken windows, past the ashes of a small fire that could have been made of the defrosted floorboards themselves, past a small pot of solidified porridge, past the padded boots of old Edgar, up his arm to his face. It was turned towards Lyle, with accusing pale eyes, unblinking like a fish.

Lyle crawled up on to the floor, edged towards Edgar, and felt along his white, twisted throat for a pulse. The skin was cold, rapidly dropping to room temperature. He sat back and looked around, feeling his stomach begin to turn and his hands to itch, the cold suddenly a thing coming from inside his bones.

A shadow moved behind him. Lyle twisted round to where it had been. But the shape that had been caught in the light, swathed in a black coat, was already bounding back down the stairs. Lyle sprang up and threw himself after it, now blind to the weakness of the floor. He heard its footsteps hammering, the wood beneath it bending, creaking and splintering as though made by not one person but twenty; in comparison his own hurried footsteps were a quiet afterthought. At the bottom of the stairs he turned, saw a figure slipping out through the broken window where he'd come in, and raced after it, ducking through the frame and out into the dull light of the wharf. The shape ran towards the river, moving with a slight stiffness, as if finding it hard to drag the weight of its own limbs.

Lyle shouted, with a sense of futility even as he did, 'Stop! Police!' and was unsurprised when no one, not even the dock hands in the street behind, stopped. '*Right,*' he hissed, and ran on. As he followed the figure towards the river the wooden walkway along the side of the workhouse became more ruinous, supported on a few struts sticking up from the frozen green mud of low tide. Swinging round a corner he saw the figure leap off the walkway on to the bed of the Thames far below, as if making the gentlest bunny hop, and heard the shattering of ice.

Lyle peered down, and made out the shape darting under the shadow of the walkway and into the mess of wooden struts and pillars, and frozen mud banks smelling of rot beneath the dock-side buildings. Black water crawled through the shattered indent in the ice where it had landed. He cursed, slithered down off the edge of the walkway until he hung by his fingertips, and let go, feet sliding from beneath him as he dropped on to the ice. Getting back up was like catching a giant wet bar of soap while covered in grease; then keeping his balance was like trying to cycle with a cat on one handlebar, and a giraffe on the other. Lyle made for the support of a pillar and looked around for the figure.

He saw a black coat lying on the ice and slithered towards it. It was heavy, lined with red silk, and had the shortness and tight waist of a lady's garment. The pockets were empty. He let it drop and turned to look for the figure.

Something caught his eye, standing on the ice, in a last out-break of sunlight.

Lyle edged towards it.

The thing was a head shorter than him, off-white, and cold to the touch. One arm was raised in the direction of the sun, shield-ing its closed stone eyes; the other was stretched to one side as if to keep the thing's balance. It was the statue of a fashionably dressed woman, with a tight face, all bones and skin, set in a cruel little smile. Lyle made his way past it, into the shadow of the wharves, then out on to the ice of the river itself, where the narrow passage of open water was shrinking almost visibly in the cold.

There was no sign of the fleeing figure. Lyle edged back into the shadows of the wharf, and knelt again by the coat, rummaging once more through its pockets, as much for something to do as in the hope of finding anything. All the while his mind raced. He was being, he felt fairly sure, stupid. Something obvious was happening, and he was refusing, without his knowing, *refusing* to see what it could be.

Lyle reached a decision. It was, he knew, totally irrational, but he had to check. He got up and slithered his way back towards the marble statue of the woman, standing in pale sunlight on the ice.

To where the marble statue of the woman had been. To where the marble statue wasn't standing any more.

Horatio Lyle turned this way and that, mouth opening and closing in surprise and dismay. He stopped, controlled himself, and tried to think logical, sensible thoughts, while the sun crawled its way beneath the smoke-drowned horizon, and the body of old dead Edgar, in the abandoned building above, slowly dropped to the temperature of its surroundings.

Thomas woke, and immediately felt guilty, but that was normal: he felt guilty about most things all the time. That was fine; guilt was all part of responsibility, he told himself. He became aware of the cold, pouring through the cab like rising night-time fog. Then he felt a momentary spurt of fear, slow to arrive as the brain suddenly questioned what on earth he was doing here anyway, with Tate snoring peacefully under his feet, outside another mansion on another street that, in this part of town, looked like all the rest.

Fear briefly flared into terror as he realized he was not alone. A shape sat by him, a large hat pulled down over its eyes, hands buried under its armpits, legs crossed and stretched out in front of it, breathing low and steady. Thomas gave an instinctive 'Eek!' making both him and the figure jump.

Mister Lyle woke up. 'What? Who?' He saw Thomas, and relaxed. 'Oh. What is it?'

'Mister Lyle!' Thomas squeaked.

'Yes?'

'You're . . . *here*?'

'Yes?'

'Erm . . . when did you get here?'

'About half an hour ago.'

'And was your visit to the docks successful?'

A flicker on Lyle's face, the slightest hesitation. 'I . . . didn't find Edgar, I'm afraid.'

Thomas opened his mouth to speak, then noticed something in Lyle's face and voice that made him reconsider.

Lyle checked the watch in his pocket. 'Past your bedtime. Where's Tess?'

There was a sound outside. A crunching of snow underfoot and a hasty pounding of footsteps, then a shadow moved in the fog. A second later Tess's shining red face appeared in the cab doorway. 'Coo-eee! Mister Lyle! You back from the docks then?'

'Yes, Teresa,' said Lyle as she climbed inside, feet stepping on feet with blind carelessness. 'And how has your day been? Was this house of any use in finding Lady Lumire?'

'It were all right,' she said, opening up a bundle on her lap. 'An' the one before. There was this man what was called Cartil . . . there was this butler-type person an' he said how I was a "poor neglected waif" an' how I clearly weren't looked after right an' . . .'

'Did you get anything useful?' said Lyle impatiently.

'I got,' Tess examined her bundle, 'three apples, a loaf of hot bread, a packet of tea, four shillings, half a plum pudding, half a bottle of brandy an' a pair of woolly socks.'

'I'll take the brandy,' said Lyle, grabbing it. 'You never know when ethyl alcohol will come in handy.'

Tess stared at him with the look of one on the edge of a profound revelation. 'Mister Lyle, you ain't never been normal, 'ave you?'

'Teresa, haven't I always taught you that generalizations within a subjective group context can never be accepted as theory? I suppose we'll have to try the next mansion and –'

'She ain't there.'

'Pardon?'

Tess was halfway through the plum pudding. 'This Diane Lumire lady ain't there. The butler said how she'd recently moved into this big house up on the hill after the old owner got arrested for conspir . . . for stuff, an' how she'd sent a card round introducing herself as the new bigwig an' he gave it to me 'cos *his* bigwigs were going to go an' meet this lady person tonight at this big gathering for bigwigs, but how they're off in this place what has lotsa things with big ... goes on the head, all pointy ...'

'Horns?'

'Yes, them with them horns.'

'Deer?'

Tess bounced up and down. 'Of course it's deer, nitwit! I just said, didn't I?'

'Teresa,' said Lyle in a voice so reasonable it crackled round the edges, 'I appreciate the effort you've been to and accept that you really are a wonderful ... character ... but you're also heading for a thick ear. *Did he know which house?*'

'He gave me a *map*,' said Tess smugly. 'But I ain't givin' it until we talk about how I'm all neglected an' how dom ... domes ... home violence ain't the right way in how you should ...'

'Teresa!' barked Lyle.

She didn't even blink. '... 'cos you know you're my favourite not-normal person ever, Mister Lyle, an' I've always looked up to you 'cos of the science and the thinkin' thing an' here you go, Mister Lyle. Hope it's all right an' all.' A thought struck her. 'You find that Edgar bloke what was in the docks?'

'He's all right, Teresa,' said Lyle, not quite meeting her or Thomas's eye, and there it was, the sick feeling in Thomas's stomach. 'He's ... got nothing to worry about, I think. Just a false alarm.'

He turned to study Tess's map, with a look of forced concentration. His eyes widened even as his eyebrows sank.

Thomas saw his expression. 'Is something the matter, sir?'

'I think I know this house.'

'Sir?'

Lyle shook his head. 'Let's get there and see if I'm right before we start worrying, shall we?'

They got there.

Lyle was right.

The mansion was part of a new terrace of grand white houses, each one no longer than London Bridge and no higher than All Saints' Church. Lights flooded out of each high window, leading on to a green area of pond-dotted grass, separated only from the mansions by the sparkling new cobbled street, as white and polished and grand as the new mansions themselves and the doors . . .

'We been here before, ain't we, Mister Lyle?' said Tess, a note of trepidation entering her voice. They surveyed the carriages moving outside the pillared monster. Lyle was quiet and tense. Thomas had turned pale, recognizing each stone and step, and fearing it more than he dared say.

'Mister Lyle?'

'Yes we have, Teresa.' Lyle's voice was reassuring, though his face was pale. Almost to himself, he muttered, 'It's at times like these that a decent sceptic begins to question his lot. They raise all kinds of interesting questions about probability against unpredictable malign forces.'

'It's Moncorvo's mansion.' Thomas shuffled uncomfortably, memories rising in a sickening tide, things he'd managed to forget or tune down, irrationalities he'd managed to rationalize, coming back to haunt him. He remembered bright green eyes, he remembered running, he remembered seeing the storm and the figure fall from the dome of the cathedral and . . .

'This ain't the right address, is it?' said Tess edgily.

'It is. It makes sense in a way: a fine address on the borders of Hampstead Heath, the previous owner mysteriously carted away, property up for sale . . .' Lyle's voice had the nervous edge of someone trying to convince himself and failing.

'But . . . the bigwig . . . what was *evil* an' did all the things with the stone thing what weren't proper stone but was all evil an' . . . an' he lived here!'

'Probably a coincidence,' said Lyle, smiling reassuringly, but speaking just a bit too loudly. Thomas glanced at him, and for a second, just a second, saw the lie behind Lyle's eyes, and the sidling fear that sometimes – rarely – raised its head from behind Lyle's determined scientific objectivity.

'Let's find out, shall we?'

CHAPTER 12

Mansion

A brief view of a house, back to front, eight p.m., winter.

Back, carriages being driven out of the rain, horses neighing, hooves stamping on cobbles, servants bustling, this bag there, that coach here, who's seen Ellen, why's Ellen never where she ought to be, snow thick on cobbles and disturbed by footsteps, baskets of fruit and food frozen in the cold, back door open, blast of hot air to pass inside, corridor, long, gloomy, kitchen white with suspended flour drifting through the air, stoves black and belching with their labours, chimney newly cleaned (the boy didn't fall this time), washing area, buckets from the pump: best to boil the water first, don't want madam's white silk to come out Thames brown; stairs up, doors opening, doors closing, thick carpet, huge paintings of heroic figures across wind-swept land-scapes (no relation, came with the house), bustling noise, darling, welcome, welcome, do tell me all, was the dance really *that* ghastly? Candles everywhere, although, darling, I hear that there's this wonderful little man researching something called a *bulb*, fuelled by *electricity*, white gloves on white hand, turn up the lamp James, do you smell gas, let the servants sort it out, up again, lay the table for dinner, silver and glass, see how it gleams and sparkles, snow piles up against the glass outside, trying to get in, a thousand cold, delicate crystal moths drawn to a hundred burning flames, race down the corridor, ever a-ringing, come to her ladyship's dance, and pull back the giant double doors and bow and straighten politely and prepare to take the coat and . . .

'Welcome, my lord, to her . . . Oh. Good evening, sir. May we help you?'

Thomas swept in. 'Well, you may take my coat, naturally; careful, *don't* crease it, and my hat, oh – and do ensure that you keep it separate from the other hats. I don't want it picking up dust. Has my family arrived yet? I was told that dinner tonight was to be rather swimming.'

'Are you here for her ladyship's gathering, or is it a private visit, sir?'

'How dare you address me in that impertinent manner? Don't you know who I am?'

'Forgive me, sir.'

'I am Thomas Edward Elwick, son and heir of Lord Thomas Henry Elwick, Order of the Magpie, Cross of the Sallow Oak, Knight of the Daffodil, and I am here to partake of her lady-ship's most humble hospitality. *Now* do you know me?'

'Why, yes, sir. Forgive me, I had no idea that . . .'

'Well, then, *announce* me. Oh, and show my man where to put my belongings.'

A man, much taller than Thomas, standing behind him, touches his forelock respectfully. He's holding a single, small bag that looks like no kind of lordly belongings that the butler has seen before and contains more lumps and bulges than can be comfortably conceived. As the butler watches, one of the bulges moves. He looks up in slow horror to the grey eyes of the servant man, who grins a bright, nervous grin.

The butler opens his mouth to speak, and . . .

'Well, are you made of stone? My God, if my father were here he'd have lost his patience already; the army, you know, trains a man how to appreciate the good and the bad among the lower orders, distinguish between those who work to become more than they were and those who are, frankly, sir, idlers!'

'Yes, my lord.'

'Well, then? What *are* you waiting for?'

Thomas's highly bred rudeness was too practised to be ignored. The unfortunate butler's heels practically snapped together as he stood to attention and said in a rapid monotone passed on from perfectly nice butler if only you get to know him to the next perfectly nice butler, generation after generation, 'Yes, my lord. Please, follow me.'

Thomas radiated well-bred insufferability as he swept down the hall of the house of Lady Diane Lumire, and into a party.

As the butler's distant voice rang out with the promptness of someone who knows he's just met power and money and is never going to have any of it, 'His lordship, Thomas Edward

Elwick . . .' Lyle moved away, walking the walk of someone who has every right to be where he is, and tried not to smile.

And somewhere near by, more floors up than would please the vertigo-struck but not quite high enough to escape the enveloping fog, in a darkened room something very quietly goes *click*.

Silence. A shadow flashes across a large four-paned window, but there is so little light from outside that the shadow isn't so much a darkening across the floor as a mere bending of the blackness that is already there; sensed, rather than seen.

There is a slow, gentle *whumph*. The window, which was shut, now opens, almost as if of its own accord. Fog hungrily trickles in, keen to explore this new and exciting place where a tiny tendril of warmth yet clings. Something slips in with it, landing soundlessly on the carpet below the window, and quickly closes the window again, sliding the catch back with another gentle *click*.

Out in the corridor, footsteps quickly pass and fade, along with a little hummed tune, sung without any particular melody or reason. '"*Oranges and lemons,*" *say the bells of St Clement's* . . .'

The shadow drifts across the floor, past the foot of a neatly made but empty bed, turns a brass door-handle and peers cautiously out into the corridor one way, then the other. The singer disappears down the stairs at the end of the hall, and stillness settles. The door is very cautiously opened, and Tess slides out into the gloom, face tight with concentration, utterly silent. She passes down the corridor, trying each door-handle, until she finds one which doesn't open. Peering at the lock, she feels in her pockets.

There is a faint sound at the end of the corridor. 'Well, since I don't do the linen cycle I hardly see how you can blame . . .'

Tess finds a slim pair of lock picks and slides them into the lock.

The voices drift nearer, and now there are footsteps shuffling along the carpet. '. . . after all, I do all the locking and all the candles every night, it's Mildred who has to make sure that the beds are . . .'

The lock gives a faint, very faint, *click*, and Tess wiggles the lock picks with more urgency.

'. . . although I suppose that since her ladyship isn't that picky about her room it's not too much to put . . .'

Tess jiggles the picks, glancing round now from side to side in trepidation, the dim orange gaslight across her face competing in her field of view with the blacker shadows.

The servant rounds the corner, and looks down the corridor.

'Who the hell are you?'

The voice was rich, imperious, deep and immediately made Lyle want to throw himself on to the floor and beg for mercy. He'd been drifting through the servants' quarters, peering through open doors and listening to chit-chat. He wasn't sure what he was looking for, but was hoping something interesting would slip into his path. What had slipped into his path, almost inexorably, had been the basement kitchens, and, moreover, their formidable mistress. He managed to stiffen his knees before they jellified, stood up a little straighter, cleared his throat and said, wishing he was quite as good as Thomas at radiating pomposity, 'Lord Elwick's man, ma'am.'

The woman who'd spoken was about Lyle's age, though

somehow he felt immediately humbled before her. She wore a flour-covered apron, had white sleeves rolled up almost to the armpits, and carried a rolling pin upright in one hand in the casual manner of someone who spends most of their days hitting squidgy things with hard objects. She looked Lyle over with suspicious grey eyes. 'You don't look like a servant from a family as well renowned as the Elwicks.'

Lyle looked down at his snow-dusted coat and single travel bag. 'I'm . . . neglected?' he hazarded.

'What's your master's name again?'

Lyle felt ready for this. 'Thomas Edward Elwick, ma'am, only son of Thomas Henry Elwick.'

'And Lord Elwick . . . what's he like?'

Lyle felt a suspicion of his own creep in. 'You've . . . worked for his lordship, have you?'

'Might've,' the cook snapped back.

'Well, then, ma'am . . . Lord Elwick is an intellectual buffoon with no sense of curiosity or wonder in any bone in his body. If only the world followed the pattern laid down by certain Eastern mythologies, he would be reincarnated in his next life as a particularly stupid broom handle, but is far more likely to be reborn as one of his stupid hounds. And his son, may I add, is thoroughly neglected, bordering on emotionally stunted, and it's an incredibly noble and hardy achievement of any man to look after him, despite his obvious, if untrained, scientific potential and a certain confused power of perception.'

Lyle realized that not only the formidable cook, but also half the kitchen were staring at him. He smiled nervously. 'That's just my humble opinion on the matter.'

The cook turned to one of her juniors and barked, 'Ellen? Does any of that sound true?'

The woman called Ellen shrugged. 'Bit long-winded, but he sounds like he's met the old toff sure enough.'

Lyle beamed. 'Ladies,' he said expansively, 'you know my story now; please, share yours.'

And, aware that he was playing his trump card, Lyle put his bag on the kitchen table, opened it, and with a flourish revealed its contents.

As all eyes settled on the mass that had been compressed into the worn travel bag, twenty pairs of hands went to twenty mouths, and twenty tongues gave rise to a single note. 'Awwww!'

And Tate, sticking his head up from the bag, ears drooping over the edge, looked round the gloomy, crowded and sweaty kitchen, the air in the corners wavering from the heat, and his eyes fell on bread and fish and meat and potatoes and vegetables and caramels and chocolates and coffees, and his already substantial eyes widened, and he started to feel a lot happier about his part in the bigger picture after all.

Thomas was not at all happy about his part in the bigger picture.

True, from the first moment when he was able to squeak, in his toddler's dress, 'Weather!' he had been bred in the art of polite small-talk. But in recent months his interests had changed, and he kept having to fight an urge to steer the conversation towards topics such as the fascinating properties of a gas diffusing through a potential difference at low temperatures or maybe even ... *even* ... the derivation of Newton's

Gravitational Constant and its application between two point masses 'M' and 'm' with a radius square of 'r' and . . .

Instead he heard himself saying, and marvelled at how different his voice sounded in this company than when talking to Tess and Lyle, 'Oh gracious, no, I haven't met her ladyship yet, but I'm told she's terribly influential in Suffolk.' A lie, but one that he hoped would give immediate rise to a passionate argument about the benefits of shooting in Suffolk over shooting in Norfolk, and thus give him a little breather to rearrange his thoughts.

However, today fortune did not favour Thomas.

'*Really?* How fascinating. I heard her money was from . . . well, I hardly dare say it . . . *manufacturing*.'

'No, that's not what I heard at all. She's a great European beauty, they say, a widow; certainly I don't see how she could have made all that money herself, although I suppose they do things rather differently over there . . .'

'I wonder how many will go after *her* fortune tonight?'

'I beg your pardon?' Several pairs of eyes turned on him, and he could see them matching his face with so many acres and so much a year. Interest started to rise among them proportional to their estimations of his income. 'I beg your pardon,' he said again, 'but when did Lady Lumire arrive in this place?'

'This place?' echoed someone, amused by Thomas's choice of words.

'As in . . . London. This mansion was Lord Moncorvo's, wasn't it?'

'Oh, what a ghastly business!'

'Such a charming man! And such a charming collection of friends! I can remember nothing but good about them.'

'More than good! They were the essence of goodness and grace.'

'Such a tragedy to hear about the accident . . .'

'Oh, I rather heard he'd been appointed to India . . .'

'No, no, Lord Lincoln definitely reassured me that Moncorvo had decided to follow in the footsteps of his father and join the army . . .'

'I beg your pardon?'

Their eyes turned again to Thomas. 'Yes?' Impatience tainted the edge of the answer.

'When did Lady Lumire arrive in London?'

'Oh . . . almost immediately after dear Moncorvo left. She's some kind of distant relative, I believe. I think Moncorvo might have left her the house in his will . . . or was it a gift of . . . well, it's all terribly mysterious, if you ask me.'

Thomas remembered a storm, and the green eyes, and felt sick. He wondered if he could go and search for Lyle, to warn him of the terrible truth; but then a creeping doubt settled in his mind. He found himself looking round the high room, all marble floors and serpentine pillars, and noticed the metal buttons, candlesticks, clocks, effigies and frames that seemed everywhere, and remembered how the people with the green eyes, the Tseiqin who had thrown Lyle from the dome of St Paul's and chased Thomas beyond the edge of his mind, had flinched from iron, and he wondered.

'You aren't as old as the rest of them.'

Thomas started, stared around for the source of the voice, and eventually looked down to where a small child, dressed immaculately in a suit far too brown for a creature with a face that round or pink, was tugging at his jacket, trying to get his attention.

'Erm, no?' he hazarded.

The child blew a fat raspberry. 'You . . . *you* . . .' It paused, looked Thomas up and down cautiously, with an almost calculating glare, daring him to be anything but what the child said he was. '*You* like the weather?'

'Well, yes.' Thomas found little reason to argue with a statement so accurately and profoundly rendered.

The child put its thumb on its nose and said, 'I'm Arthur.'

Since etiquette had no guidelines for this kind of situation, and since the adults of the room had spontaneously and mysteriously all found something better to look at than the child, who'd clearly spent the evening endearing himself, Thomas mumbled, 'I'm Thomas,' and dreamt of inverse square laws and radial fields.

The interrogation wasn't over. 'You tell stories?'

'Well, no, not really.'

'What you do?'

'Well, if you must know I'm . . .' For a moment Thomas hesitated, thinking of all the possible things to say, such as, 'I'm Thomas Edward Elwick, I'm to inherit my parents' estate, I recite Greek verbs, I . . .' and replied, 'I'm a detective.'

The child's face split into a delighted grin. 'A detec . . . detect . . . one of them! What sort of . . . thing?'

'I'm a . . . *scientific* detective.' The fatal words rolled out. Thomas stood up straighter, stuck his shoulders back and his chest out and repeated, louder, 'Yes! I am a scientific detective!'

'What's 'at mean?'

This nearly stopped Thomas short, but he recovered quickly and declared, 'I use science to detect things!'

The child flapped its arms impatiently, stamped its foot and announced, 'I wanna . . . I *wanna* . . .' then hung its head and mumbled, 'I dunno what I wanna, but I wanna now!'

'Science is very good at detecting things,' went on Thomas, feeling his face start to turn purple now with the effort of keeping up this cheerful line of conversation. 'It can detect whether blood has been spilt, even if you clean it up after! Or if it's human blood, or whether there's arsenic in something or if you drowned before or after being shot or if a gun's been fired or . . .'

'How's it do that?'

Thomas stared into the round, pink, childish face, probably no more than five or six years old, staring up at him with big, bored, impatient eyes, and felt all the wonderful things slip out of his mind. 'Well, I . . . it's all to do with *elements*, you see. All you need is a little iron and a little lime water to pass the carbon dioxide through and then . . .'

'*Why?* Why why why?'

'It's . . . well, you see, if you . . .' Thomas stared into those uncomprehending eyes, and let out a little sigh. 'It's elemental, really.'

The child thought about this, long and hard. Then put one finger in its ear and one in its mouth and mumbled, 'I wanna be detective.'

Thomas couldn't help feel that two scientific detectives with a grasp of the useful applications of lime water and carbon dioxide might be one too many, but found himself saying kindly, 'Maybe if you work hard at it, Arthur . . . ?'

'Doyle. Me mam wanted me to be called Ignatius after the priest what has the thing with the cross and goes to the place where the men who study the things learn about stuff. But me dad calls me Conan.'

Thomas patted Arthur gently on the head. Arthur mumbled, 'I can do this thing with my ears . . .'

However, what Arthur Conan Doyle could do with his ears, Thomas never had a chance to find out, although he was probably not the sadder for the loss, because at the far end of the room, the doors swung open.

'Who the hell did this?'

The servant marched down the hall and picked up the lantern that had fallen on to the floor, plunging the corridor into darkness. She picked it up and shook it gently. Inside, something rattled in a distinctly broken way. She hissed in irritation and scanned the darkness for something to take out her annoyance on. Then she frowned: for a second she thought she saw a shadow where there wasn't usually one, a little area of darkness darker than the rest of the corridor; but a blink and it was gone. She advanced a few cautious paces and looked again. There was the tiniest suggestion of a shape, the faintest outline of something alien and odd, something that shouldn't have been, something like . . .

'Where are the damned sheets?' The muffled voice drifted up from the stairwell.

The servant sighed, turned, glancing behind her in case something moved there, then left, clutching the lamp. At the stairwell she quickly looked back, but the darkness had thickened in her wake, and not a flea breathed.

Sighing, then singing under her breath, ' *"When I grow rich,"* *say the bells of Shoreditch . . .*' the servant went downstairs to sort out sheets.

Tess counted to sixty in her head, then pulled herself up from where she'd been lying, pressed into the wall of the corridor. She felt her way past the place where the lantern had stood, the wood under it still warm, ran her fingers down the door until she found the lock, and gave the lock picks wedged in it a damn good thump.

The lock clicked. The door swung slowly open. Tess peered into the room beyond, lit by a single candle burning on the desk, and started to smile.

And somewhere, not as far away as the coward in Lyle would have liked it to be, but close enough to alert the copper in him, someone, maybe even something, looked up slowly from its contemplation of black stones in a black darkness behind a black door, and said in the voice the earth would use if it talked, or the deep rumble heard in the mines when you've gone too far down, 'Yes.'

And it stood up, and looked at the door, and began to smile.

CHAPTER 13

Earthquakes

The whole kitchen staff, half the housemaids and one or two footmen who should have been on duty had congregated in the kitchen. Their combined attention was fixed on Tate.

Tate ignored them, and focused whole-heartedly on eating his way through a substantial plate of cold meats that had appeared before him as if by magic as he'd scrambled out of Lyle's bag and on to the table. The dusting of flour on the table showed his paw prints running directly from Lyle's bag to the plate, and on either side of them ran a long, straight line where the tips of his ears had dragged.

The more Tate ignored everyone around him, the more they

tried to get his attention. Every hand vied for the chance to scratch his chin or stroke his glossy coat.

Lyle all this time had been edging cautiously away. He reached the door, peered left, peered right, made a break for it, got two paces and . . .

'Are you leaving so soon?'

Lyle turned. The head cook stood behind him, and *still* had the damn rolling pin in her hand.

'I was just going to see if everything was all right.'

She advanced towards him slowly. 'All right where?'

'Down there?' he hazarded, pointing down the corridor.

She smiled. It took him by surprise – the smile was light, warmer than her stern, determined gaze suggested, and almost made him want to smile back.

'We aren't allowed down there, Mister . . . ?'

'Lyle,' he replied quickly. And then, not knowing why he said it, 'Horatio.'

She held out a hand. He found himself taking it in a daze.

'Marley,' she said. 'I suppose I could tell you that my first name is Margaret, but that's jumping into intimacies a little fast, isn't it?'

'Erm, yes . . . Why aren't you allowed down there?'

Marley looked past Lyle at the gloomy corridor beyond. 'It's the cellar down there. Mistress said we weren't ever to go in. And considering how well she pays, I thought maybe it would be better to let curiosity slip on this one. Wouldn't you, Mister Lyle?'

Lyle hesitated. 'Well –'

'It's a nice dog you have.'

'Thank you.'

'What's its name?'

'Tate.'

'You clearly spoil it.'

Lyle bridled. 'Actually, it's young Teresa who spoils Tate so shamelessly. I am *always* the one who has to tidy up afterwards and look after the children with, may I say, heroic temperance and . . .'

'You're not very good at being a servant, are you?'

Lyle turned red. 'I'm new.'

'It shows. In fact, if I didn't know better, I'd say that you were more of a poli—'

And the ground shook.

Earthquakes and London have never coincided, except on a minor scale whose tremors barely have force enough to ripple water.

What shook the house that had once belonged to Lord Moncorvo, now gifted to his distant relation Lady Diane Lumire, was different. It rose up from the stones of the cellar and ripped through the kitchen, sending pots and pans tumbling, making old nails creak and water splash and pool. It wobbled its way up the stairs, hummed down the brighter corridors of the house, shimmered up the walls, made the windows creak and the glass crack, caused the curtains to flap and each chandelier to jingle like a drunken percussionist; it thrummed its way up higher and higher, making old stones hum and new metal sing a gentle little tune, *hark, hark,* whispered under the toes and up the legs, and stretched its fingertips luxuriously up to the roof, sending showers of snow tipping down the side with a wet, heavy noise, before fading into silence.

The vibrations passed under Thomas's toes, and shook him from his scrutiny of the lady who had just entered the room. As the nervous titters of the guests faded, he looked up again and saw *her*, Lumire, the lady of the house, the object of their mysterious search, standing serenely in the doorway. She was smiling, unperturbed by the sudden vibration which had shaken the guests and made each wineglass tremble in its holder's fingers. Her skin was marble white, her hair was volcanic basalt black, her eyes were granite grey, and she wore a sapphire blue dress that seemed to light up the elegant monotone of her appearance to a new radiance. He had never seen anyone quite like her. When she moved, it was like watching the world glide around her. If anything, the tremor which had just shaken the house brightened her face with an almost childish glee. She surveyed the room, and for a second her eyes settled on Thomas's. At that moment he knew they weren't the eyes of a Tseiqin: not the bright emerald eyes that delved through your helpless mind. These eyes reminded him of the seashore on a cool misty morning; and like her lips they held a smile.

She raised her hands in greeting to the room, waited for the assembly to fall into stillness, and said in a voice Thomas couldn't have described, 'Friends. Welcome.'

And looked once more around the room, and this time her eyes met Thomas's, and stayed.

He felt his heart race, and heat rise to his face, and tried to think of Gravitational Constants and cabbage.

Tess glanced up, as the vibrations passed through the soles of her feet. She paused, shrugged, and went back to examining the contents of a desk in the corner of the room.

She had struck gold, she knew it. If the large crucifix hanging on the wall by the bed hadn't given her a hint, then her opinion was sealed by the giant Bible on the pillow. With scrupulous care she was now rifling the desk by the glow of a single candle.

The first drawer had been disappointing: pen and paper and a pamphlet entitled *Thy Damnation Cometh? St Paul and St Peter compared (revised)*; Tess resisted the temptation to tear it up for sheer spiritual satisfaction.

The second drawer, however, was full of papers. She pulled one out. It read, in huge letters, *I am the vessel of change, the Lord maketh and . . . WOE to her that is filthy and polluted, to the OPPRESSING CITY!*

She turned it over. On the back, someone had doodled a couple of crosses, and a smaller note read, in the same hand, *Her ladyship has been most generous. BEAUTY. Weakness in men, thy damnation . . .*

She put it to one side and opened up a huge sheet of paper. It was a map. At the top, in a curly script, was written 'London'. But it was no London she recognized. The streets were neatly laid out, and seemed to lead in together, with a series of circular roads spreading out from the core of the city. Here and there public buildings had been marked, like 'hospital' and 'church';

she noticed many churches, some of them in a stranger hand than the one which had originally marked them.

She opened the third drawer, and with some trepidation, as well as a sudden horrified fascination, pulled out the object inside. She didn't know much about such things, but she was sure no one should have a gun quite *that* big in their bedroom. She peered at the chamber, and saw six bullets already loaded. She put the gun down quickly, turning it to point away from herself, feeling suddenly afraid of it, and tried not to look too much at it, on the off-chance it took offence.

There were footsteps in the corridor outside.

Tess slammed the Bible shut, stuck the paper in her pocket, bounded over to the desk, grabbed everything she could carry, blew the candle out and was halfway to the window as the handle turned in the door.

The tremors had caused chaos in the kitchen. Boiling pots had spilt, pans had fallen, plates had shattered, and the younger and less practical of the staff were still buzzing. Marley strode back and forth, restoring order with a look and a command that couldn't be disobeyed, glancing around and surveying the damage in an instant, taking everything in her stride. She knew where everything was in the kitchen, could look at a bulging drawer of cutlery and tell how many teaspoons were missing, and who was most likely to have them. She could bake a pie with one hand and boil jam with the other, and stoke a fire to get an oven to exactly the right temperature; she knew how many coals it took to increase the heat given off by how many degrees and how many minutes more or less to cook the pastry. It took her less than five minutes to get the staff back to their rightful places, after which she paused in the doorway, looked round and saw everything as it should be.

Although Lyle and his dog were now nowhere to be seen.

CHAPTER 14

Marquis

'Master Elwick?' Lady Diane Lumire simpered, one hand going to her mouth, and her shoulders shook as her eyes crinkled up. 'Master Elwick, I think – I hope – I'm right. But you are Master Elwick, aren't you?'

'Erm . . . yes, m'lady, you are correct.'

'I'm so glad you could call – I hadn't hoped for such an honour as an Elwick visit.' She simpered again, and, for just a second, there was something unsettling about it. Then one of her arms was linked through his – Thomas could feel how cold she was even through his jacket – and she was leading him to one side, talking all the way. 'Please, you must tell me everything about yourself. I've heard so much.'

'What do you want to know, my lady? What have you heard?'

Before Thomas knew it he was sitting on a padded chair against one of the walls of the room, and she was next to him, gesturing with excitement at each new question. 'Do tell me about this medal. What was it for?'

Thomas almost choked. 'Ah . . . well, it was . . . there was . . .' Memories flooded back. It felt wrong to talk about it in this house, at this time, to a lady who he knew Lyle regarded as a suspect, to someone with such eyes and such a voice.

'It was . . . nothing.' The words killed him to say it. 'An accident at St Paul's Cathedral. It was my privilege to be able to assist in some small measure.'

'Oh, it can hardly have been *small*, surely!'

'Well . . . I say small, but . . . naturally . . . I mean . . . well . . .' Thomas took a deep breath. 'So tell me about yourself, my lady.'

'Me?' She laid her fingertips over her heart, as if astonished that anyone could want to know. 'Oh, I'm hardly interesting at all. Not like you. I travel a lot, I *love* to explore and meet new people. I think it's what I live for, you know.'

An idea struck him. 'Have you ever been to America, my lady?'

'Why, yes, I have. Are you interested in America? Terrible state at the moment, of course, such problems. Oh, it hardly bears speaking of . . .'

Thomas felt as if he had struck gold. 'My family has an interest in America. Some people we once met were terribly keen on cotton, although,' he almost bounced up and down with excitement, desperate for Lyle to see how clever he was being, 'I'm told that in some areas they can be very unsound on religious matters.'

And then, to his shock, Lady Diane Lumire, the most mysterious lady in London, or at least that part of London which could buy Somerset and have change left over, giggled, 'Oh, my dearest, you are absolutely right! What terrible dears these Americans are.'

Darkness. Lyle's footsteps sounded hollow and lonely on the stones. Tate's snuffling somewhere in the gloom had grown into monstrous proportions. Every few paces Tate would stop and something warm would brush against Lyle's feet as though to say, *no, this isn't wise, let's go back now . . . please . . .*

When the darkness became so thick that it seemed to stop all senses beyond sight, and it was impossible even to guess where the walls were or where to move to carry on in a straight line, Lyle dug into his pockets. His fingers passed through layers of glass tubes and rolled fabrics and tools and bits of stray wire and loose change and the occasional compromising paper wrapper that at one time had hidden a secret, guilty caramel. One day, he promised himself, he'd organize his pockets.

He found what he was looking for in his inner pocket, the bulb trailing wires and, deeper yet into his voluminous coat, a small magnet, encased in a cylinder of tightly wrapped wire. A handle was attached to one end of the magnet. He twisted the wires leading to the bulb around the small nodes at either end of the coiled wire, and started turning the handle. A glow dawned inside the fat bulb, the thick black filament giving off acrid smoke that clouded the yellow light.

The light didn't exactly illuminate the corridor he stood in so much as merely give gloomy definition to where one wall began and another ended. The floor was stained with puddles of dirty water, frozen over, and Lyle's breath fizzled off the hot bulb where it touched it. Tate began to whine.

They walked carefully down the corridor. It took an eternity. Tate grew quieter as they neared the blackness towards the end where the faintest of lights seemed to stop, until even the padding of his paws was inaudible. As Tate grew quieter, Lyle walked slower, until they stopped dead at the end of the corridor. The hand that turned the magnet fell to his side. The bulb went out.

Lyle listened.

He could hear himself breathing. And if he strained, he could hear Tate taking shallow, scared breaths. Beyond the door that shuttered the end of the corridor, he could hear nothing. Not a breath, not a murmur, not a creak. He reached out in the darkness and felt the rough, thick wood of the door and the pocked iron. His fingers danced across a locked padlock, a closed bar.

He could smell something old and dry. It reminded him of baked clay, or dry loam, but it was subtle and hard to place.

A little sound behind the door. The tiniest of chinks. The sound of something pushing against the flagstones. Lyle dug hastily into his pocket, pulling out a little clouded glass sphere and a box of matches. He struck a fat match on the wall and, in the dull yellow light, he held it underneath the sphere. The sphere began to smoke and turn white before, with a sudden hiss, it exploded in burning brightness, almost too hot and too bright to look at. Lyle shook the match out, raised the sphere up to eye height and peered through the keyhole.

For a second, just a second, two stone-grey eyes stared,

unblinking, back at him. Lyle gave a cry and jumped away, dropping the matches, just as the eyes retreated from the sudden and blinding light into the darkness again. Tate started barking furiously, but from behind the door there wasn't a sound. Lyle, not taking his eyes off the door, bent down to pick up the matches, still holding up the light. As his fingers closed over the matches, the ground shook. It was more powerful this time, a deep, low humming that travelled right up the toes and came out at the ears. It knocked Lyle off his feet, and he landed with an undignified thump. Without glancing back, Tate exploded past him, heading away from the door at speed. Lyle crawled towards the buckling wall and clung to it for support as around the door the stones bent and twisted, grinding in their old mortar, which erupted in a shower of dust, as if squeezed out by unbearable pressure. Lyle heard a low, painful creak, saw a couple of stones splinter, then watched as cracks began at ground height and raced upwards towards the ceiling, crawling into the roof like poison ivy, running over his head and onwards, chasing after Tate's vanishing tail.

Frozen with fascination and horror, Lyle turned and looked at the doorway. With a final heave, the stones around the hinges shattered, flew outwards, taking with them a large part of the wall and the door itself, and flung themselves down the corridor, before exploding into splinters just beyond Lyle's head.

The rumble died. Then the cracking of tortured masonry, a slow, drawn-out sound. Lyle stared up at the ceiling by the dying light of the globe in his hand. A tiny crack snaked a few cautious inches from the main river of destruction through the ceiling, stopped, snaked another inch, stopped again to creak luxuriously in an agony of indecision, and stayed, giving off a shower of dust that rained down on Lyle, turning his sandy hair grey. The light in his hand went out. In the darkness something moved laboriously. Lyle froze. He heard another long, slow creaking, and the trickle of falling masonry. He forced himself to take gentle breaths, utterly silent, utterly still, as if his heart weren't racing in his chest and every nerve didn't scream for air and relief.

He felt something move just to his right, and knew it wasn't Tate; *felt* something huge and heard a hard footstep, as if the owner wore shoes made of steel or stone. Long, slow footsteps. He counted them, tried to calculate the stride by how long it took, relatively, for each step to get closer proportional to the sound increasing and how, if the sound increased at a rate of so many micro-decibels per step and the distance was, say, ten metres between here and there, divided by steps taken and . . .

There was a movement right by him. He glanced up in the darkness, and imagined he saw a shape looming above him. He looked into the darkness, and felt that it was looking back. As quietly as possible, pretending not to move, he slid his hand into his pocket.

Where there hadn't been anything, there was suddenly a hand round his throat. The shock was, if anything, worse than the sudden pressure, as he gasped, letting out what little air was in his lungs anyway, and grabbed at the arm which dragged him up as if he were a shuttlecock. With just one hand. He had never felt a grip like it, and hoped he never would again, if there was to be an 'again'. He thought, *About six foot three and horrendously strong, kills without qualms, what a stupid way to die . . .*

Still in his pocket, he loosened a match from the box, moving the tips of his fingers only and very, very determinedly not looking down, not that there was anything to be seen in the dark. He found to his surprise that he could still breathe: tight, shallow breaths that came in gasps through a wall of fire. He slid the match out of the box, turning it this way and that until he felt the phosphorus end, dusty under his nails.

When the voice finally came, it sounded like a deep rumble right in Lyle's ear, although he felt no breath. **'What. Are. You.'** Whoever owned the voice clearly wasn't impressed.

'No one!' squeaked Lyle. 'Lost! Misguided! But essentially well-meaning!' And then, because in all circumstances his natural sense of curiosity had an unhealthy power over other instincts, he added faintly, 'Who are you?'

The grip tightened, and Lyle realized that what little air he'd had before had been luxury.

'I am someone. And you are not.'

Lyle felt another hand move near by, and thought of twisted necks. 'Can I just . . . ask a question?' he croaked as the hand moved towards his head.

'Ask.'

'Are you Lucan Sasso?'

The question seemed to take the man by surprise. The grip lightened for a second, then tightened. Lyle heard a slow, uneasy shuffling in the dark, and felt the sudden confusion, almost fear, rolling out of the gloom. Then, quieter, but no less menacing for it, **'I was.'**

'You murdered Captain Fabrio and Mr Stanlaw?'

'Punishment.' Then, almost uneasily, '**How do you know . . .** that name?'

'Little birdy. Will you come peacefully?'

Silence, followed by an incredulous, '**Would you die so?**'

'Thought not. One last question.' Lyle's eyes were watering, his face bulging, turning blue in places. 'Are you right-handed?'

The hand closed against the side of his head, fingers tightening, pushing against bone.

'Thought so.'

Lyle dragged the match out of his pocket; and even that was a movement too much. He'd always meant to take other exercise than the obligatory five hundred metres legging it, and now he realized why. He twisted the match round and slashed it against the wall behind him. Dull yellow phosphorus light erupted, singeing his fingers. For a second, taken by surprise, the hand around his throat relaxed. Lyle kicked out at whatever was there, and nearly broke his toes. In the dull light he saw, just for a second, a pale face, grey eyes and steel-grey hair. He stabbed upwards at the cold eyes with the flaming match and the man reeled back. Lyle slid out of his grip, threw the match towards his face, turned and ran, following Tate's furious howling at the end of the corridor.

From the first step, something was wrong. He kept stumbling, tripping over rubble, and in the darkness something seemed to be moving: not footsteps, but a prolonged drag. Something bumped against his ankle and he tripped, catching himself on the wall. The stones were warm to the touch despite the bitter cold, and almost hummed under his fingers, a little rhythm that reminded him of a nursery rhyme long forgotten . . .

He kept running, fingers trailing the wall to feel the way. Overhead, there was a hideous creaking noise that grew louder and louder and seemed to be racing him, until something long, dark and deep passed him by above, showering dust as it went.

Lyle was already pulling out a match and a little glass sphere, swinging round into the turn at the end of the corridor, before the whole ceiling collapsed on top of him.

CHAPTER 15

Priest

'Who the hell are you?'

Tess, caught halfway between the desk and the window, froze in the candlelight, her jacket bulging with stolen papers. For a second she stayed that way, face twisted and pensive, eyes on the door. Then she straightened up, folded her arms and said, 'Ah, yes, well, you may ask that.'

'Yes,' said the American voice like maple syrup, 'I may, this being my room.'

'*Ah*. Well . . . since you're clearly ignorant, I'll tell you.'

The shadow in the door was blacker than the gloom outside, and outlined a tall, well-built man standing with utter confidence. Tess began to move cautiously, putting the bed between her and him.

'Yes. Do tell me,' said the American voice.

'Well I . . . *I* . . . am Lady Teresa de . . . Stepney! And I have been sent by the Pope! To see if you're doing your priesting proper.'

The shadow drifted into the room. She saw a man with burning auburn eyes set in a dark face of a consistency achieved only by practising the same fervoured look for hours in front of an eager audience. He was wearing black. Quietly and carefully he shut the door behind him. Tess backed away until she was standing at the head of the bed, the huge Bible on the pillow beside her.

'You'd . . . be Ignatius, right?'

'I am Ignatius Caryway,' said the auburn voice as the man advanced, 'but I don't see how a little lady like you should know that.'

'Well, as I was saying, I was sent by the Pope to make sure you weren't doing anything evil, like bringing killers or suchlike to London 'cos of dark and mysterious forces and . . . you ain't heard of *them*, have you?'

'I don't know. Who are "them"?'

'See,' said Tess, wagging a finger, 'if you have to ask, you don't know. That's 'cos they're all evil and mysterious.'

'I'm not. I have a vision.'

Tess scowled. He was a few paces away, so that her back was pressed against the wall. 'Mister . . . my friend says how you should never trust visions. They cloud your judgement, he says.'

A hand reached out for her. 'Would this be a certain Mister Lyle?'

Tess didn't hesitate. In a single movement she turned,

grabbed the Bible, spun, inelegantly dragged down by the weight of the book, and threw it at the window. It wasn't a very strong throw, and the Bible more flopped than flew, but it was a heavy book, and the glass was thin. The window shattered in a storm of frost and silver shards. As Ignatius lashed out for Tess, she ducked under his arm, ran for the window, and threw herself out.

A little later there was a soft *thump* from the snow below, and the sound of frightened pigeons making for the sky.

Ignatius looked out of the window. A long way down, small against the snow and barely illuminated by the candlelight seeping out of the windows, was the Bible, and a lot of broken glass.

Some way above that, dangling by her fingertips from a gutter, was Tess.

'You'll fall, little lady. Your kind do,' called Ignatius.

'Thank you,' she snapped back, 'professional at work here.' Tess began to swing her legs, pushing against the icy stone.

'Assuming you make it down, I'll have already summoned servants.'

'Ah, but that means you're going to go an' have to stop lookin' while you do the summ'nin'.' Tess's voice was both weak and smug. 'That means you'll 'ave to go away and when you come back, for all you know I might have dropped through an open window and got back into the house, or done somethin' all clever and got out, an' then won't you feel stupid?'

Silence from the window above. Tess peered up and saw the black shadow still watching her. She gritted her teeth and tried to pull herself up into the gutter, the sharp metal, made sharper by the cold, digging into her fingers. Her arms buckled and nearly jerked free of her shoulder blades. She dangled over a long drop, and wondered how deep the snow was below.

From above, Ignatius's voice drifted down. 'I can offer absolution, if you wish.'

'Is that like a very long rope?'

'It's so you will not burn through all eternity for your sins.'

'Can I let you know?'

Tess looked down and saw, dimly, a window ledge, just wide enough for a few toes and nothing more, somewhere below. She looked up, looked down again, reached a decision, took a deep breath and let go.

Lyle picked himself up from the rubble, and groaned. Above him, a voice rumbled, '**See your own weakness, little man. Once I was weak, but I learnt through cold and patience how to be great, and will be greater still.**'

Lyle crawled up on to his hands and knees. He still clung to the match and the glass sphere. He staggered a few paces – even the darkness seemed to be spinning – and leaned against the nearest wall. He tried to breathe, tried to ignore the pain of a dozen bruises. 'Sasso?' he rasped into the darkness. 'You still alive?'

The voice was just a few paces away. In the darkness, he half-imagined he could reach out and touch it. '**Yes.**'

Lyle scrambled backwards, leaning his shoulders into the wall to stop himself from falling. His ears were filled with a high-pitched whine, from somewhere uncomfortable behind the eardrums, and his hands shook as he struck the match and held it up to the sphere. 'Keep back!' he barked. 'Or I'll oxidize!'

There was a sudden and prolonged silence. In the dull yellow light, he saw the black shadow, a few paces away. Finally, **'Is that what threats are in this time?'**

'Oxidize,' explained Lyle, feeling he was losing a certain control over things. 'As in expose to oxygen. Combustion in an oxygen source, i.e. air. As in changing the charge on a metal, by the process of a reaction which bonds the metal to . . . to oxygen.' Lyle's voice faded away. Somewhere, there was the clicking of light pieces of falling masonry. 'The technological revolution just passed you by, didn't it?'

Finally, **'Tell me: has this revolution changed hearts as well as minds? Should I have . . . felt fear, little man?'**

'Well, something would have been nice,' mumbled Lyle.

'I feel nothing.'

'That's just terrific.'

He heard the movement, rather than saw it, and instinctively ducked, dropping the match. At the same second, the sphere, burnt almost carbon black underneath, exploded in white light.

Later, Lyle wondered if he hadn't half-imagined everything; would play back what he saw, image by image, as if flicking through a book of drawings and watching them change, picture melding into picture as the story progressed, pausing here or there to take one image out and turn it every which way, see if from any other angle it could tell the same story, but from a different perspective. Later, he'd say there was too much magnesium in the sphere to be entirely safe. Later, he'd probably think of a logical explanation.

The white light, too bright and too white to look at directly, burning brighter than any winter sun, exploded in his hand like the opening eye of some demi-god, looking out on the world for the first time. It burnt through the darkness like a sword through cobwebs and lit up, bright and white, the face of Lucan Sasso.

The Marquis screamed, an unnatural, high-pitched wail that seemed to be resounding at three pitches at once, hiding his face from the light with his hands, twisting away. Lyle staggered back, the sphere of hot fire and magnesium burning his hand, but he clung on to it for dear life and squinted past the light at the Marquis.

Where Lucan's hands were in front of his face, the light fell full on them, and the skin changed colour. It seemed to drain of all life, to become hard and flaky, with the texture of sand-blasted stone. Joints froze up stiffly, each movement seeming to be a fight against some great weight, and as he watched, the hands and all areas exposed to the brightest of the light turned, inch by inch, to stone.

'Oh, *bugger*,' muttered Lyle, as Lucan laboriously dragged his hands away from his face, the skin underneath also darkening, the mouth set now in a fixed grimace of anger and hatred; and Lyle turned and ran.

Behind him, Lucan Sasso roared. **'I am stone, my heart is stone, the stones hear my heart as no other mortal ever shall, and they answer to *me!*'**

And the stones of Old London Town roared with him.

Thomas, wineglass in hand, felt the sound start beneath his feet. It rose up in a hum that twisted candle flames in odd directions and made the curtains brush nervously against each other. It was a long, deep, howled whisper that reminded him of an animal in pain, heard far off: the injured wolf, its cry muffled by the forest.

'Good grief,' said someone at first. 'I do declare this weather is simply awful.'

When the sound went on, a furious, pained howl that seemed to be most audible through the toes, the room began to fall silent. Lady Diane Lumire giggled. Suddenly Thomas found this previously charming habit very, very irritating.

Someone else said, 'Do you think it's getting louder?'

With a start, Thomas put his head on one side, and heard now a sound underneath the pained hum of the stones, the thrumming that came up through his feet and bounced off the eardrums in a low, agonized howl; it was the sound of a human voice, but a human voice distorted beyond recognition, that seemed to be sounding three deep notes at once, rather than the standard one, screaming in expressionless hatred and rage. And just beyond it, getting nearer and louder, the sound of running footsteps.

All eyes, as if sensing an imminent spectacle, turned towards the sound of the running feet, and the door. Accompanying the feet, but half-drowned by the general racket, came a voice, shrill and frightened, rising from an incoherent babble to a loud exclamation as it drew nearer: ' . . . whatthehellareyoupeopledoing here don't you realize HE'S UTTERLY MAD HE'S GOING TO KILL YOU STUPID IDIOTS!' The voice and the footsteps passed by the door, stopped for a second as if the owner was hesitating, then began again, briefly, right outside. The door was thrown open, and a bedraggled, wild-eyed figure stared in, covered in mortar dust, blood and bruises, clinging to a dying sphere of light in one hand as if his fingers had fused to it. There was a general gasp of high dignities in the face of the unwashed.

'Well, don't just stand there, you bloody fools!' Lyle snapped. 'He's utterly mad and *you're* not helping!'

With this, Lyle turned and started running again. Thomas hesitated for a second, then began pushing his way towards the door. Seeing this, other people, perhaps with a greater pragmatism than their breeding implied, started pushing and shoving in Thomas's wake. Thomas exploded out of the crush, the floor still humming under him, and looked towards the centre of the roar.

A man, his skin changing slowly from hard grey to more natural off-brown in the dim light, was marching down the corridor towards him. As he walked, the stones around him seemed to ripple, bending before and behind his feet, cracks spreading all around through the screaming masonry, candles and lamps toppling as the fabric of the building tried to twist in on itself. From his mouth came a low, furious roar, and the stones themselves seemed to grow mouths to share in it. Thomas felt he knew against whom that anger was directed.

He stood frozen with fear, staring into the eyes of the oncoming man. He was *huge*. His unstoppable bulk made Thomas feel like an unfortunate earthworm in the path of a rampaging ox. The man didn't seem to have seen Thomas, so focused was he in his hate, but he saw the crowd of people racing from the room, and his face twisted into a cruel smile. He lifted his hands up to the ceiling, and Thomas followed the curve of those raised fingers with horrified fascination. A crack started above the man's head, began to spread, racing along the high ceiling like a hungry, feeding, growing snake. Thomas saw the ceiling sag.

A hand snaked out of the air behind Thomas, grabbed him by

the scruff of the neck and nearly lifted him off his feet. He saw Lyle's filthy face behind him, almost unrecognizable for the dust, and heard Lyle say through gritted teeth as he dragged him bodily out of the front door, 'Time and place for everything, lad, but not now.'

Behind him, Thomas heard the slow, inexorable grind of the roof hesitating, sagging and giving in, just as Lyle threw him out of the door and on to the gravel beyond. He fell heavily into a heap of terrified aristocracy. Dust and darkness rolled out of the door behind him, along with a low rumble.

Dust settled. The rumble died. Thomas pulled himself carefully up on to his feet on the hard gravel, and listened. There was a sound, so tiny it was hard to tell whether it was real or imagined. A little crunching noise, like the sound of gravel underfoot, but he hadn't moved to crunch it. It grew louder, rose to a roar. He glanced at his feet. All the fragments of gravel were bouncing furiously, like sand on a tambourine. He turned round and saw that Lyle too was staring down in horror. As they watched, the gravel bounced higher and higher, until it was rattling against Thomas's knees. He looked round for Lyle, and saw him already on the grass. 'What the hell are you waiting for?' snapped Lyle.

There was already an exodus of people off the gravel, screaming ladies and white-faced men. Thomas scrambled clear, almost falling on to Lyle and the safety of the lawn as, with a roar, the gravel seemed to coalesce, dragging the stones from its edges into a thick central pillar, then rear up and form a mouth, which opened.

This time, Thomas didn't need to be told. Running by Lyle's side, he threatened to overtake him as the giant head of stone wheeled around, snapping at anything within its reach, stretching out long and thin to snap at the ankles of fleeing women. And still the gravel bounced and chittered in a thin storm, its sound like the laugh of a rattlesnake, lingering after the two retreating figures.

Tess had landed on the edge of the sill when she fell. For a second she teetered, arms wheeling like a windmill as she struggled for balance. With a mighty push she toppled forward, and pressed her palms into the side of the window to hold herself there, gasping for breath. Under her fingers, the walls felt odd: warm, almost humming. The glass seemed to be vibrating before her eyes, tiny cracks spreading in it from the edges, as if it was being compressed between the walls that held it.

From above, she heard a slow clapping.

'Well done, little lady! Lyle really does pay for professionals, doesn't he? Now what are you planning on doing?'

'Busy here!' sang out Tess, scrambling for another hold. The humming noise was now loud enough to make her nervous, inching its way into her skull, to bounce around, doing damage inside. She quickly swivelled and sat down on the edge of the sill. There was another, a storey below. Clinging on, she eased herself out on to the edge of the sill, turned and lowered herself. Even when dangling by the length of her arms, it was a long drop. She took a deep breath, closed her eyes and let go. This time, her feet slipped on the ice of the sill, and dropped out under her. She flailed wildly and her fingers closed round something large protruding from the wall.

It was a cherub, small and ornamental, hiding a gutter spill.

She almost sobbed with relief, her aching hands scrabbling for better purchase around its chubby neck.

From quite a long way above, Ignatius's voice drifted down. 'You're doing well, little lady. But I think the next drop will be harder.'

Tess risked peering down. There weren't any handholds, not even a decent toe hole, not a chip in the wall nor a window ledge to cling on to, not a pipe nor a drain in sight. She whimpered. Somewhere below, a dark shape moved.

'I think Mister Lyle should have been more noble and rescued you by now,' called down Ignatius. 'If I were in your position I would resent his abandoning you. Perhaps he really is a cruel man. Just using you, and leaving you to fall alone.' Tess squeezed her eyes shut and tried not to shiver in the cold. Her grasp on the cherub was slipping; she could feel it. Below, she heard a thoughtful snuffling noise, then a sudden series of barks, short but insistent.

Ignatius didn't seem to hear it, or if he did, he didn't care. 'Tell me, little lady, if you had a chance, would you go back to the life you led before? Sinful, perhaps. But surely better?'

Tess felt her fingers sliding apart, and tried to brace herself against the smooth, cold walls. She could feel something humming up through her toes, and from somewhere in the distance came a chittering noise, like the laughter of a rattle-snake.

'Perhaps, if you weren't already unredeemable, lost in sin and ignorance, I would mourn the passing of one so young. It's almost a shame.'

Below, the barking grew louder, and there was a sound in the snow which she recognized as panic, running. 'Mister Lyle!' She half-screamed. 'Mister Lyle!'

From below, a reasonable but breathless voice drifted up. 'Yes, Teresa?'

The sob got caught up in her gasp of relief. 'I'm slippin'!'

'I'll save you, Miss Teresa!' Thomas's voice bounced off the stones.

'There's that Ignatius person up there!' screamed Tess.

Lyle looked up at the dark outline in the high window, and his voice turned to an indignant squeak. '*You're* the stupid idiot who thought it would be nice to turn loose a homicidal madman. Well, you're in for it now, because I'm telling you . . .'

'Mister Lyle!'

'Yes, Teresa, just a second.'

From below Tess, there was a conspiratorial murmuring, punctuated by Lyle's occasional cry of, 'Don't be daft, lad!'

Tess looked up. Ignatius had vanished from the window. Somehow his absence, and not knowing where he was, made her feel worse. Below, there was a shuffling sound. 'Mister Lyle! I ain't goin' to be able to hold on much longer!'

'Just . . . formulating . . . a method of decelerating . . .' came Lyle's breathless answer. The shuffling noise went on.

'Mister Lyle!'

'Teresa,' came the sharp reply, 'gravity is not the only problem we have at the moment!' From somewhere round the front of the house, there came a long, primal roar.

'What the hell was that?' squeaked Tess.

'Language, Teresa!'

'Sorry, Mister Lyle,' she quavered. 'What the hot fiery place with demons was that?'

'We think . . .' The shuffling was now very loud, and punctuated by a little flapping noise, 'that it's a mad, rampaging monster imprisoned for an unknown amount of time by the Vatican on a small dumpy Italian island . . .' A mutter from below. 'All right, on a small Italian island the dumpiness of which we currently lack any evidence to determine.' Another mutter. 'Thomas! Anyway, we think it's a mad rampaging monster made of stone who controls stones in a manner yet to be determined, with murderous intent.'

'Oh. So which's worse? The gravity or the monster?'

'Depends where you're standing.'

There was another long, animal roar. It sounded a lot nearer. Tate started whimpering.

'Tess?' Lyle's voice was suddenly changed, burning with fear and concern. 'You need to let go.'

'You takin' the . . . you havin' a laugh, sir?'

'No. You have to do it *now*.'

'I ain't just droppin'!'

'It's all right. We've . . . we've come up with a very clever, scientific way of slowing your fall.'

'Yeah? Tell me 'bout it!'

'Well, we've . . . we've rearranged white crystalline matter in such a manner that the compressive force of the fall will be largely absorbed both through energy transferred thermally by work to cause a little . . . change of state, and through compression of the flexible crystalline structure to . . .' There was another roar. It was much closer. 'Tess, dammit, just drop!'

'No!'

'I mean it! Right now!'

'I ain't . . .' Tess's voice trailed off. Under her fingers, she felt something move. She froze, not breathing, not moving, as very slowly the stone cherub flexed its neck, turning this way and that in a slow, sleepy way, and opened its eyes. A pair of stone-grey eyes, without iris or pupil, fixed on her, and the huge, chubby smile on its face changed, twisting at the edges. Its lips drew back, revealing neat stone teeth. It drew its head back slowly, writhing in the wall, and then jerked it forward, right towards Tess's skull.

Tess let go, and fell.

The actual falling wasn't that bad. There was a moment when it was even enjoyable: the feeling of air rushing by and pressing against her, of the dark world streaming past with no prospect of ending. Then something cold and hard slammed into her, curled up round her, folded in over her head, her face, crawled coldly into her mouth and tried to suffocate her. Every nerve faltered as the breath and warmth were knocked out of her, and her head felt as if it was made of ringing brass. Then hands were pulling at the stuff over her face, brushing snow out of her eyes and she was coughing and spluttering while Lyle grabbed her, plucking her off her feet and clutching her to his chest, muttering frantically, 'You're all right, Tess? For God's sake, tell me you're all right!'

'Let me go an' I'll tell you,' she said, pushing at him.

Lyle put her down again, brushing self-consciously at his coat. 'Well, yes . . . well . . . I'm glad to hear it.'

Tess turned to look at the thing which had broken her fall. It was . . . a mound of white crystalline matter, now squashed in a Tess-sized shape and a little bit wet where energy had been transmitted thermally by work being done against it.

Tess thought about it. 'It's . . . snow. Piled snow.' Then the indignation kicked in. 'An' I were up there thinkin' how you'd come up with summat clever, summat smart to stop me, I thought how you'd use *brains* and maybe some kind of spring with coats and a trampoline or small gas balloon from Mister Lyle's pocket an' . . . an' you just stuck *snow* there?'

'No, no!' said Thomas quickly. 'It's snow that was arranged in a manner to maximize its capacity to absorb the energy of your fall by collapsing as much as possible under your weight without actually allowing you to hit a more solid surface.'

'It's very *cleverly* piled snow,' added Lyle helpfully.

Next to him, Tate sniffed at the wall of the mansion, then in his very special way, made it a tiny part of his own little world.

The roar came again, and it was much closer. 'And now,' sighed Lyle, 'we're going to have to run like a hot fiery place with demons.'

CHAPTER 16

Flight

The bells are ringing across Old London Town. They ring from St Giles's to St Clement's, from St James's to St Mary's, and around them the sounds of London rise up through the night and the fog. When the sellers of hot nuts, tepid soups, warm coffees and brief pleasures slip to bed, the poor man who eats watercress from the market at Spitalfields or the old woman who sells violets at Covent Garden are only just waking. The city doesn't sleep, only parts of it sleep, which never need meet the other cogs in the clock that make it tick. The sounds of the city never die, and tonight a new sound has been added: a low, deep resonance that whispers through the new sewers and the old, hums across the bridges and makes even the thick, deep ice, tough enough to support the dozens of sledges that the children drag across it, whisper the stories that usually only the stones whisper.

Somewhere, a child in the suffocating twists of the black, crooked rookery sings, in the shrill, hungry voice of the frightened and alone, in the dark and the fog:

> *'When will that be?' say the bells of Stepney.*
> *'I do not know,' say the great bells of Bow.*
> *Here comes a candle to light you to bed,*
> *Here comes a chopper to chop off your head.*
> *Chip chop chip, the last man's dead.*

And the bells still sing on quietly to themselves after the ringing has stopped, rocking gently back and forth in contemplation:

> *Hark, hark, the dogs do bark,*
> *The beggars are coming to town.*
> *Some in rags and some in tags,*
> *And one in a velvet gown.*

It is said by some that the stories of Old London Town make its people who they are, that the stones which make the city, make the man. For those who have walked through the smoke and the fog, felt the shiny new cobbles of Regent Street or the old mud paths of Bow, who have smelt the river upstream of Woolwich, and seen it glow at Richmond, the city changes them. Each street, it is said, makes a new person out of itself. You cannot leave it unchanged, and nothing you do will ever change it back, merely change the people who will come after. Old London Town will always have its stories.

It is said by some that there are forces beyond any mere man's control. Very few know what this really is. And they're the few who it, whatever 'it' may be, will never change. Unless the stones that made them who they are change first.

And now the fog is rising through the snow. It crawls through the narrow alleys of Bethnal rookery, down the plugged, black iron gutters of Holborn, and clings to the timbers of Clerkenwell and the stones of Mayfair. It laps against the walls of Hampstead, pressing down against the sights and sounds of the city on this night. It finds a little voice in the night, and tries to snuff it out, indignant that anything should break the stillness and quiet.

'Mister Lyle?'

'Yes, Teresa?'

'Where we goin'?'

'The Heath.'

'Why?'

'So that we can get out of this place.'

'You ain't scared, are you, Mister Lyle?'

'Teresa, there are some situations where an acceptable blood rush can simulate the most improbable emotional characteristics.'

Tess dropped lightly down the other side of the mansion wall, on to clean snow and soft grass. Thomas followed more carefully, lowering himself inch by inch. Lyle glanced down, scowled, and jumped quickly, eyes half-shut, Tate cradled under one arm. The Heath was only visible beyond the snow as a place where the darkness was thicker, and could be felt underfoot as a gentle downward curve of the land. Behind the wall there were footsteps and voices.

'Come on,' muttered Lyle, patting his pockets. 'Let's get out of here before someone finds us.'

He dropped Tate on to the ground, and immediately the dog started sniffing, padding this way and that. 'What's he looking for, Mister Lyle?' asked Thomas.

'Either something to eat or a scent.'

'Whose scent, sir?'

'Ours, I'm hoping.' Lyle had the little spinning magnet out of his pocket and was fumbling with the handle. As the magnet whined and spun in its cage of wire, the bulb slowly lit up again. The light didn't penetrate the fog, hardly even reached the ground beneath their feet, but cast an odd, luminous orange glow across the faces of the three as they scampered on as quickly as caution would allow. Between the snow, areas of rough, black brush appeared, snapping at their ankles, then their knees. Tate suddenly barked and started scampering forward. Lyle's face split into a grim smile as he muttered, 'Quickly, children!'

They ran, chasing the shadow of Tate and his muffled bark, the bulb in Lyle's hand flickering erratically as he spun the magnet round and round inside the dynamo. Thomas could see how his fingers were unnaturally red from more than just the cold, and thought of chemicals burning. To Tess, the quiet and the stillness of the fog were more unsettling than a murderous mob; it left the imagination free to create monsters out in the shadowy unknown, and her imagination duly filled the picture until she could almost feel tentacles tickling at her face.

They seemed to run downwards through the darkness for ever, until the shape of the land began to change and Tate led them uphill. Tess stumbled and almost fell; she struggled to get back up again, her legs aching almost beyond belief, her arms sore from her fall, her back bruised and head still groggy. Lyle caught her under the arm as she scrambled on to her feet, and half-carried, half-dragged her across the Heath. The land dropped abruptly into a crater-like impression, and then climbed again, filled with the tatty remnants of deciduous trees, all colour drained by snow.

And then, almost without warning, they rose above the fog, and saw for a moment the city spread out below them. It was huge, sprawling, black and white with soot and snow. There were no clouds above the fog, and the moon shone full down on it, making every rooftop sparkle where the snow was only slightly stained with the ever-present overhang of smoke and dirt. They could see the miniature lights of carriages and carts still moving through the streets, tiny streams of fire through the cobweb of narrow streets and alleys. Running out from the city were the railway lines, stretching on silver rails towards an unknown destination, with their trains steaming like angry whales venting water. The river was a snake through the heart of the city, still and frozen, except out in the furthest eastern reaches where the estuary began among reeds and swamps and where the passage of the largest ships, and the sheer depth, width and salty dirt of the river had shattered the ice into little islands moving through a moonlit mirror. For a second, they paused, contemplating this, before Tate's insistent barking drew them away.

Outlined in the moonlight, at the top of the Heath, was a familiar box-like shed. Lyle scrambled towards it and struggled with the lock on the door. It had frozen solid. With a hiss of frustration, and giving the shed door a kick that made Thomas jump, he pulled a tube of clear liquid out of his pocket, uncorked it and dropped a few careful splashes into the padlock. The liquid started to hiss, and a thick, acrid smoke rose up from inside the lock. Lyle dragged at the lock again and, almost burnt through by the acid, it snapped open. The three of them yanked the doors back.

Inside the shed, crouching in the darkness, was Icarus.

A howl split the landscape. It made the branches of the black trees waver, sending avalanches of snow down with a little *crack-splash*, dripping white crystals. Lyle was inside the shed in a second, striking a lamp and inspecting every joint and strut of the slumbering machine.

Tess had turned white. 'We ain't seriously usin' that?'

Thomas's eyes when he looked at her could have illuminated Mars. 'We're going to *fly*, Teresa,' he whispered breathlessly.

'But . . . we ain't never flied before.' Tess sat down heavily on the ground as if not noticing it was there. 'I thought how we was going to . . . not . . . fly?'

'Well, now,' came Lyle's voice, ringing with forced joviality, 'what would be the point of constructing a pressure-differential-velocity aeronautical device of quite such high calibre as this one, and not use it?' His arms were full of long, narrow tubes which widened at each end to two sharp metal fans inside the container. As Tess watched in horror, he slid the tubes into slots on the back of Icarus, locking them into place with a precise click.

Thomas sidled up to him. 'Mister Lyle? Are you sure . . .'

Lyle spun, grabbing the astonished boy by the shoulders and staring intently into his eyes. 'Thomas? You did the maths, you know every bolt and every strut of this thing better than I do, the science is *beautiful*. Every number melding into every answer, every plus leading to every equals, every part honed to within a millimetre of accuracy, everything tried and tested and *real*. Real science, beautiful science, numbers that fit so neatly into reality it might have been a child's puzzle designed for our exploration and delight. It can work. It *will* work.' There was another howl in the night, closer, rippling through the trees. 'And dammit, it's probably safer than staying down here.'

'But the lift . . .'

Lyle gave him a shrewd look that lingered for a second. Then he smiled. 'I know, lad,' he muttered, patting him on the head. 'I thought of that too.' Before Thomas could answer, Lyle sprang away, strapping down the long tubes and kicking the stocks out from underneath the wheels. 'Teresa!' he barked.

Tess, pale-faced, looked up from where she sat. 'Yes, Mister Lyle?' she quavered.

'Your job is to look after Tate and make sure the tubes don't stop burning, got it?'

She nodded dully. Lyle picked her up easily and swung her into the cradle of wood and straps that made up one of the two seats in the complicated wooden plane. He strapped her in briskly while Thomas scurried to check every cranny, every gear and every joint.

'Tess?'

She stared into Lyle's calm grey eyes.

'It's going to be all right, you understand?' She nodded again, hands shaking with terror. A warm shape was deposited in her arms, stopping their trembling. She looked down at Tate, and Tate looked back up, tongue lolling. His tail wagged eagerly.

'Hold on to him.' Lyle held out the dynamo, the bulb pulled out. 'Use the wires to make a spark. It'll relight the tubes if they go out.'

'These'd be the things what went bang?' squeaked Tess.

'That's them.' He patted her gently on the head. 'It'll be all right, understand?'

She tried to speak, but her mouth was dry, so she just nodded once more, clinging on to Tate.

Lyle turned to Thomas, who was already halfway into the front of the cradle, where ropes and pulleys ran together towards a series of stiff-looking cogs and gears. They ended in a tangle of levers and more ropes, the function of which almost any mere mortal wouldn't have dared speculate on. 'You think you can do this?'

Thomas nodded. 'Yes, sir.'

'Good.'

Lyle hopped down from the side of Icarus, patting it gently on one long, curved wing with a sad expression, as if saying farewell to a friend. 'Brakes!'

Thomas kicked a lever. Something banged inside the machinery, and struts moved, visible from outside, like the workings of an exposed heart. Tess leant out. 'Wait! Mister Lyle, you've got to . . .'

Lyle was already running towards the door. 'Not now, Teresa!'

Icarus jerked forward, following the gentle incline of the land that dropped down towards the sleeping city, visible behind the settling fog. Matchbox in hand, Lyle knelt down at the top of the slope. There were three matches left. He swallowed as Icarus started to roll, nose beginning to pitch forward as it slid down over the snow and ice, wings bending slightly to catch the breeze of its passage. Inside, Thomas, Tess and Tate were just shadows. Lyle struck a match. It flickered in his hand, guttered for a second, then caught. He scrambled through the snow until he found a thin length of string, soggy and smelling of old oil, sticking up from the ground. He held the match to it. A faint blue flame began at the tip of the string, clinging, tantalizingly, to life, then went out.

Lyle swore, struck another match and held it to the string. This time it caught, flickered, held, and with a sudden hiss started to burn with a bright orange flame. Lyle leapt back as Icarus drifted slowly by, the wheels squeaking under the weight of stretched wood and canvas, Thomas squinting into the darkness. Beneath Lyle's feet, the flame raced along the string, divided, raced along two strings, three, four, down the slope and into the fog.

Inside Icarus, Tess was shaking Thomas's shoulder. 'What you doin'? We got to stop for Mister Lyle!'

'Icarus won't build up enough lift to carry us and *him*,' replied Thomas stiffly, eyes fixed on the darkness ahead.

'What's that mean?'

Ahead, without warning, something went *whumph*. The flame leapt from the lit string at Lyle's feet, to a series of half-buried candles, which hissed, spluttered and exploded into white fire, beacons of hot sparks leaping feet off the ground. Two parallel lines of flame raced downhill, burning through the fog, out-lining a long, sharp drop towards the city below.

And the shapes that filled it.

They were . . . almost people. Some of them. The shapes were indistinct, even in the sudden white glow in which they basked. But Lyle saw the outline of angel's wings, the flash of demon's claws, the tilt of an immaculately triangular chin, the shuffle of a scrupulously folded robe. They were all around him, above, below, behind, a perfect stone circle. Some were the statues of angels who guarded the tombs of the dead, some the cruel gargoyles who clung to the churches, some the chubby cherubs who watched over the gardens of the rich. Lyle half-imagined he saw a garden gnome, squatting with a snotty expression on the edge of the ring, no higher than his knees, looking into the lines of flame.

'Holy hell!'

He looked down the path of fire defined by the candles, and saw shapes on that, too. And one shape, larger than the rest. As his eyes fell on the stone wall of living monstrosities, risen from their sleep in front of it, Icarus pitched forward, tail rising and nose dipping, and began to power downwards, straight towards Sasso.

'Thomas!' Lyle started running, oblivious of the shapes surrounding him on every side, fumbling in his pockets through glass and wires. At the back of Icarus, there was a crackle, and sparks began flying from two of the half-dozen tubes that lined the back, followed by the slow hiss of air being sucked in through the fans. 'Thomas, get off the bloody ground!'

Thomas was struggling with the controls, pulling back on everything with all his might, the wings stretching and snapping as they twisted to catch the wind. Lyle raced down towards Icarus, hands coming out of his pockets with a fistful of test tubes. He threw them without looking to see what they were, and somewhere ahead there was an ugly chemical bang as acids and ammonia smashed into each other, sending up dirt, snow and smoke around the feet of the nearest stone figures.

The whine of the two sparking tubes turned to a screech as they ignited, flame spouting out behind them, fans screaming. Icarus lurched forward with a sudden new thrust, dropping almost vertically down the slope of the Heath, wings twisting to catch the air. The front wheel lifted for a second, a foot, two, above the ground, sagged again, and hung suspended gently in the air as Icarus wheeled downwards. Directly ahead, face lit dimly by the burning candles on either side, Lucan Sasso folded his arms, and looked unimpressed. Lyle felt in his pockets and pulled out another tube, an ugly brown-purple, and screamed, 'I'll show you bloody oxidization!'

Sasso looked up sharply at the sound, distracted momentarily from Icarus. Lyle threw the tube, a long overarm straight at him. Instinctively, Sasso threw himself to one side, rolling easily as the tube shattered in the snow, directly in front of the screaming shape of Icarus.

A little puff of smoke went up, twinkling merrily, as Icarus, trailing fire and screaming with strain, rushed straight through and onwards, towards the city. Sasso stared in surprise as Lyle ran straight past him, following Icarus, coat flapping clumsily behind him, down the aisle of sparking roman candles.

'We'regoingtodiewe'regoingtodie!' screamed Tess.

'We'renotgoingtodiewe'renotgoingtodie!' Thomas screamed back.

Icarus pitched and wheeled clumsily as it fell. Thomas could feel the pressure against the wings, pushing it back up, dragging it away from the dropping ground. He saw the nose rise, hanging on the air, but the back wheels remained firmly attached to the ground. Ahead, he could see the trail of candles down the Heath getting shorter and shorter, a heavy, somehow very solid-seeming blackness ahead. 'Tess?' he screamed. 'Light another tube!'

Tess peered over her shoulder. The air being dragged past her face tugged at her skin and hair, sucking with a hungry pressure, and she could feel the heat coming off the tubes, even though they were set back further than she could reach. 'You having a bloody joke?' she screamed back.

'Light it, Tess, we need to go faster!'

Tess peered past Thomas. In her lap, Tate was leaping gleefully, trying to raise his head enough to see, tail wagging like grass in a gale. She cursed under her breath with all the colour that ten years in the East End thieving business could teach a girl, turned, wrapped the two wires of the dynamo round one of the fuse lines that ran from the tube to the cradle, and twiddled the magnet quickly. A spark jumped between the wire ends, almost lost in the wind, and fizzled across the fuse, which hissed and exploded in orange fire. She watched it crawl down the fuse and disappear into another tube, which puttered weakly, and started sparking. She saw the fans begin to turn, then explode into a blur of motion as the tube lit, the inside bursting with sudden fire that trailed out of the back of the tube. Icarus lurched forward, the world blurring on either side. 'It's working!' she yelled, almost bouncing with excitement. 'It's *working*!'

Thomas felt Icarus lurch under him, the nose suddenly rising up, pointing straight towards the moon. 'Fly, dammit!'

Behind him, he heard Tess shrilling, 'Why ain't it working, *why ain't it working?*'

The line of candles ran out. For a second Icarus rattled through perfect, unstoppable darkness. Thomas closed his eyes, and felt something small and vital go *clunk* under him. He clung to the controls until they cut into his hands and made his arms shake. Death didn't come. He could hear a hissing roar in his ears and feel a sickening pressure in the pit of his stomach.

There was something missing.

It took a few seconds to realize what, in the rush of wind and pressure of the air and bite of the cold, was incredibly absent.

Tess's high-pitched squeak had fallen suddenly, inexplicably, silent.

Thomas opened his eyes.

Below, the lights of London spread out smaller and smaller across the moonlit, fog-stained, snow-stroked landscape. He half-turned, and saw the narrow path of the candlelit runway dropping away, already just a small arrow of fire on the ground, and saw Tess too, leaning out of the cradle and peering at the stretching black and white landscape with an expression of surprise and something else: a strange and thoughtful look he'd never seen there before, something alert and intelligent that had begun to understand what no one had ever understood before.

Inside, an odd feeling, unfamiliar and strange. It wasn't a spectacular firework, a burning revelation. It was still and quiet and looked out at all that was below, and he saw himself above it all, and said, simply, *yes*.

He pulled at a control lever, and at the end of the wing, a flap dipped, and Icarus responded, leaning into the wing, turning gently, like a swimmer dancing under the sea, circling round over the blackness of the Heath. Below, the small parts that composed the life of the heath seemed to be moving slowly, dragging their limbs with a weight that Thomas no longer felt. The candles were guttering, the fog crawling sullenly back into the black space burnt clear by the fire, and the dark too was a stillness, and a quiet contentment and quiet certainty that Thomas found, for the first time in his life, he could accept, and *almost* begin to understand. A perfection unutterable.

Below, something new was happening. The crowd of monstrous stone shapes was parting, lumbering uneasily aside to let something else through. It was long, spindly and, at the best of times, aerodynamically unsound. It looked up at the sky with black marble eyes, opened a jaw the length of Thomas's arm, licked dry sharp teeth with a dry sharp tongue that flicked hungrily at the air, stretched ancient, solid, slow joints and, with an inexorability equal to the setting of the sun, fixed its gaze on Icarus.

Tess began to turn white. 'Bigwig?'

Thomas didn't answer. 'Bigwig, it's ... startin' to run. *Bigwig!* It's got wings!'

'Don't be absurd, Teresa! The probabilities of something weighing that much with such a small wing surface area ratio ever accumulating enough lift to get off the ground is so small it's practically negligib—'

'*Bigwig! It's not runnin' on the ground no more!*'

And below, although getting closer with each moment, the

coiled stone dragon that had guarded a tomb or maybe a spire while it slept unstretched, spread its unimpressive wings, and leapt for the sky. Incredibly, improbably, the sky let it stay as, twisting like a snake caught in a trap, it rose above the fog, catching the moonlight on its shiny, polished stone surface, and turned, jaws agape, straight for Icarus.

CHAPTER 17

Chase

And, without warning, Lyle was running blind, in fog and darkness.

He slowed, stopped, looking around, searching for a sign of life this way or that, his only sense of geography given by the slope of the Heath and an instinct that somewhere, that way, a long way off, was the river. It was at times like these that Lyle almost wanted something to pray to.

He felt in his pockets. They bulged less than before. The dynamo was in Tess's hands, somewhere overhead, and the little glass spheres that burnt so brightly were almost gone: two left out of the handful he always carried. In the darkness, he ran his hands over the tubes that filled his pockets, feeling the shapes and sizes of their corks, the tiny indentations in each one suggesting what might be inside. His fingers brushed the matchbox, slid it open, felt inside. One match left. He closed the matchbox and shuffled onward through the dark, hands held out clumsily, feet feeling the way, like a blind man.

There were things around, in the darkness. He couldn't see them, but he could hear through the fog the definite crunch of hard snow underfoot, faint but close, and was aware of the shadows keeping him company. He stopped again, listening for the sounds, and they stopped, all around. He moved a step, and so did something else. He peered into the dark. The hint of a shadow too deep off to the left, the tiny suggestion of a flash too bright off to the right, the sense of an exposed back and an unknown front. Lyle swallowed and once again ran his hands through his pockets, feeling the limited remains of his arsenal of chemicals and tools. 'Come on,' he muttered under his breath. 'Come *on*.'

As if in answer to his prayer, the shadows deepened all around. Lyle turned white. 'I didn't mean it!' he hissed, feeling slightly embarrassed and extremely resentful that for once in his life he hadn't followed his basic principles, which had always suggested that loose talk really *did* cost lives.

And ahead, far away, muffled by the fog, there was a new sound, a sudden familiar clatter: horses' hooves and iron-bound wooden wheels, fading into darkness. Lyle thanked whichever theologically unsound and scientifically impractical non-entity was watching over him that night, bent his burnt hand into a fist, took a deep breath, and ran faster with the blind speed of a man who had nothing left to lose.

Around him, on every side, the gargoyles of London Town also started to run.

Tess lit another fuse and another tube started to spark. Five were burning already, propelling Icarus forward with an unsteady jerkiness that made it buck like a ship in a storm, and still the stone dragon was following, still it rose behind them, teeth snapping ready for the kill. 'It's gaining!' she shrieked.

'How close is it?'

'About . . . some . . . maybe a few . . .' Tess wished she'd paid more attention to measurements when Lyle tried to explain them. 'Close!'

Thomas looked down. Below, half-obscured in the fog, were the uneven chimney stacks of London. The moonlight gleamed on a host of railway lines, converging into a single silver arrow racing towards the city. He banked the plane and shouted, 'Hold on!'

'What?' screamed Tess over the roar of the wind.

'Hold on to something! Cling! Grab!'

'What?'

He shook his head and muttered under his breath, 'Just don't let go.' He kicked a lever and felt, behind him, flaps in the wings turn and rise as, writhing round the guttering flame of the burning tubes, the stone dragon twisted, reaching out a claw for their tail, which snapped up past its grey snout as the head of the ship tipped forward and plummeted down towards the silver of the railway lines. Icarus dropped like a stone, describing almost a straight line as it fell, the wings screaming and creaking, trying to grab at the air. The railway lines grew and grew, until they seemed to fill the world, the fog over the track half-broken by the passage of the trains and their burning engines. Tess heard the angry whistle of a steam train somewhere through the wind and the darkness, saw the railway lines so close she half-imagined she could jump now and land easily on her feet, heard the *clunk* as Thomas punched a lever and a gear slid into place somewhere in the mass of cogs and levers that held together the wings in all their parts.

As the wing slid back to its natural shape, she felt the cradle shudder beneath her, and thought that she could feel the wood stretching, see it bend under the sudden pressure. She looked back and saw the stone dragon, wings tucked in to almost nothing, diving after them, snout forward, marble eyes unblinking. Her stomach lurched as, laboriously, Icarus twisted, wheels almost scraping the railway, and righted itself, the world a blur merely a few feet below. Fog and cold and fast-moving dark air stung her eyes as Icarus raced along just above the railway line. Behind her, one of the tubes gave a little whine and died, the flames slowly retreating at its back. But Icarus was moving so fast now it hardly mattered, with Thomas struggling to keep the nose level as the whole contraption hungered for higher air and space. Ahead, Tess saw lights, dim and yellow, rising high above the track. An almighty shudder shook Icarus; the dragon was there, its claws blackened by the flames bursting out from the back of Icarus; blackened but not even scratched.

'Bigwig!' she screamed, but he didn't answer, or if he did, the answer was lost. She heard the whistle of the train again, and this time it was closer, and this time there were other sounds coming with it, the steady *cump-humph-cump-humph* of the engines and fat belchings of steam. She looked with a sort of inexorable certainty towards the lights ahead and saw one growing larger and larger, bringing with it a vague blackness that cut out the lights behind it. '*Tho-maaassss!*'

Thomas let go of a lever and Icarus, its wings nearly flapping loose with the strain against them, exploded upwards almost vertically, catching the rush of air with open wings and accepting it like the release from the pressure of low flight that it was. Another tube was whining and giving out, and then Icarus began to slow, hesitating, drifting. Tess looked down. Below, the railways were lit up with orange light on either side of the rush of a train, and, running along its roof, stone claws digging through the frail wooden ceiling, was the stone dragon, eyes still fixed on them. Icarus slowed and, for a second, seemed to hang in the air. The dragon leapt, stretching to its full, incredible length, claws open, teeth ready. Tess stared at it in rapt horror, unaware of Thomas's shout in her ears, just feeling the sudden stillness of Icarus and the hypnotic steadiness of the black eyes.

Something cold and wet struck her face as Tate brought her sharply back to the high-speed rush of the present. He bounced in her lap, ears flying out behind him like a flag, and Thomas's words formed into a coherent exclamation in her mind. 'Light it, light another or we're dead, light it now!'

She spun round and struck a light to two more fuses, just as a third tube was dying. They began to spark. Below, the dragon rose up with an almost luxurious ease, turned towards Icarus, and, claws outstretched, charged for the heart of the ship. It stretched hard, immovable death towards the belly of Icarus, and the two tubes exploded in flame. Icarus lurched forward, twisting on to one side unevenly as, with a bang that shook the ship, the dragon missed by an inch, and scraped along underneath, sending splinters flying as it scored the hull. Icarus dived back towards the light, and Tess heard something go *clunk*. She looked up.

Two gears in the mass that controlled the wing were jammed, warping around the bolts that held them. She hammered at them with her fists, but they were wedged, trapped between each other. Icarus began to bend, one wing twisting down uncomfortably below the other, pulling the nose round with it in a spiral that brought them lower and lower. Tess half-stood up in the cradle and beat at the jammed gears with an elbow, but that just hurt her elbow. Below them, the slightly surprised dragon was rising again, tail writhing. Tess almost screamed in fury and frustration, grabbed the nearest dead tube, still sparking occasionally and, with utter disregard for the heat that seared her fingers, slammed it as hard as she could against the gear. It clunked, bent, wobbled for a second, and slid back into the whirling mass of cogs, which clattered happily on.

Icarus lurched to the right, nearly throwing Tess out and pitching Tate against the side. The tube fell away from her hands, spinning leisurely down into the blackness, still sparking, trailing its burnt fuse line. Below, she saw the dragon spin automatically and catch the tube in its claws, snapping it in two and throwing the jagged metal pieces away, in a shower of black dust from the clogged and burnt up chemical fuel. Tess began to frown. There was . . . a feeling. A sudden, calm stillness inside. Just for a second.

She found herself looking thoughtfully at the tubes.

Chase

And Icarus was diving again, twisting easily through the air towards the lights ahead, which became clearer through the fog and formed, in quick succession, a large arch across the darkness ahead, then an arch full of steaming black shapes, then a giant arch full of shapes and people and lamps and luggage racks, then an arch full of shapes and people and lamps and luggage racks and bridges and steel girders and clocks and whistles and noises and trains and then became, in an instant, the giant iron arch of King's Cross Station, into which, with utter ease, Icarus flew.

Lyle was running. It was in many ways a liberating feeling. His legs had hit their stride and he was bounding blindly along, his direction given only by the slope and the gravity that pulled him towards its base. Thorns and brush and shrubs lashed at his ankles, snow spattered up around his shoes, ice slid under his heels, but he was moving so fast he hardly had time to register any of this. The noise of pursuit was all around, a constant rush of air and crunching of snow, no cries or thuds, but the unmistakable sound of heavy stone feet. And still Lyle kept running, face burning in the cold, breathing fast and shallow but keeping a steady rhythm. He'd passed the point of pain long ago; now there was just a throbbing in his legs that pushed him to run faster, if only to escape the burning of his own blood. He flew down the Heath, coat flapping, shoes soaked through, toes itching and burning from the melted snow and the weight of the run. The sounds of pursuit seemed further off, or maybe his own breathing was louder. Lyle hardly cared now, the run had turned into everything, his world, nothing else was important, all that mattered was the speed and the freedom and the darkness that stripped you of thought and fear and left behind a sudden, internal stillness, a perfection unutterable . . .

The Heath stopped so suddenly under Lyle's feet that he tripped over the brush at its edge and landed on his hands and knees on the hard stone road, new and barely disturbed either by the passage of traffic or by the dirt of the city. A single lamp burnt at the corner, casting a dull light on the snow at its base. Lyle shuffled towards it, and pressed his burnt palm into the ice that clung to it, gasping for air, ears ringing with the effort of the run, and looked back into the fog. He could see nothing, hear nothing. He began cautiously to sidle down the edge of the road, following the tracks of carts in the snow, away from the light. The Heath dropped away, to be replaced by the high walls of new mansions for the rich and privileged, gleaming with ice. He kept walking, four hundred yards, five hundred. The streets were empty, but he followed his nose and instinct through the thinning fog, smelling the dirt of a more familiar, older city somewhere ahead, the smoke and sewage that, even out here in the rich suburbs, was faintly noticeable on the air, and in many ways all the sharper for its subtlety – enough to notice, but not enough to get used to as the smell drifted in and out of perception.

Lyle thought, *A priest pays a fortune to smuggle from a Vatican madhouse a man made of stone who controls stone, and who may or may not be utterly mad, messianic and murderous. In* my *city* . . .

Nearly a quarter mile, walls on all sides; and the faintest noise. It was the wet, hissing sound of snow falling. Lyle stopped and listened. The noise came again, just a little bit louder. He advanced another cautious pace. The sound grew, and underneath it was another, a hard, heavy clattering. With a sense of weary dread, he turned.

Snow was pouring down the street, a tidal wave of it, being pushed ahead of a moving wall of cobblestones that grew higher and higher as he watched, the cobbles building on top of each other, pressing against the walls on every side, rushing down towards him, the hardest tidal wave he'd ever imagined. Lyle turned and ran. He reached for the nearest wall and was leaping for the top with an agility lent by terror, slipping on snow and ice as he scrambled at it. He clawed his way over the top, bracing his legs against the side and leaning his weight into the cracks between the bricks, as the wall rushed down, showering snow and dirt around, the street behind just a muddy mess of torn soil.

Lyle threw himself off the top of the wall and down on to the other side as the wave passed by, snapping at his coat tail and sending cobbles showering this way and that. He landed badly, on one side, crooked, legs flailing and arm going under him. Beyond the wall, the wave of cobbles collapsed, useless, a deafening roar of stone crashing down. Lyle scrambled away from the wall, limping slightly, across the darkness of a lawn. The grounds seemed endless, trees neatly laid out, the glow of a house somewhere in the distance. A stone house; Lyle didn't dare approach. He felt his way to the darkness of the wrought-iron gate and struggled to pull it open.

Something brushed against his shoulder. He jumped, pressing his back against the iron gate, clinging on to it. His eyes now fell on two empty stone pedestals on either side of the gate, then moved slowly to the two figures standing before him. They were shorter than normal men, wore tunics in a classical Greek style and each had a laurel wreath in its hair. They were, in brief, the kind of ornamental statues Lyle told himself he should really have expected. They looked at him quizzically, a boy and girl, with tranquil faces. Lyle's fingers tightened in useless fear round the iron of the gate; he didn't move, didn't breathe.

Slowly, thoughtfully, one of the statues reached out and ran its hand down the side of his face, starting at his hair, leaving a trail in the blood, sweat and dirt that stained his face, running its cold stone fingers under his chin, down his neck, stopping, two fingers lightly resting on the side of his neck, so that he could feel his own pulse against its cold touch. He swallowed, tried to speak, couldn't think of anything to say, fell silent once more. More cold fingers slid down to touch his throat. He thought, *What a waste,* and closed his eyes.

And something exploded through the gate.

CHAPTER 18

Friends

People scattered as Icarus exploded into the arched metal tube of King's Cross Station, screaming and running for cover as the wooden ship passed overhead, trailing fire and sparks on the waiting trains. Those who had stayed and watched, the intrepid who gaped and pointed and clapped and frowned as the machine rattled overhead, joined their neighbours in wild flight when, with as much confidence as Hannibal faced with a mountain, the stone dragon dipped easily down under the iron rafters of the station. Tess was struggling with an unlit tube at the back of Icarus — not trying to light it, but pulling it out of the clamps that held it down, freeing it and the fuse wire that ran to it, oblivious to the screams of people below and the rapid shrinking of the platform's length. She dragged it free just as the stone dragon roared and dived, tearing at a train below with its claws before lashing up and towards Icarus. Looking up, for the first time she registered where they were. 'Bigwig!'

'Miss Teresa?'

'What the hell are you doin'?'

'We can fly out through the entrance!'

'You ain't never been 'ere before, 'ave you?'

'How can you tell?'

'I mightn't know about distances, but I know if summat's bigger than summat else and we're *big*!'

A slight hesitation. For a second there was just the rush of wind. 'The entrance . . . isn't small, is it?'

'What d'you think?'

Thomas's eyes flew round the iron-arched prison, flickered up to the giant yellow brick wall at the end which was getting closer faster, and faster, and *faster* and . . .

'Tess, get down, hide your head!'

Tess looked up too and saw the wall, the two huge windows set in it. 'You gotta be havin' a laugh!'

'Too late now!'

Tess threw herself forward, pushing Tate underneath her legs and covering her head with her hands as, with a jerk, Thomas pulled on the controls. The wings dipped and rose, pitching the shell of the ship over on to one side, so that it arced through the air in a long curve that dragged it towards the wall. Thomas grabbed another lever, the gears slamming into reverse. One wing rose, the other dropped, lurching the ship on to its other side, into another curve away from the far wall and straight towards the window. Tess closed her eyes and, an instant before impact, so did Thomas, diving forward, hands over his head. The nose of Icarus ploughed straight into one of the huge, semi-circular windows in the front of King's Cross, smashing it into a million pieces which flooded down like snow in an avalanche, shattering into smaller and smaller parts off the hull of the ship. For a second Icarus travelled along in a cocoon of falling glass, small shards snagged in the wood or sliding along the wings, showering all around before it was free and spinning out towards the wall of a machine shop. Thomas opened his eyes, saw giant, friendly letters painted on the wall – 'Machines, Weights and Scales, Gray's Inn Road' – and kicked at the nearest lever. The nose of Icarus swung upwards, arrowing for the moon. Behind, the great stone dragon slithered out of the shattered window, hesitating as it tried to find its prey again, then leaping forward with silent determination, claws stretched for Icarus.

Lyle threw himself on to the ground out of instinct, covering his head with his hands, as something fast exploded through the gate. He heard two loud, sharp bangs and felt snow shower around him, then heard the whinny of horses and the stamp of hooves. He felt something a few inches away skidding in the snow and coming to an eventual stop. He slowly raised his head.

A man, dressed all in black, face hidden in a burgundy-red scarf, looked down at Lyle. Lyle raised his head and peered past him, at the cab that had been driven through the gate behind a pair of wild-eyed horses, then beyond, to where one of the statues was already back on its feet. Cracks showed around its neck and arms where the stone was thinnest, but it was struggling inexorably towards them nonetheless.

'Erm . . .' began Lyle, pointing a trembling, burnt, filthy finger in the direction of the statue. Without looking up at it, the man in black bent down, grabbed Lyle by the back of his collar, and dragged him on to his feet and out of the gate at a brisk pace that left Lyle scampering feebly through the snow, slipping and sliding, half concussed and extremely confused. The cab was waiting under a lamp post, with the driver dismounted and holding the horses. Both were well-fed, sleek black stallions, not the average beast of burden that shuffled round the streets of London all the days of the year.

Lyle found himself pushed up next to the driver's seat and squeezed in beside the man in black, who grabbed the reins, nodded once at the driver holding the horses and murmured softly, '*Xiexie.*'

The driver nodded back, turned and ran off into the darkness. The man in black snapped at the reins, in a few seconds urging the horses into a trot and then a gallop. Lyle clung desperately to the side of the seat with the last ounce of strength and willpower he had left. He felt in terrible need of a comfortable chair by a good fire, of answers and explanations and maybe a decent curve of direct proportionality squared with which he could feel at home.

Instead, as they clattered through the streets, the man in the burgundy scarf demanded, 'How many chemicals do you have left in your pocket?'

Lyle patted them, in a daze. 'Some,' he muttered.

'How many of them are acids or explosives?'

'A few. Why?'

'You'll need them before this night is out.'

'I thought you'd say that, Feng Darin.'

The man in black hesitated, then smiled behind the scarf. 'How long have you known, Horatio Lyle?'

'Ever since you fed Tate one of those damn ginger biscuits. You're the only spy I know with such a weakness for them. What piqued your interest this time? The mad priest with an intellectual deficiency? Or the madder man who turns to stone in bright light?'

'A bit of both.'

'And are you here out of personal attachment to the noble cause of self-preservation, or were you sent again by your employers?'

Another smile, slightly wider. Amusement in his voice, though his eyes never left the road. 'A little bit of both.'

With one hand Feng Darin swept the scarf away from his face, and in the dull light that burned on the cab, Lyle saw the familiar worn features, dark walnut brown from both his origin and his occupation. Lyle said quietly, 'You disappeared without a word after St Paul's.'

'No. I visited you in hospital, while you were still asleep, after your fall.'

Lyle nodded, then frowned once more. 'We're in the poop this time.'

'Tell me everything when we're safe.'

'There seems to be no safety.'

'I know a place.'

'And you'd know what's happening, too?'

'Some of it. But if I knew everything, Horatio Lyle, I wouldn't need you. What explosives are you carrying?'

'Ammonia compounds, and reactants, one or two things that can oxidize very rapidly when exposed to heat, but nothing that does severe damage.'

'I always wondered why you carried them.'

'You never know when you'll need to blow something up. Why do you ask?'

'Because we need to survive long enough to have a private conversation.' They spun round a corner, rattling down towards the lights of the city, following the railway lines towards Euston and Marylebone. Lyle watched the cobbles racing by beneath them, saw the lights getting brighter and the squalid little houses that clung to the side of the railway lines growing thicker as the real city began to intrude on the false city of the suburban mansions. In the shadows, he saw something moving among the roadside slums, keeping level, and felt a shudder down his spine, and imagined a cold touch at his throat. Feng lashed at the reins again, eyes flickering this way and that, and Lyle knew he wasn't the only one watching the shadows. And with that realization came the sudden awareness of a tune, hummed almost inaudibly under Feng's breath. '*London Bridge is falling down, falling down, falling down. London Bridge is falling down, my fair lady . . .*'

Lyle clung tighter to the side of the cab.

'What are you doing?'

'You don't just try an' hit nothin', bigwig!' Tess was leaning over the side of Icarus, almost on her feet, holding a loose tube in one hand. Icarus raced over the roofs of Gray's Inn Road, over yellow-brick houses selling weights and measures and old clothes and broken furniture, sending the ladies who haunted the area, and the men who pretended they didn't, scattering below. Seven of the tubes were now blazing at the back of Icarus, and still the stone dragon was keeping behind, twisting its way through the air with a snake-like movement. Gravity clearly had decided to look the other way, rather than deal with those claws.

'Can you get higher?' Tess yelled.

'Why do we want to go higher?'

'Who's givin' the orders round here, bigwig?'

Thomas tugged at a lever. Icarus jerked, flaps moving in the wings, the area facing the wind of their passage growing larger, pushing Icarus bodily upwards. Tess had the outer casing of the tube stripped away, revealing the packed, staged chemicals compressed around the central fan, like a second casing to the tube. She grabbed at the fuse, which ran from the end of the tube into the heart of the fan, passing through one chemical and one only, which was to burn at a constant rate, heating the air that passed through the small inner fans to provide thrust, and started wrapping the fuse tightly not only round that chemical, but round every other weird, compressed chemical pack that surrounded the tube, so that only a small part of the wire was left free as she slid the tube back into its casing. She turned and screamed, 'Bigwig?'

'Yes, Miss Teresa?' Thomas's teeth chattered and his voice wheezed with effort. Icarus was still climbing, the air growing thinner and colder as they rushed for the moon, trailing sparks and fire.

'You need to let the dragon get close!'

'I need to *what*?'

'*Who's in charge here?*' snapped Tess. 'I want you to let him get real close, so close he can touch us, and then, when he's close, an' I give the word, I want you to dive, go right back down the way we was, and don't stop for nothin' 'cos we need to be a real long way away very quick!'

'Why?'

Tess looked down at the tube in her hands, the tiny nose of the twisted fuse peering out from the end. ''Cos there's goin' to be a real big bang.'

'Miss Teresa?' Thomas's voice was a faint wheeze in the air. 'I don't think this is a good idea.'

Tess looked down. Below, the city lay black and still, half-washed in the fog, a misty outline of dull fires, eclipsed by the rising shape of the dragon. 'Well . . . there ain't nothin' better, is there?'

For a second, she had the feeling of eyes on her, and looked up, and saw the moon filling the sky, rocking from side to side in front of her. She realized that, just for a moment, she was a shadow across its face, a blackness blotting out its light. It was a feeling she'd never had before, and it was both frightening and wonderful. Briefly she smiled and wondered who, a long, long way below, might be watching.

'That's them!'

Lyle almost stood in his seat, pointing at the moon. 'Look!'

Feng glanced up from the reins, and then half-leant round Lyle to see properly, eyes widening.

'What is *that*?' The silhouette of Icarus, stretched across the moon, seemed to hang overhead like an eclipse by a tiny planet across the face of a watery sun. It didn't visibly move, but they could see the faint haze below it, where the sparks and flames of its passage floated towards the earth.

Lyle laughed. 'It's them! It's working, it's *working* – look at the height, look at it! They're all right, it *worked*!'

'Lyle, get *down*!'

Lyle ducked automatically. There wasn't any disobeying a voice like that. The gargoyle sprang off the roof to his right, missed his head by an inch and slid down the side of the cab. Stone claws hooked into the wood of the cab, which lurched as Feng slapped the horses into a wilder and faster gallop. Lyle looked and saw the gargoyle, all odd angles and bent, sharp limbs, climbing, talon over talon, up the side of the cab. He scrambled on to the roof, belly down, swaying with the speed, his feet dangling over one side, and as the first claw reached the top, he drew out a tube from his pocket and slammed it on the claw. A howl split the night, and it didn't just come from the gargoyle. The streets hummed with it, the houses swayed with it, everything of stone or clay or brick offered its own unique noise to the overall cacophony.

The contents of the tube spilt out on to the talon and the wood of the cab; it hissed, smoked and gave off white, obnoxious vapour that stung Lyle's eyes. The stone of the claw began to dissolve, melting away to leave a thick black scorch mark, and where the acid had missed the stone, wood bubbled and dissolved. Lyle shoved at the gargoyle and, with one claw boiled away, it fell back, tumbling with a clatter into the road.

The cab swung round a corner, nearly throwing Lyle off. He saw lights ahead, recognized them, heard the bleating of sheep and the mooing of cows coming in from the west along Marylebone Road for the early morning market at Smithfield and the rattling of carts laden with vegetables and fruits for Spitalfields and Covent Garden; heard too the clocks ringing out the hours between night and morning when all decent folk should be abed.

'Where are we going?' he yelled at Feng.

'Hyde Park.'

'Why? What's at Hyde Park?'

'Safety!'

The cab clattered on through the thick traffic, sending horses neighing and shying as it belted along, while men shouted abuse. Lyle looked up and saw the Greek columns of a church, four huge stone ladies supporting the giant stone roof, turn their heads ever so slightly, eyes fixed on him, on *him*, before the sight of them was whisked away in the rush of the cab. He could feel something more than just the swaying of the cab, and see it too. Trees were twisting in pain, snow trickled off rooftops in avalanches, the light in the lanterns flickered and stretched itself thin. He half-closed his eyes and sensed the hum rising up through his shins and fingertips.

'Feng!' he yelled.

'What?'

'We need to get off this cab!'

'Why?'

Lyle opened his mouth to answer, and behind, just a few inches behind, the street exploded. Cobbles and dirt and brick and snow ruptured out and upwards, luxuriously reaching out for the sky like a mouth opening its jaws hungrily for its prey, the edges bending back like lips, eating up all that might be above it. Then, with an almost languorous air, the mouth closed around the space where the cab had been, sucking in the air and snow, and slid back down into the street.

'Because of that!' yelled Lyle.

He felt another rumble in front of the cab. He saw the cobbles bend and yelled, '*Feng Darin!*'

Feng pulled at the reins, swerving the cab off the road and into a side-street that ran between a wall of factories and sweat shops and smelt of coal and mould and stagnant water turned to solid ice. At that moment the street behind them erupted into another mouth that kissed at the air. And there was something else too. Looking back, Lyle saw two faint bulges in the street, saw the stones peel back like eyelids, saw the mouth bend, before it collapsed again, into a cruel, unnatural smile.

Feng stopped the cab so suddenly it nearly threw Lyle off.

'Can you ride?' Feng had already jumped down and was unharnessing the horses.

'I'm a bloody scientist, not Sir Galahad,' snapped Lyle, scrambling down from the roof of the cab.

'It's incredible that you've survived as long as you have, Horatio Lyle,' muttered Feng, swinging easily on to the bare back of one of the horses, before pulling Lyle up behind him. 'Just try not to fall off.'

Feng dug his heels into the horse's sides. It leapt forward with an angry snort, and pounded off down the street with utter disregard for the discomfort of its riders. Lyle clung on, trying not to let his fear show, listening to the sounds of a city coming alive around him.

CHAPTER 19

Escape

Icarus reached the top of its flight and, for a second, hung there. The last tube went out. They drifted gently through the cold air.

'Miss Teresa?' Now that there was just the gentle humming of the wind across the still shape of Icarus, gliding past the moon, Thomas's voice sounded clearly, and Tess could hear the fear in it. She could also hear the wind being beaten out underneath the dragon's wings below them, a thick *whumph*, *whumph* sound.

'Yes, bigwig?'

'What was your plan, precisely, from this point onwards?'

'Mister Lyle was tryin' to tell me about this thing to do with work,' said Tess calmly, leaning out and peering down at the rising shadow. 'An' . . . an' how heat and work were really kinda part of the same thing, I mean, just like another way of moving energy about. Do you see?'

'You mean the laws of thermodynamics, the transfer of heat to do work?'

Tess frowned. 'Ain't no need for words that big, bigwig.'

To his surprise, Thomas heard himself say, 'I'm sorry, Miss Teresa. Please, carry on.'

'Well . . .' Tess's voice had a thoughtful quality to it, a distant maturity. She had changed, Thomas realized, in the few months Lyle had been looking after her. She'd learnt to read, for a start. '. . . Mister Lyle was sayin' how it ain't just heat what can be used to do work, but work what can be used to do heat. How . . . if you work *on* something like . . . like a smith banging away with his hammer . . . then that thing gets hot. I pretended I weren't listenin'. But sometimes it almost seems peaceful, just listenin'. Like . . . quiet an' warm. Safe.'

'And how is this relevant to us, Miss Teresa?'

Tess snapped sharply out of her train of thought. ''Cos,' she hissed, as if talking to a child, 'that *thing*' – as the dragon rose up level with them, and swung round the gently gliding Icarus as if it was a toy, flexing its claws – 'could crush us into a little bitty piece of goo.'

And as Icarus slid along under the stars, the dragon stared straight into Thomas's eyes, and for a moment, he too felt as if he was stone, felt as if a greater intelligence, an old and ancient force, was watching him, and him alone. Then something sailed past his head, swinging through the sky, tumbling one end over the other. It was the tube of compressed chemicals and a fan, so simple and scientifically elegant, something where he'd seen the numbers that made it the shape it was, running together towards the equals sign, to make up a perfect, satisfying answer to a question he'd never even thought to ask. Cold air comes in, hot air goes out, and it goes out fast.

He saw the dragon spin, the tube bouncing uselessly off its stone side. It looked almost bemused, as if wondering whether any intellectual being could really be foolish enough to think it could hurt an entity made out of stone and improbability. Thomas watched the tube fall away, slightly bent where it had bounced off, saw the dragon reach out a luxurious claw and catch it lightly, holding it up towards Icarus as though to say, 'This? This is the best you can do?' It tightened both claws around the tube; squeezed. He saw the end of the tube give off a single, fat, embarrassed spark. Behind, he heard Tess say, quite casually, 'This is where we goes down, bigwig.'

He saw the dragon look at the tube compressed between its claws with a surprised expression. Thomas pushed at a lever, tipping the nose of Icarus earthwards. The tail rose slowly, the wings dipped, presenting a smaller and smaller line to the wind. Creaking gently, Icarus began to dive. As it dropped, pulled down by sheer gravity, it picked up speed and began to rock from side to side. Cogs started to rattle, wood to creak and bend. They were already travelling fast when above them a high-pitched *whiiinnnggg* sounded, like a child's whistle. They were a blur when the tube, still suspended in the dragon's grip, started to spout fire at both ends: flickering, angry red fire. They were an unstoppable rush through the sky, just a black shimmer against the moonlight, when the tube, compressed and twisted, every chemical inside igniting at once in a deadly inferno of reactants, exploded.

Stone rained down, spinning through the air as it tried to catch up with Icarus, shards that here or there contained the image of an eye or the shape of a wing or the half-impressed outline of a scale, spattering down like rain, with fire and smoke and twisted metal mingling in the overall ruin. Even propelled by the force of the explosive blast, it fell too slowly to catch up with Icarus.

Below, getting closer with every second, Tess saw a white pool of frozen water, rising up to meet Icarus's dipped nose. She heard the sound of cogs grating as Thomas struggled with the levers, kicking against them furiously to make them shift in their gears. The giant whiteness rose up to fill the world: thick ice swept clean of snow by enthusiastic skaters. A lever slid back and Icarus lurched to one side then the other, rocking like a ship in a storm. Tess heard something go *clunk* above her, and, looking up, saw the gears warping, splinters flying off the top and bottom of the wing, heard something else give, saw something small but vital pop out of the central core of gears and cogs and spin away, flying into the night. Icarus seemed to back-pedal in the air as the wings swung round to catch the wind, almost pushing its nose backwards over its tail with the force, and slamming Tess back against the cradle. They hit the fog that hung over London, and the world filled with thin greyness, turning the outline of all things distant into mere blurs on the edge of perception. As the world rose up to meet them, Tess put her head in her hands and closed her eyes.

Icarus hit the ice, bounced back up, landed, bounced again, one wheel jerking, ready to snap, landed again, and spun like a confused ballerina, the ice pulverizing under the sudden force of their impact, leaving a long wet pool behind as they wobbled and shook, wheels screaming with effort, and the cradle almost shaking loose from the wings. Underneath, Tess heard something snap; Icarus tipped sharply on to one side, almost throwing Tate out. She half-saw in the darkness one of the wheels, sparking madly, flying away, and now they were spinning around one point, the leg of the wheel, dug deep into the ice, scraping and screeching like nails across a blackboard. They spun until her vision whirled and her ears buzzed and her stomach churned, and stopped.

Tess crawled out of the cradle, and collapsed on to the ice, shaking with relief and terror. Thomas followed. Where Icarus had spun round, the remaining wheel had defined a perfect circle scraped over the ice. Thomas looked at Tess, Tess looked at Thomas. Tate slunk out, sat down with doggy determination on firm land just beyond the edge of the ice, and stuck his nose in the air with a look of profound indignation. Something tickled Tess's head. She looked up, then held her hand out to the sky to catch whatever it was that was falling. Thin grey powder settled lightly in her palm. She rubbed it, then let it trickle away between her fingers on to the ice. Stone dust. She smiled.

Behind, in the shadows, a voice exploded. '*What the hell do you think you're doing to my ship?*'

A few minutes before Thomas's and Tess's descent from the sky, any persons who happened to be in the vicinity of Soho Square might have been startled to see an unsaddled black stallion explode out of Charing Cross Road and gallop in a westerly direction with two dark riders on its back. Their surprise would have been increased by the extraordinary swaying motion of the riders, as if they were trying to avoid something unseen from sneaking up unawares. Surprise would then have converted to amazement if the perceptive viewers, seeing through the fog and gaslight and general fatigue of the hour, had noticed the quite remarkable manner in which the cobbles seemed to ripple behind them, like the wake after a ship, and how unnaturally the trees bent in their passage, and how oddly the buildings suddenly looked, as if they were things alive, monsters shuffling in for the kill.

Ahead of Feng and Lyle, the shadows moved, and behind them too. Lyle could hear something on the street: hard, ponderous sounds thudding through the snow, which only slightly muffled them.

'What's behind us?' yelled Feng as the horse twisted its way through the streets.

'I don't know!'

'You're the detective!'

'I hear . . . four legs, moving . . . very heavy, at a gallop!' Lyle saw a shadow getting bigger, rising out of the fog, growing from small to horse-sized to a towering shape that filled the street, its shoulders pressing against the walls of the houses, which seemed to make space for it to pass, leaning away from its giant form. 'Get us somewhere narrow!' he yelled. 'Do it now!'

Feng made no answer, but pulled on the reins. The horse twisted round a corner and dived down a dark alley, just as the lion, one of four usually swarmed over by children and pigeons, that guarded Nelson's Column, slammed its shoulders against the old, crooked timbers of the alley, sending splinters and shards flying after them, its shadow cutting off the light from the lanterns in the street beyond. The horse galloped down the alley and out the other side. Lyle looked back the way they had come, and saw the lantern light again, unobscured by any shape. He looked ahead, and there were no lights burning, except for the occasional glimmer from under a rotting door.

'This is the rookery!' he yelled.

'I know!'

'You really want to go in there?' Above, something roared. The lion looked down at them from the roof of a house, claws unsheathed, and snarled.

'Never mind!'

Feng kicked the horse into action again as the lion drew back ready to spring, tons of rippling stone poised to kill. It didn't need to get at them with its claws or teeth, thought Lyle. It just needed to sit down and that would be the end of them. The lion reared up, but the roof it stood on, buckling with age and rot, couldn't take so much weight on such a small area. With a roar, the old timbers parted, sucking the stone lion down. Lyle saw the frames of the glassless windows shatter and explode outwards, flying after the retreating horse and riders, saw the walls of the house, already bent and crippled like the narrow winding streets, bulge with the passage of the beast through its floors, and give out, flying in every direction, and emerging from it all, the lion shook itself free, spitting stone dust.

The horse lurched, pitching Lyle forward. Ahead he saw a cellar door, tall and open, and ducked as Feng urged the horse down into it. In the rookery, you didn't use streets to move from place to place; every house was an open road, every cellar a sewer, every rooftop a public tavern, every room a hovel for ten, every shadow a thief. They rode through the stultifying darkness of the cellar, mud and dirt and old straw flying up from the horse's hooves, and then up on to a winding street closed off at both ends by houses that had grown like cancers out of their limits, shattered walls and piles of refuse combining into something almost solid and sentient.

Behind them, the end of the road exploded as the lion walked straight through the shoddy, crooked house that blocked it, shaking itself free of dust and shattered timbers, and fixed its eyes on the horse as it swerved into another house, tore through a room of ten, twenty sleeping shapes huddled on the floor head to toe, and out of the door at the end, into another alley.

'Lyle?'

'Yes?'

'Can you do anything about our pursuer?'

'Do I look as if I carry *that* much nitroglycerine?'

'Can you do anything else?'

'Do you know the St Martin's brewery?'

'Yes?'

'You know it has a crane? And a vat in the basement.'

'Yes?' Feng thought about it. 'Heaven have mercy – you can do that?'

'Are you asking about the legality or the scientific practicality?'

Behind, the lion exploded over the next house, and landed in the street with a shudder that sent snow pouring off the rooftops and the horse's hooves sliding on the unstable cobbles. 'Neither!' snapped Feng. He pulled the horse round in a new direction and they thundered on.

A pause, a moment, another place, another sight.

A stillness. A stillness so certain and so constant, it is almost hollow and empty, for there is no sign of movement or life in it to give it character.

A man stands, eyes closed, a statue, on Hampstead Heath, and lives through the stones of London Town. And though Lucan Sasso's mind is cast through the streets and the stones, though it hums with power as it warps the streets themselves to its will, though the cobbles twitch when his finger does, though he remains still, is in control, aware of all the feet that trample all the stones below him, he is not aware that he sings a little song as he bends the city of London to his will.

And he sings, in a sad, strangely human voice, from his inhuman throat,

London's burning, London's burning,
Fetch the engines, fetch the engines,
Fire, fire! Fire, fire!
Pour on water, pour on water.

And still, though they twist and live anew to the mind of one man, the stones of London sing their songs, whisper of their past and their people, of the future, and maybe, in just a little way, they bend back against the will that bends them.

London's burning, London's burning . . .

Perhaps the city was always alive.
It just never showed it until now.

*

And somewhere off St Martin's Lane, a pair of huge double doors, barred on the inside, shook, rocked, thundered. Then opened. The giant stone lion sprang inside the St Martin's brewery, finest distiller of deadly alcohols, gin for the ladies who clustered round Covent Garden and clawed at the coats that passed them by, deadly spirits so heavy in alcohol they were only drunk by those who had burnt away their taste buds, and trained for weeks in advance to repress the gag reflex. The floor was in darkness, a few sheltered, very secure lanterns burning in the corners. The building was long and high, cranes reaching from floor to ceiling, a stairway snaking round the wall to the top floor, barrels stacked against every wall.

The lion edged forward, and looked down at the giant central hole in the floor. Below, a full vat sat, not a ripple disturbing its dark surface, ready to be turned into a true mind-melter. A taut rope led from the ceiling up through an open trapdoor, beyond which something orange glowed and a crane waited to take delivery, then down to the vat. This was the crane that lifted the barrels out through the roof and swung them down into the courtyard, dozens at a time, gently swaying.

The lion looked at what hung from the bottom of the rope, a few inches above the vat of alcohol. Lyle, the rope tied round his middle, pale-faced, clung to the side of the vat by the tips of his fingers to stop himself from being dragged up by the tension in the rope. He smiled wanly at the lion. 'I hate heights, you know.'

Above, something went *whumph*. The lion raised its head as Lyle let go of the side of the vat and was dragged, lurching, spinning, up through the centre of the giant building in a blur, all flailing limbs and coat. Heading the other way, the weight that dragged him up by its falling, a barrel plummeted down from the skylight. And it was on fire.

The lion, or at the very least the mind which controlled the lion, clearly wasn't familiar with the basics of combustion. Lyle, passing the downward barrel as he shot upward, already had his hands in front of his eyes and was waiting for the blaze. The flaming barrel struck the vat of alcohol just as Lyle spun through the open skylight and slammed into the crane that overhung it, nearly falling free of the rope that held him, as the flame crawled cautiously from the barrel into the still pool of liquid, discovered that it was alcohol, and duly exploded.

Feng, standing by the crane, had snatched at the helplessly hanging Lyle, dragged him to the edge of the roof, grabbed hold of the rope that supported him, and thrown himself and Lyle off the side of the roof before the blue-orange flame had even reached the lion's knees. As Lyle and Feng dropped down, swinging by the crane rope, falling together towards the street a long way below, the fire and the tattered remnants of the barrel raced each other for the ceiling.

The blue flame ruptured out of the barrel in a thousand flying spatters of boiling alcohol, pushed every window out of its frame, gobbled through every strut and bolt, melted glass in a second, boiled leather and metal, crawled up the walls and into every corner and then, finding that there was nothing there but wood and darkness, reached into the middle of the building and crawled up the air itself, as if it were a ladder to the moon, pillowing up in a flame so bright and so hot, every inch of snow around turned to slush and steam rose up from the street outside, burning away the fog in an angry hiss. The flame reached the skylight and exploded through it, found the crane, found the rope, ate through both in a second, gobbling them up in a hungry explosion of heat and pressure that shattered icicles and made the sky shimmer.

When the flame consumed the rope they clung to, Lyle and Feng were only a few feet above the ground. Feng sprang up in an instant, hurrying away from the fire that already lashed through the windows, roaring for more to fuel it. Lyle lay where he'd fallen, blackened and bruised. Feng cursed, ran to where he lay, and dragged him further from the fire. 'Lyle! Lyle, dammit! Get up!'

Lyle groaned and tried to cover his blackened face with a blackened hand.

'Horatio!' hissed Feng. 'We can't stay here!'

Lyle tried to say something, but the words dissolved into a fit of coughing. He rolled over, hacking black spittle on to the snow. Feng swore, and dragged him up by the armpits. Lyle's eyes opened on to the inferno, whose heat was almost unbearable, even from across the street. People were grouped at windows, bells were starting to ring out through the night, footsteps sounded through the dark. 'My God,' he muttered. 'Did we just do that?'

'Yes, come *on*.'

Lyle looked past Feng, and his eyes widened. He didn't have time to call out, but pushed Feng to one side without a word, and ducked. The lion, blackened almost beyond recognition, missing its back legs and tail, dragging itself forward on one half-shattered paw, roared painfully in the night, dust and pieces of stone crumbling off it, and lashed out again with its one paw. Even as it did, cracks were spreading through the stone. It caught Lyle, lifting him off the ground and spinning him through the air.

Feng pulled himself on to his feet in time to see the lion heave itself painfully another inch forward, the cracks in it growing, running up its forelegs towards its head as it raised its paw above the still shape of Lyle. Feng leapt forward, reaching into his coat as the lion brought its paw round. His hand came out holding something long and black that gleamed dully in the night. He scrambled up on to the lion's ruined shoulder even as its dust slipped away beneath his feet, clung on to the still-smoking, hot stone mane and brought the blade down as hard as he could into the lion's skull.

It slid in like a knife through treacle. The cracks rippled across the lion, reached their very limit, and split. The lion collapsed gently into dust, which spilt across the street in a little storm that billowed into nothing before it reached the corner.

Feng lifted the half-conscious Lyle on to the horse's back, swung up behind, and kicked the horse into a gallop, heading towards Hyde Park.

And in the darkness of the Heath, Lucan Sasso's eyes fly open in surprise and horror. For a long while he just stands, frozen, mute with amazement. His mouth soundlessly moves, trying to speak, trying to find an emotion to match what he thinks he should feel. He remembers how to be surprised, remembers how to be hurt, worried, pained, angered, and he clings to these memories, gives them a face, gives them a name, feels the shock of the lion crumbling into dust, sees the face of Lyle swept away into darkness, and thinks, a roar of thought louder than any speech, making the city's bells sway in their towers and the pigeons start up in surprise, *The blade! Selene's blade!*

CHAPTER 20

The Great Exhibition

'*What the hell do you think you're doing to my ship?*'

Tess recognized the voice instantly. Half-supported by another man, a dark shape in a burgundy scarf, Lyle was staggering away from an exhausted black horse. She gave an irrepressible cry of delight, ran towards him, reached out to hug him, saw that he was covered in soot, thought better of it, stood back and bounced with joy on the spot.

'*WeflewMisterLylean'therewerethisbigdragonthingwhatcameafter usan'IsaidhowIhadthisplanan'howwecouldjustuseoneoftheexplo-sivetubethingstostopitan'thebigwigdidallthesteerin'althoughIwerethe realbrainsbehindtheplanan'* . . .'

'What the hell happened here?' demanded Lyle, limping towards the stricken shape of Icarus.

'Sir! You're all right!' Thomas exclaimed as Lyle paused on the edge of the ice.

'I'm *fine*. I've been chased, burnt, battered, bruised, stared death in the face, experienced heights at speed, blown up half of St Martin's, rushed through a series of cellars on horseback, met an old friend, caused thousands of pounds of damage and been half-eaten by the Marylebone Road: I'm perfect! But what the hell have you children been doing to my pressure-differential device?'

'*OhohIcantelllletmetellitwasallfastandscaryan'Isaidhowweshould dive'costherewerethisthingan . . .*'

'All right!' Lyle raised his hands defensively. 'You can explain later. It doesn't look as if the damage is irreparable. Thomas, though, I'm surprised you couldn't land it better than that. Incidentally . . .' Lyle glanced at each disappointed face. 'You two are all right, are you?'

'*Allright?Allright?MisterLyleyoushould'veseenusalthoughIsayus Imean . . .*'

'Yes, Mister Lyle,' said Thomas.

'Well . . . good,' mumbled Lyle. He hesitated and then, to Thomas's and Tess's complete surprise, knelt down, put an arm round each of them and hugged them close, touching their messed-up hair and brushing their faces with his filthy fingers, which if anything left them more dishevelled than before. And to their respective surprise, each child clung on, digging their fingers into his coat and hair and holding him close as if he were the last thing left alive on the planet.

A second later, he was back on his feet, brushing himself down self-consciously and muttering, 'Well, yes, glad to hear it, good thing, carry on. Yes . . . well . . .'

There was an embarrassed silence, broken by the sound of Tate whining.

The three of them turned to look at Tate. He was sitting squarely in front of the dark stranger, tongue lolling, tail wagging, looking expectant. The stranger's hand went into his pocket and came out holding something square and large, wrapped in a handkerchief. He unwrapped it carefully, to reveal a ginger biscuit.

'Don't feed him that!' snapped Tess.

The hand paused, biscuit halfway to Tate's mouth. Tate, sensing difficulties, leapt up with surprising agility for a dog of his refined laziness, grabbed the biscuit and swallowed before anyone could protest.

'It ain't good for him!' Tess stamped a foot, thwarted in her motherly instinct.

'Children,' said Lyle with a little smile, 'a friend.'

Feng Darin stepped forward, and bowed politely to each of them. Thomas bowed back automatically, though he wasn't sure why. Tess put her head on one side. 'Oi! You chink spy; you been trailin' us?'

'I am delighted to see you well, Teresa,' replied Feng with a smile, 'and must confess that, drawn by your incisive detecting skills and radiant charms, I have been for a few days your faithful shadow – with, naturally, the purest of intentions.'

Tess tried to translate this, then gave up. 'You got any more of that biscuit?'

Lyle said, 'Just hand it over now; don't give her an excuse to go for your pockets.'

Feng passed a ginger biscuit to Tess, then brought them back to serious matters. 'We can't linger here. It's not safe.'

'Where is?'

Feng pointed towards an incandescent shape in the near distance. 'There.'

Thomas's father had once described the Great Exhibition as 'a wonderful thing, my boy! British power at its most spectacular, a demonstration of why our nation has been appointed to greatness above all others!'

Tess's friends had called it 'a place full of things what no one ain't never going to go an' fence'.

Lyle now described it as 'This monkey house?' adding, 'What about this place is safe?'

'Horatio, I'm surprised at you,' chided Feng. 'Aren't you a man of cultural curiosity?'

'This place isn't about cultural curiosity,' snapped Lyle. 'It's about cultural snobbery.'

And such had been the Great Exhibition. Encased in a huge glass and iron haven, it had stretched across Hyde Park, galleries and galleries of the strange or spectacular, dragged from every part of the world to be gawped at by the British public: the most extravagant masks from the Indies, sweetest fruits from Asia, brightest clothes from Africa, latest inventions from America, strangest religion from India, and largest fish from Indonesia. Many booths contained people, long-limbed black women who stood in their cultural costume and were examined like specimens in a zoo; dwarves forced into clown costume to parade up and down all day long; giants who carried children on their shoulders; and singers who told tales of their homelands in mournful voices to the uncomprehending crowds. Up in the rafters, sparrows and pigeons had made their nests, along with stranger, wilder fowl, bright flashes of colour, parrots escaped from their cages and birds with tail feathers that stretched longer than their wings and who blinked with emerald eyes.

The birds were awake, squawking nervously, although all the people, both spectators and spectacles, were long gone. Feng led the way round to a small wrought-iron door in the glass, difficult to spot as anything other than just another piece of framed ornamentation, and unlocked it with a key from his pocket. Inside, the air was cold and heavy. He showed them all through a maze of silent booths to a small area where hung silk flags, sewn with Chinese symbols. They ducked under these, past a window through which the crowd could stare and gape at the Chinese world displayed for them, through another small iron door, and into a tight, windowless room. Feng closed the door behind them and lit a lamp. As the light rose, it fell on heavy leather armour, spears gleaming for the kill, pistols, letters covered with neat Chinese script, several long sofas, and a couple of armchairs.

These were already inhabited.

Tess gave a yell, and jumped back to hide behind Lyle. Feng Darin slipped across to stand next to the two figures in their chairs.

Lord Lincoln said, 'Well, I'm glad to see you made it. Please sit down.'

Thomas did so, heavily, on the nearest sofa. Tess cautiously sat down next to him. Tate sat at her feet, looking up imploringly towards the hand that still clung to the biscuit. Lyle stood, a dishevelled mess of a man in a small room made entirely, he realized, of iron. Surprised, he reached out and touched the wall, running his hand down its smooth surface. 'What is this?' he asked.

'A place of safety,' said Feng, concern written on his face.

Lyle glanced sharply at him, then down at Lord Lincoln and across at the man in the other chair. 'Hello,' he said. 'Are you a scheming manipulator of men too, or do you just keep bad company?'

The small, wizened Chinese gentleman sitting in the armchair grinned an astonishingly wide grin at Lyle and said, 'I believe it is necessary to master all skills for a fruitful life, *xiansheng*.'

Lyle smiled wanly and said, 'I see. Please excuse me, gentlemen, but a roof collapsed on my head a few hours ago.' Tess realized he was swaying gently, and saw fully for the first time the blood clinging to his hair, his skin, the burn on his hand, the bruising that seemed to be everywhere, the soot and the dirt and the scorched coat. She started up to help him, but Feng was there first, supporting Lyle under the elbow and guiding him on to a seat. He poured water from a jug and helped him drink; Tess saw how Lyle's hand shook as he swallowed the water down.

The silence was broken by Lincoln. 'Are you well, Mister Lyle?'

Six pairs of eyes gave Lord Lincoln the same look Napoleon had given his generals when asked if he *really* thought invading Russia had been a good idea. Lyle carefully put the cup to one side, took a deep, shaky breath, and said, 'As well as can be expected, following an encounter with a man made of stone who controls the living stones and kills without qualm.' He gave Lincoln a weary, crooked look. His voice was low and calm. 'And, my lord, if you ever put me and the children in a position like that ever again, it won't just be a brewery that blows up.'

'You've blown up a brewery?'

'Gravitational inevitability. Anyone who decides to put a combustible liquid at the bottom of a long drop is simply *begging* for gravity to take up the challenge and find something flammable to fall. I just happened to be in the vicinity.'

'Good God. Is there anything else I ought to know about?'

Tess and Thomas exchanged guilty looks. 'Well . . . there was this window . . .'

'Which window?'

'It was quite a big window . . .'

'But I accept full responsibility!' added Thomas hastily.

'Where was this window?' snapped Lord Lincoln.

'Erm . . . King's Cross.'

'What happened to it?'

Tess thought about it. 'Sort . . . of gravi . . . gravitat . . . what Mister Lyle said.'

Lord Lincoln turned incredulous eyes on Lyle, who shrugged and said coldly, 'Don't look at me. I was busy being eaten by Great Russell Street.'

'I see. There wasn't, I imagine, a damage-light alternative to all these actions?'

The silence that met the question could have been used to cut granite. Lord Lincoln sighed. 'Well, that's all useful to know.'

'And what should *we* know about, my lord?' There was ice in Lyle's voice. It scratched against the iron of the room and made it shudder; it was the voice of a man who had seen Hell and been unimpressed. 'What *exactly* don't we know about?'

'That is such a general question I hardly know where to . . .'

'*Tell me the truth about Lucan Sasso or I swear I'm going straight back out there, dancing a tap-dance on the roof of this place and singing "The Ballad of the Cheerful Shepherd" with a loud voice and a gleeful expression until half the city of London is knocking at this door with writs for damages and an inquisitive expression!*' Lyle hadn't moved an inch, but his voice sent a shudder down Tess's spine, and made Tate curl up on the floor. It took even Feng by surprise, who leant slightly away from Lyle and stared into his face, as if trying to work out whether this was the same man he had just helped to a seat.

Lord Lincoln coughed politely, unfazed, and glanced at his companion. 'Shall you tell it, *xiansheng,* or shall I?'

The Chinese man nodded. 'My lord,' he said, 'I think Mister Lyle's over-developed sense of moral certainty won't be appeased, unless he hears it from you.'

And Lord Lincoln turned to Lyle, nodded once briskly, one professional man to another, and for possibly the first and last time in his life, told all.

CHAPTER 21

'What I know is fuzzy, distorted by the blur of myth, memory and bad reports. It is important that you know that, and understand that it, among other reasons, contributed to my earlier silence.

'Lucan Sasso was, in his time, a remarkable man. Raised to the level of marquis from an inauspicious birth, in Italy, he was honoured for his skills and bravery in battle, and was accepted to be, though perhaps lacking in strategy, a noble warrior. For such, he was rewarded. He was a poet too, a man of culture and passion. He devoutly believed in the Roman Catholic Church, and on one occasion went to Rome to seek the personal blessing of the Pope. He also, however, had a weakness for women. At the time when he was still a young man, there was a lady in Europe, who moved from country to country without regard for the borders of nations. Some said she was an Austrian princess, some said she had come even from the realms of the Ottoman, some that she was a Spanish beauty raised in the south by Moors. As with all mysterious, beautiful women, the reports were naturally unreliable. What we do know is that her name was Selene.

'Lucan Sasso met Selene in Rome, and was struck with her instantly; she, however, did not return his interest. She led him on while he followed her to Vienna, to Paris, protesting his love for her. Finally, here in London, she said she would accept him, and swear to him a secret love. Myth and rumour mingle, but the fables say in typically melodramatic style that somewhere in this city he spent seven days and seven nights with her, at the end of which she turned round and announced that she was leaving for ever, sailing somewhere across the seas, and they could never meet again. She left him a blade made of a special stone to remind him of her. He swore he would kill himself with it rather than be parted from her, but she was unmoved, and left that night. Surprisingly, for a man of Lucan Sasso's reputation, he was as good as his word, and the same night, on Westminster Bridge, he stabbed himself through the heart with the stone blade.

'As I suspect you have begun to surmise, it was a death with . . . complications. There are various doubtful but very colourful descriptions of his death: the earth shook, towers toppled, the bridge cracked, bells rang, the heavens opened, at the moment of death he could control the tides and so on. But what can be said for certain is that something . . . not entirely explicable by your science, Mister Lyle, took hold of Lucan Sasso. He is stone. His heart is an empty space under his skin; his skin is hard marble; his eyes do not dilate in bright light; the moonlight and the sunlight burn away the illusion of life that is half-real, half-imagined by all who see him, and reveal him for what he really is. We, all who look on such things, are very good at telling ourselves that they are not so but, in the brightest of lights, even we cannot deceive ourselves. Consequently, he hides from the daylight, has no power in it. Once he was beautiful, now he cannot bear to look on himself, or have others see anything but the hard, illusionary beauty that still clings to him. His blood is clay, and if you can cut through the hard stone of his skin, hardest most when seen for what it is, clay merely slips back in and heals the wound. A geologist once took a sample of this clay that Sasso bleeds, compared it with other minerals of the land, and finally declared that it was London clay, the clay that is taken from the riverbed, east of the city.

'I can give no explanations; that is neither my concern nor my role. You have seen how he kills, how ruthless he is; how did you put it? "Without qualm." He is heartless indeed. He has plagued cities, manipulated and twisted the stone they are made of; but this city has remained always a pull to him, his love and his hatred, as if some of it entered his blood when he died – for I firmly believe that Sasso is no longer alive nor human in the sense of the word.

'Following his . . . transformation, he travelled across Europe, murdering, mostly women, although anyone who irritated him was a target, anyone who looked and saw. His victims were all of a type, resembling Selene, all beauties in their ways. It took a long time to find him, to catch him, cage him like the monster he has become. The Church took responsibility for him, put him away in Isalia, where he was studied and kept. He eats the stone, Lyle. He eats it to control it; they sealed him in a coffin of stone, strong enough to contain him, but of a mineral he had never tasted and could not control, and left him to weaken, to grow powerless, together with his own demented mind.'

'They sealed him alive?' Lyle's voice was low.

'Indeed so.'

'For how long?'

Lord Lincoln didn't answer.

'*For how long?*'

'Sixty-three years.'

'And Ignatius Caryway let him out? *Here?*'

'So it would appear. My agents were unable to prevent it.'

Lyle shook his head. 'My God,' he whispered. 'No wonder he's mad.' He looked up sharply. 'All right, now the honest answers, because you have deceived me all the way and now we're all going to pay the consequences. First, who are you?' An accusing finger pointed at the quiet Chinese man sitting in the armchair.

The man smiled. It was an unnerving smile, wide, bright, friendly and somehow shark-like. 'I am Mr Lingdao, sir. I was invited here by his lordship because I and my people also have an interest in the activities of Mr Sasso.'

'Who are your people?'

Feng Darin cleared his throat and said, 'We represent the interests of the Emperor overseas. His more . . . unlikely interests, shall we say?'

'You were involved with the Tseiqin,' snapped Lyle, not taking his eyes off the amused face of Mr Lingdao. 'You came here to destroy the Fuyun Plate, the only thing that could give them power. But you weren't working with Lord Lincoln then; why now?'

'On the contrary,' said Mr Lingdao. 'If you consider, you will find our aims were the same. We both desired to prevent the Tseiqin achieving a power that was not rightfully theirs, and both realized that your kind co-operation was beneficial to this aim. Our methods were disparate, but we have never found any cause for disagreement, his lordship and ourselves.'

'Is Lucan Sasso such a threat you would have Feng Darin trail me across London, again, and risk his life, again, in the shadows?'

'Not immediately a threat to the Emperor,' replied Mr Lingdao, 'but in this matter, Lord Lincoln requested our assistance.'

'*Why?*'

'Because,' said Lord Lincoln mildly, 'Mr Lingdao and his associates have the stone blade of Selene.'

CHAPTER 22

Darin

Lyle stormed through the Great Exhibition, Tess, Thomas and Tate struggling to keep up with him, Feng Darin in flustered tow. 'Horatio! You don't know what you're doing!'

'I know exactly what I'm doing! I'm putting Tess and Thomas on the first train out of this damn city, going back to my lab and cooking up enough nitroglycerin to turn *bloody* Hampstead and its *bloody* occupants with their *bloody* good manners into a giant smoking crater!'

There was a little 'hurrah!' from Tess, hastily muted.

Feng Darin thrust himself in front of Lyle as they neared the door. 'Listen to me! *Listen!*'

260

Lyle stopped, an unimpressed look on his face. 'Yes?' he snapped.

'If you go out there, it will be a matter of minutes before Lucan finds you. You heard what Lincoln said: that . . . creature . . . kills without compunction. He will feel your feet on the stones and hunt you down.'

'Then we'll bloody fly! It won't take long to fix the plane. We'll launch it from Greenwich in hours, if we have to.' Lyle started forward, pushing past Feng Darin.

'It's not like you to run away, Lyle.'

Lyle froze, hand on the door, then spun round and grabbed Feng by the collar, dragging him up with surprising strength. His eyes were burning, his hands shaking with anger and fatigue. '*You* listen to *me*. Lincoln thinks he's won me, knows me, understands what pushes me into each new farce or danger, thinks he knows how to make me bend left or bend right. But you, *you* should know better.'

He pushed the door open, hurried the children out into the cold, dim air, took a deep breath of it after the enclosure of the dome, looked up at the sky, and let out the long breath he hadn't realized that he'd been holding. At his feet, Tate sniffed the air, his tail beginning to wag.

'How will you survive the night?' asked Feng quietly behind him.

Lyle looked back, smiled an odd smile and said, 'That is the wrong question, Feng Darin. The question should be: how will Sasso survive the day?'

And across London, the bells began to ring, declaring the hour, singing their brief songs to anyone who would listen, who would care that the city was alive, coming alive, had always been alive, buzzing with sound and noise day after day, the inhabitants making up a whole so huge, each part had to tick away in harmony with another part which ticked with another and another so that for just one part to bend and break would change the rhythm of the city, a thousand thousand lives living together by a single beat, the heartbeat of the city, the *living* city, and the bells rang out and proclaimed the hour, and Lyle turned and looked towards the east and saw, glimmering over the docks of Rotherhithe and the grasses of Greenwich and the ships of Westferry, the first, seductive trace of daylight, burning through the fog.

Dawn across London. The dim grey light crawls through the glass of the Great Exhibition, turning the blackness of the night to a tantalizing warm orange glow as the glass bends the light, its impurities shining as thin shadows across the floor, making a mystic map to another land in the play of light.

In the darkness, shut away from the dawn, sit Lord Lincoln and Mr Lingdao.

'Will Sasso wait again until nightfall?'

'Yes. And now Lyle knows. I suspect Sasso will want to know more of our Mister Lyle. I suspect Lyle will solve our problem, without our . . . mutual interest . . . being endangered.'

And in the darkness, Lord Lincoln smiles, and feels, just for a moment, confident, ready to face the world, the city, the stones. A tune drifts into his mind, into the empty space shaped by the city that made him, into the place where the heartbeat of his home keeps a steady time dictated by the winding alleys and rippling waters of the city, and he purses his lips, and hums quietly, ' *"Oranges and lemons . . ."*' And stops, surprised, and tuts quietly to himself, shaking his head to free it of the tune, and returns to thinking about more important matters, while outside, the bells ring on.

And in another darkness, hiding from the sun, a door opens, and something is pushed into black gloom, thick and cold and stultifying. And a frightened voice, used to speaking English, but not as it is spoken in England, says, 'Who's there? What's happening?'

'Priest. You thought to tame me. You gave me the stones, to feed on their power, their age. I fed. I grew powerful. You had a vision, a dream; you wanted to change this city. I said I shared the dream, to feed on the power. But my dream is purer, simpler, the stillness that waits inside. This city will tremble and die, the blackness you feared will tremble and die.'

And Ignatius Caryway whispers, 'I *made* you! I brought you here, it was a mission appointed by God, I am the vessel of Our Lord, I am the Way, I am the . . .'

'The sun shines on the city, priest. It is painful to me. It shows me what I am. I prefer to be seen for what I was. You have until nightfall, then, to live.'

'And the Lord sayeth, "I am the Lord thy God and thou shalt have no . . ."' Voice trembling, terror in every word, a salvation that isn't forthcoming.

'The scientist, Horatio Lyle, he scurries home through the daylight, knowing that I feel his footsteps as if he walked on my grave. He has something I want: a black stone blade. Bring it to *me*.'

Fatigue had caught up with Thomas and Tess, springing on them as they passed through the streets of London. Somehow, though neither of them understood how, the day brought safety and, for the moment, everything was all right. Relief at the incredibility of still being alive had begun to mingle with the realization of what they had achieved, and each mind slipped in and out of the closed doors of sleep.

'Are you sure it is wise to go back to your home?' asked Feng Darin quietly as they each carried a child in their arms up to the doors of Lyle's house.

'Nowhere is safe,' replied Lyle. 'But daylight is as frightening to some people as the night is to us.' He stared into Feng Darin's dark brown eyes and his worn, openly foreign features, exposed now in the sunlight. 'It shows some of us, who would rather not be reminded, what we really are, inside.'

Feng met Lyle's eyes for a second, then followed him uncomplaining through the door.

Seven a.m. in London, and Thomas lies asleep and dreams of flying through the sky, of the world below being all his, of being freer than the ship on the sea or the rider on the horse, dreams of escaping it all, dreams of making a dream come true, and smiles in his sleep, and rolls over, to sleep and dream again.

Seven a.m. in London, and Lyle sits quietly by Tess's bed as she rolls over in her sleep, shivering in half-real, half-dreamt winter's cold, kicking unconsciously at her blanket. Lyle pulls it back over her feet and, for a reason he can't quite explain, sings softly under his breath, with no particular tune or sense of time, '*Hush-a-bye, don't you cry . . .*'

And Tess sleeps the peaceful dream of safety in daylight, and dreams that, somewhere, in the shadows, a vague shape sings a song to her, as no shape ever did when she was awake to hear. '*Blacks and greys, dapples and bays, coach and six of little horses . . .*'

And she smiles, and dreams of a dream come true, and rolls over, to sleep and dream again.

'Tell me about the blade, Feng Darin.'

Feng reached into his coat and pulled out, wrapped neatly in black silk, a long, slim black object. He laid it with some reverence on the table and gently unwrapped it. It was plain, unadorned, and also, Lyle noticed with some surprise, very light to handle, smooth and slightly warm to the touch. It was definitely stone; no metal felt as the blade did, but it had been carved down to a point that was sharp to the touch, and had a deadly gleam at its curved end that looked as if it had tasted more than its share of blood.

'This is Selene's blade,' said Feng. 'Stolen from Sasso while he slept. He treasured it above all things. It is said that a man who drives it through his own heart and longs to die will not die. That it does not kill the man, merely the heart, and that where the heart was, there is an emptiness, waiting to be filled. Do you recognize its material?'

Lyle glanced up, then down at the blade again, running his

fingers over it with a more intense expression. 'Good grief,' he muttered. 'Don't tell me it's magnetic?'

'This is hyresium, the stone that the Tseiqin once knew how to manipulate, when they were a great people and mankind was still learning how to light its own fires. The knowledge is now dead, but some of the artefacts they forged live on. The Fuyun Plate was one, until it was destroyed. This is another. It is suggested . . .' His voice trailed away.

'Suggested that?'

'Supposition . . . suggests that Selene was once Tseiqin, once had the green eyes that could burn through a mind. But for some crime against her own people she was banished, lost her power, and took with her into exile only this blade. Lingdao *xiansheng* does not hold with the theory, but I myself have always had an affection for it.'

Lyle sighed and put the blade down gently, as if afraid of either touching it or breaking it. 'Just what I needed for a logical and rational lifestyle. Another scientifically uncertain object of implausible power. I assume it's the kind of thing we can't let fall into the wrong hands?'

'Absolutely.'

'Typical,' muttered Lyle, slumping down in an armchair.

Feng sat down opposite Lyle, and said nothing. The grandfather clock ticked on. Lyle stared up at the ceiling, brooding.

Finally, 'Tell me about yourself, Feng Darin.'

Feng hesitated, looking across the cluttered sitting room as Lyle prodded the fire. All sense of time had dissolved after the rush through the night; the room had the comfortable feel of a place ready for supper, not early-morning breakfast.

'I . . . cannot, Horatio.'

Lyle shrugged, and stretched, from toes to fingertips. Washed, in a clean shirt and trousers, he looked like a more acceptable member of society, but washing had also unveiled the bruises and cuts that clung to his face and hands, one of which Feng noticed was tightly bandaged. Lyle saw his eyes lingering on the bandage, smiled and said, 'Never cling too tightly to a rapidly oxidizing magnesium compound. The reaction, you discover, is distinctly exothermic.'

Feng raised his eyebrows enquiringly.

'Things get hot,' translated Lyle, and then in the same breath, 'Who do you work for?'

Instant reaction. 'The Emperor.'

Lyle grinned. 'That's a bit of a fib, isn't it?'

Feng shifted uncomfortably. 'I am . . . forbidden. Knowledge may prove dangerous.' He saw Lyle's expression, sighed and leant forward, fingers interlaced, shoulders hunched like a tiger ready to spring. 'Have you ever . . . no, that isn't how to begin. Do you believe that there are forces beyond man's control, Horatio?'

'Yes. But not necessarily beyond man's explanation.'

'How rational of you,' said Feng, smiling faintly. 'Let me put it another way. There *are* forces beyond . . . at least most men's . . . control. Everyone has a different way of calling it; some say fate, some magic, some God, some luck. No one really knows what it really is. To know what "it" is, this inexplicable force that pushes us towards change, from the past and into the future, is to be suddenly beyond its influence. Once you know what "it" is, you can control it; it cannot control you.'

'And you know what "it" is?'

'I am simply a servant of a greater plan, of a force pushing us towards the future. I have been so all my life. I was born a peasant boy in the mountains of Tibet. The Chinese took me, showed me the possibilities of science, of progress: things you would appreciate, I feel. They taught me . . . but that is not for now. I am a servant of my Emperor, and of a future which, when I was just a boy in the mountains, I could not have begun to understand. I will die for this future, Horatio. Would you do such a thing?'

Lyle almost laughed. 'Die? For something intangible, for something that I cannot see, taste, feel, measure? Die for someone else's dream taught to you when you were probably too young even to understand the lines between which the *real* text was drawn? Absolutely not. I am a firm believer in keeping all my limbs attached, thank you kindly. And you talk, Feng Darin, as a man having a religious experience.'

Leaning forward he added, in a conspiratorial tone, 'Religious experiences, I find, can lead to irrational thought. Now' – reaching down to a table – 'what do you make of these?'

He tossed a wrapped bundle of papers at Feng, who caught them instinctively and opened them out. Feng leafed through the pages, eyebrows drawing together. 'These are . . . just maps.'

'They're not just maps. They're maps that Teresa stole from Ignatius Caryway last night, from out of his bedroom, no less. They're drawn by Sir Christopher Wren, the man commissioned to rebuild London after the Great Fire, almost two hundred years ago. He was going to build a dream city out of stone, with broad streets and absolutely no flammable bakeries in strategic positions. He designed St Paul's Cathedral and many of the more luxurious houses you see along the river. Sadly, his plans didn't get much past Trafalgar Square before the city's own natural growth and practical demands caught up with him, and here we are now.'

'What do you think it means?'

'I have an idea,' said Lyle with a little shrug. 'But to confirm it I really need to talk to a man in the grip of a mad religious experience.'

There was a hammering on the door, so loud and sudden it made even Feng Darin jerk in his seat, his hand darting towards his coat pocket.

Lyle sighed. 'Just a moment.'

'Are you sure that's wise?'

'Could it get worse?'

Lyle sauntered out of the room. Feng waited, heard the sound of the door opening, followed almost immediately by a thud. He heard Lyle's indignant exclamation. 'Oh, good grief.'

'What is it?' Feng glanced round the door.

With a cautious toe, Lyle prodded the body that had fallen at his feet. The shape groaned and twitched. 'The heavens seem to be prompt in answering my call today,' he sighed. And bent down over the unconscious shape of Father Ignatius Caryway.

CHAPTER 23

Blade

They put Ignatius on the smallest, dingiest spare bed Lyle had, in the dustiest, greyest part of the attic. Feng leant over him, and slapped him gently a couple of times round the face. The priest groaned, but didn't move. His skin was bright red and unpleasantly hot to the touch, his face was a mass of bruises, and a number of his fingers looked bent at an odd angle. Lyle examined the bruises with the dispassion of a geologist examining a sample. 'He's been hit a few times by a very strong right-handed man with a fist like stone,' he announced coldly. 'He's running a high fever, probably the result of too much running round in cold weather without suitable clothing.'

Lyle thought, seemed to reach a conclusion, then disappeared from the room. A few seconds later, he reappeared, carrying a bowl of water with a thin layer of ice on its surface. He tapped the ice to break it and tipped the water over Ignatius.

The man's eyes flew open. The pupils were wide, and slightly out of focus. Blood vessels stood out, alarming and ugly, around the rims of his eyes, which swivelled in terror and confusion. He wore the drained, watery aspect of a man who'd looked his nightmare in the face and been swallowed whole. He saw Lyle and whimpered. His voice was barely above a whisper. 'I am the vessel of the Lord thy God, I am the . . .'

'I am on the edge of asking Feng Darin to shoot you,' said Lyle. 'Are you Ignatius Caryway?'

The man nodded quickly. 'I . . . I have . . . it is . . .'

'Did you bring Sasso here?'

'I am the vessel, I am the way, I am . . .'

Lyle's hand shot out so suddenly that even Feng looked surprised. He grabbed Ignatius by the ear like a disobedient puppy and twisted it sharply. 'Mr Caryway,' he hissed, 'I am so close to committing an immoral act that I can practically feel my immortal soul counting its assets and preparing to pack up shop. Did you bring Sasso here?'

'Yes, yes, I was –'

'You paid Captain Fabrio to collect Sasso from the island of Isalia?'

'Yes, I . . .'

'You arranged with the abbot to release Sasso, and leave him in a sealed stone coffin on the beach?'

'Only one of the faith, a servant of the Lord, can communicate with Isalia. I am a servant of the Lord, I am a vessel of . . .'

Lyle twisted his ear harder. Ignatius's words drained away into a gurgle. 'You stood by while he murdered Fabrio and Stanlaw?'

For the first time, Ignatius's eyes managed to find Lyle's and stay. In the cold air and grey light his face was glistening unpleasantly with sweat. He smelt of disease and sickly convictions. 'They were in the way, sacrifices to the cause . . .'

'And what is the cause? *Tell me*. What are the maps about? Why did you bring him here?'

For a second, Ignatius was silent, hands shaking, eyes fixed on Lyle's, though not necessarily seeing what he looked at. Then his eyes narrowed, and his voice changed, ringing out with fervour. 'This city . . .' The words almost seemed to choke him, twist him round a sudden fit of coughing, which he forced his way through in a rush. '. . . is a slaughterhouse, a den of sin. Black, the fires of hell burn constantly in every house, every factory, on every porch. Smells of filth and mould and smoke and fire and refuse and despair and hunger and craving and desire and anger and hatred. The poor sleep next door to the rich, fifty to a bed in a house made of crumbling wood where the worms feast richer than the children who die in the mud of a cellar, and they hate, *hate* the man in the house next door who lies luxuriously pillowed in a cushioned bed. Throw every creature, every sinner and every saint together, and to survive in the black streets between the Church and the factory the good man must learn the ways of the bad, learn how to live the evil lives of the twisting alleys and the broken windows. The city *makes* you evil, makes its people part of the filth, until all that you know, all that the people of this place can see, is the dirt and the squalor in which they live, and that constitutes home. Hell that I was sent to change! The city makes the man, it is a force so powerful it cannot be denied.'

He swivelled, grabbing Lyle's wrist, trying to pull himself up. His voice dropped to a hiss. 'Sasso will change your city, Lyle. If the city is clean and pure, the people will change; it is inevitable. I brought him here to destroy the old and make the new, a new city, a new place, a new people.'

His strength failed him and he fell back, coughing, his face twisting in pain. Lyle stood, looking coldly down at him. 'You were going to re-make the city? Using the old designs and Sasso's power over stone; make a city that had never been?'

Ignatius, too lost to answer, managed a nod.

'What about Mrs Milner and Edgar? Did you stand by while they died?' Lyle's shout sent dust drifting down from the low rafters.

The question, and Lyle's rage, seemed to take Ignatius by surprise. 'I don't know them,' he whispered. 'I never sent anyone . . . no one . . .'

Doubt flickered in Lyle's eyes, but was quickly gone. 'What about Lady Diane Lumire?' he asked, quieter, hardly able to look at Ignatius for fear of his own anger. 'What's her part in this?'

'Lumire?' Ignatius almost spat the word. 'A fool! A weakling! She serves the true faith, so she will not burn when you do, but she is virtuous only in much money and little perception! A servant of the Lord . . . and an unwitting one, as so many are.'

'You used her?'

A hesitation, then a short, almost defiant nod. Lyle ran his hands through his hair, across his eyes, and let out a long, calming breath. 'And why have you come here now?'

Panic flared in Ignatius's eyes. His lips began to move, though only the faintest whisper came out. 'I shall fear no evil . . .'

Lyle leant forward, grabbed Ignatius's ear again, and yanked on it sharply. 'Enough! Tell me *now*, or I swear I'm going to develop such an interest in anatomy you'll wish you'd been born clumsy in a butcher's yard!'

Ignatius's hands shook, his eyes grew wild once more, a little bead of salty sweat ran down the side of his face. 'Sasso sent me. He's . . . he's a devil. I thought . . . I could control him but I let him out and now he speaks of destroying and revenging and trembling and dying . . . and he talks of a woman called Selene, of a blade. I thought I could tame him, and now he's the Devil, a creature of sin and darkness, a—'

'*Enough!*'

'A message . . . he has a message . . . in my coat . . .'

Instantly Feng was digging through Ignatius's coat, coming out a second later with a sheet of folded paper. Lyle took it, opened it carefully, sniffing it first and holding it up to the light as if afraid it might contain a small army, and read it slowly out loud, for Feng to hear.

'"You used her blade to escape me, but I am the city and I am the stones. You will bring me the blade, alone, tonight on Westminster Bridge, and I will not shake the city to dust. If you doubt my power then . . ."'

Lyle's voice trailed off. He dropped the paper and was

Blade

running out of the door, coat flapping behind him, before it
even hit the ground.

A voyage through the city, for as long as it will remain the city.

Fires burn constantly in every house, every factory, on every
porch, trying and failing to burn their way through the darkness
of the thick green fog and the falling heavy snow that hisses and
splutters in the fires, trying to extinguish them but not quite
managing to kill the last, hellish red glow of the embers.

In Lyle's house, two children sleep, deep, peaceful sleep, and
dream of nursery rhymes sung in a more innocent time, and not
of stones that watch you as you pass, and whisper underfoot.

And here comes the tremor: very, very slight, hardly audible
except in the chinking of glasses and the gentle, sucking slosh of
water trapped under the ice of puddles, trying to resonate in time
to the land.

Lyle burst through the door to Tess's room, calling her name.
She sat up blearily, blinking in the grey light, and mumbled, 'It
ain't lunch already?'

Lyle didn't answer, but darted out of her room and into the
room next to it, slamming the door back against the wall, calling out Thomas's name, and recoiled sharply, hand in front of
his eyes and arm across his mouth.

The stone dust, picked up from a dozen masons' yards and
crumbling walls, and forming a mass so thick and seething it was
practically solid and alive again, made a noise like bluebottles as
it flew round the room in a grey cloud too dense to see through,
stinging the eyes and choking the throat, drying up every drop

of moisture in the air and stinging against the skin like a million needles.

Lyle screamed out, 'Thomas!' and half-imagined through the horrific, deafening roar that he heard someone answer back, faintly, calling out his name in a dry, terrified voice that immediately disappeared into a suffocated cough. Feng tried to hold Lyle back, but was shaken off as Lyle threw his arms up in front of his face and dived blindly into the cloud. He navigated by guesswork and memory, eyes shut, until he stumbled into the bed, tripping over it.

Thomas was curled up into a tiny ball, head buried against his knees, hands over his head. The skin of his hands and the back of his neck was red and raw, as if sandpaper had been dragged across them, and his clothes were torn from the abrasive dust. Lyle threw himself over the boy, cradling him in his arms as the storm knocked them this way and that, tearing at him with a million tiny nails. Dust filled his mouth even as he screamed, 'I'll do it! I'll do whatever you want! Let him alone!'

Still the storm raged, if anything harder, forming a veritable tornado that tried to pull Lyle's hair out by the roots. 'I'll give you what you want!' he screamed, almost unable to speak for the dust that burnt his throat. 'Do you hear me? I'll give you Selene's blade!'

And abruptly, the storm was over. Dust fell to the ground in a thick grey drift, with a little patter like the lightest drizzle when it first bounces on a roof. It fell on Thomas and Lyle, turning them both grey from top to toe. Lyle sat back slowly, stunned and shaken. At the door, Tess and Feng stood and watched in silence.

Thomas looked up into Lyle's face, the picture of his own — grey with dust and too numb to assume any expression other than dumb shock. Thomas's lips shook, as did his hands, but he tried to stand anyway, feet crunching in the dust as he put each one carefully down on the floor. He took a few uncertain steps; then his knees buckled and he twisted, grabbing at the bed. Lyle caught him under the arms and held him up, half-carried him to the door. Thomas buried his head in Lyle's shoulder and — not because he must, not because he was going to all along, but because for the moment he was safe and unseen, and it was expected, and it was all right and not weak, as he had always been taught — he cried, in silence, and without moving, except for where the salt water tickled as it passed through the dust clinging to the end of his nose.

Feng stared at Lyle as he emerged from the room. When he spoke, it was quickly, as if not sure that he should. 'Horatio . . .'

'Not a word.'

'If you give him the blade . . .'

'Not a word!'

'You *cannot* give him Selene's blade! If he gets power over that element, over the first element, the one the Tseiqin revered, then . . .'

'Feng Darin,' snapped Lyle, 'If you have any respect and faith in me, then you'll stop talking right now.'

Feng hesitated, then closed his mouth and slowly folded his arms.

'Thank you,' said Lyle. 'Now, we have maybe twelve hours. Tess, Thomas, get your clothes. I'm putting you on the first train out of the city.'

Tess folded her arms. 'You ain't.'

Lyle glared at her. 'Teresa, do you see this expression of firm-eyed will and determination?'

Tess peered up at him. 'You mean the kinda slitty-eyed one?'

'That's the one.'

'The one what has the kinda wrinkle at the end of your nose and makes your ears seem funny?'

'That sounds very likely.'

'I'm seein' it.'

'It means you're on the first train out of this city.'

'Ain't.'

'Are.'

'Ain't.'

'*Are.*'

'Ain't.'

'Ain . . . *Are*, dammit, Teresa!'

Thomas's voice, dry and dusty, cut in. 'Mister Lyle?' he croaked. 'We can help you.'

Lyle scowled. 'I'm not having children's blood on my hands!' he snapped. 'Dust and nitroglycerin, but not children's blood!'

'Mister Lyle,' said Tess, 'you ain't got enough hands to stop us. You need us.'

For a second, fury leapt up behind Lyle's eyes, and he flushed an angry red. He looked from Tess to Thomas to Feng and back again. Several times he opened his mouth to speak, saw their expressions, and changed his mind again. Finally he let out a furious hiss and, turning to Feng, snapped, '*You.*'

Feng raised his eyebrows politely.

'Get me all the ammonia you can find. And Tess?'

278

'Yes, Mister Lyle?'

'Get me the spare wheel from the basement, and get up to Greenwich Hill. If you stay, you stay above the stones, all right?'

'Yes, Mister Lyle.'

CHAPTER 24

Bridge

To Tate, who watched from the security of his basket in the kitchen, the day went quickly.

He was woken early by an unusual buzzing sound from upstairs and a lot of shouting, but decided it wasn't worth investigation. He opened another torpid eye a little later when Lyle, covered in dust and looking very, very angry, exploded into the kitchen. A little strategic whining distracted Lyle long enough for food to be provided, before he stormed out again, carrying an armful of saucepans and some very thick gloves.

A little later, Thomas, also covered head to toe in dust, entered the kitchen, carrying a bundle of foul-smelling rags which he began to soak in lamp oil. Tate whined at Thomas, and was promptly fed.

Tess was the next to come in, wearing an alarmed expression and carrying one of the saucepans that Lyle had earlier taken away, only now it smelt sickly, a mixture of alcohol and the kind of chemicals Tate associated with large scorch marks and dirty smoke. Tess washed it in the sink, with frozen water and the care of someone who's just been given a grenade instead of a cricket ball and told to 'go play'. Tate turned his attentions to Tess, who in leaving, fed him.

It was turning into a good day.

The afternoon brought new and interesting odours from outside the kitchen, but they were that class of smell which Tate knew well enough to avoid, and which put him in mind of a hairless mouse with a scorched tail. He had a brief bout of exercise chasing his own tail, before Feng Darin walked in carrying a handful of test tubes, into which he poured a lot of sugar. Tate tried whining at him, saw Feng's expression, and quickly went to hide under his blanket. When Feng was gone, Tate climbed up on to the table and helped himself to some of the food Lyle had forgotten to tidy away. Though it was technically against Tate's policy to go out of his way to feed himself, desperate times did call for desperate measures.

Evening brought all four of them back. Tate whined at Tess, who gave him a biscuit. Dissatisfied with his prize, he whined again at Lyle, who muttered guiltily, 'We have been neglecting you, haven't we? You can't have eaten since breakfast . . .' and promptly fed him.

After dinner, Tate watched Tess and Thomas get into one

hansom cab, Feng get into another and Lyle linger in the hall, uneasily waving goodbye. He was surprised at the way Thomas and Tess ran back and hugged Lyle in a rare show of affection. In Tate's mind this suggested either deep concern on their part, or a mind-controlling experiment on the two hapless children, which would, Tate reasoned, go some way to explaining the smells that had been drifting out of the basement all day.

He regarded his master carefully, as Lyle waved goodbye. The odours coming off Lyle's battered overalls were almost too thick and noxious to separate one from another, but Tate smelt evidence of ammonia, salt, sugar, carbon, soot, ammonium, various magnesium compounds, clay for some reason, maybe a dab of silver nitrate, a few iron oxides here or there, some of the foul electrolytes Lyle liked using when extracting elements from compounds in order to acquire certain otherwise unobtainable products, and, through it all, something that combined in many ways the worst of the smells and might, indeed, explain why Lyle was moving so cautiously, with one hand firmly over his left coat pocket, to stop its contents from moving about too much.

Tate reached the obvious conclusion.

It was terrifying.

Later. The kind of later that might be the last later ever recorded, or might just be the first of many, many laters yet to come.

Midnight in winter. No traffic crosses Westminster Bridge tonight, which is hardly unusual, considering the lateness of the hour, the depth of snow, the steadily falling white flakes which drive even the toughest horses back to the stable, their metal bits too cold to bite on. The gas lights burn dully on the freshly painted bridge, trying in vain to force their beams just that little bit further into the darkness.

Alone on Westminster Bridge, pacing under a lamp, and flapping his arms against the cold, Horatio Lyle thinks: *It is said that there are forces beyond any mere man's control. Some call it magic, some call it God, some call it luck, some call it fate. They give the random empty things names, and then fear them. How silly.*

And Horatio Lyle looks down across the silver of the frozen river, snaking west past the Houses of Parliament and Big Ben, past the wharves and docks and barges and ships trapped upright or at odd angles in the ice, out towards the edges of the city, burning gaseous yellow and snowy silver. And Horatio Lyle looks down across the silver of the frozen river, winding east past Charing Cross and the giant mansions of the Embankment, great government buildings and huge terraces for the wealthy and the indulged, past the piers and frozen walls of the river, past the burning chimneys belching their smoke into the sky, past the moving lights of the bridges where men carrying lanterns wind their way through the fog, towards the torches that burn among the stones of the Tower and around the city wall, as it runs rings through the heart of the city: here a Roman piece of masonry, here medieval, here Tudor, sometimes forming parts of buildings incorporating the ancient wall into themselves, sometimes snaking through the buildings or stopping on a street corner, to resume on the other side where the old gates had stood on the bridges or at the edge of the city, now sprawling beyond the old limits;

torches burning with a million lives and a million fires that over the centuries have tried to eat up the fog and drive back the darkness . . .

Horatio Lyle looked across at London, and smiled. Just now, just for this instant, so inexpressible, everything was . . . perfect.

'You have my blade?'

Lyle jumped, the voice right behind him, and instantly remembered the feel of a hand round his throat and the sensation that the earth was trying to swallow him whole. He backed away hastily a few steps from the shape of Sasso, half-visible in the fog. 'I brought the blade,' he stammered, trying to get control of his heart, which had suddenly decided it wanted to be somewhere else, quickly.

Sasso looked different. The mad gleam was gone; now there was just steely determination. In many ways, that was worse. 'Then give it to me.'

Lyle hesitated. Instantly Sasso advanced a step, and the bridge seemed to lurch with him.

'You'll leave us alone?' Lyle's voice was barely above a whisper. 'You'll not hurt anyone?'

'Do not presume to judge me! You cannot imagine the things I have seen, the things I have done. You cannot imagine how it . . . how it *feels* only to *remember* feeling. To know that here should be joy and here should be happiness and remember the pull of your features as each emotion swept through you, but be deprived of the heart that should most relish them! Do not dare to judge me, little man!'

Lyle heard a little clinking sound behind him, and half-turned to see the two gargoyles, clinging to the rail of the bridge with long claws, leering brightly at him.

'Well, yes . . . right,' he muttered, reaching into his coat. He pulled out a long object, wrapped in cloth and, handling it as if it might explode at any second, held it out to Sasso.

Eagerness flaring on his face, he grabbed the blade from Lyle's hands, dragged the cloth away and held it up, turning it this way and that, his face twisting into a smile. '**Selene's blade**,' he murmured. '**Her gift, her power, to** *me*.'

Lyle backed away, hoping no one would notice, as Lucan Sasso held the blade up to the light.

'**You make me a god, little man.**'

'Well, I . . .' Something cold and hard closed over the back of Lyle's neck, holding with an unshakeable grip, dragging his head back so that all he could see was the fog where stars should be, and the gently falling snow stung his eyes. The hand was cold as the night air, but was definitely a human hand, four fingers pressing deep into the left side of his neck, a thumb forming a tight loop that dug into his vein. He thought, *Someone with a left hand?*

And then there was the voice, like marble warmed in the sun, and the hand was like marble, the left hand that had a grip no mere mortal should have possessed, the *left hand* . . .

And Lyle felt just a bit foolish for not working it out sooner.

'Lucan,' hummed the voice. 'Do not do that.'

Lucan Sasso froze, and stared in horror and surprise at what-ever stood behind Lyle, the hand that held the knife dropping slowly to his side. His mouth moved as he tried to form words, although none came.

'The knife is not real,' continued the warm-marble voice in Lyle's ear. No breath, he noticed, no warm air touching his ear, though the lips that moved were right beside him, and seemed to have a coldness all of their own. 'Lyle had it made during the day, out of plaster. I am disappointed that you cannot tell. The real blade hums with *power*.'

The hunger in that word made Lyle sick, made his stomach churn. The grip tightened on his neck, became painful, dragged his head back so that for a moment, out of the corner of his eyes, he saw marble-white skin, basalt-black hair, granite-grey eyes and a smile that could have conquered the world. 'What did you do with the real blade, Lyle?' whispered the voice in his ear.

He didn't answer. The grip became more insistent, with a sudden rushing in Lyle's ears and a hammering in his head which suggested that if it was any more insistent, it would be terminal.

'Hidden!' he gasped.

'And this false blade? I imagine you've done something cunning with it.'

'Hollow!'

'And what's in the centre?'

Lyle saw Sasso looming over him, face still set with wonder and surprise. He hissed, 'I think, Lady Lumire, we're about to find out.'

And Lady Diane Lumire, her marble hand clamped round Lyle's neck, looked past him and down at the blade in Sasso's hand and he, rapt, followed her gaze and noticed the little drip that seeped through the very top of the blade, the tiny shimmer of clear liquid that fell in a steady, silent splash on to the snow. And, because Lucan Sasso hadn't had a chance to catch up with the modern technological revolution and didn't really understand these things, he stood back in surprise, and dropped the blade.

If he'd bothered to ask Lyle, he would have known that dropping anything containing nitroglycerin was the last thing a sensible man would do.

CHAPTER 25

Selene

The explosion shakes Westminster Bridge. It sends the pigeons starting for the air, rattles snow off buildings, hums through the ice of the river and, for just a brief second, burns away the fog that shrouds the centre of the empty bridge.

Somewhere, not too far away, Feng Darin looks up from loading his revolver, sees the flash, looks down at the ice of the river, and hears something stomp very quietly in the night. He feels for the weight of Selene's blade, at his side.

It is said that fortune favours the brave. Horatio Lyle, as the world filled with fireworks, smoke, noise and confusion, was of the increasing opinion that not only was this statement wrong, it was possibly spread by malignant people hoping to prove by elimination that cowardice was the more favourable Darwinian characteristic.

As the blade hit the ground, Lyle threw himself back, which worked fine, for Lady Diane Lumire clearly had a stronger grasp of science than Sasso, and was also diving for cover, Lyle utterly forgotten. He hit the cobbles and curled up, head tucked in deep below his shoulders as, behind him, the world filled with fire and flying stone. He felt the heat of the blast singe the back of his neck, turn the soles of his shoes slightly soft, scorch his coat, and instantaneously vaporize several gallons of snow so that it hissed and stung his eyes as it rushed out from the centre of the blast. He felt his ears go *pop*.

He opened his eyes. Loose bits of stone fell around him. He touched one. It was almost searing to the touch. He staggered upright. Sound was odd, out of place. He felt as if he was hearing the world through water. Light seemed a little bit too bright. Something was ringing in his head. He looked down at the ground. There was no sign of Sasso. He looked towards Diane. Where she had fallen, the stones were bent oddly, rising up above the normal level of the bridge to form a cocoon shape, large and long. They appeared to have blended, forming a smooth, almost uninterrupted slab. Lyle edged towards it. He prodded it with the tip of his toe; it felt solid enough. He bent down and touched it. The stones were warm to the touch. He moved away again, trying to work things out. Perhaps if . . .

He saw something move. The stones seemed to ripple. He backed away faster, until he bumped against the parapet. The stones bent, twisting, then rising up abruptly and melting together, until they formed the irate shape of Lucan Sasso, standing tall as ever. At his feet, where she had been covered by the cocoon of masonry, Diane Lumire sat up, looking only slightly flummoxed. The pair of them turned to Lyle with an ice-hard stare.

'Ah,' muttered Lyle. 'Well . . . it seemed a good idea at the time.'

Diane was back on her feet. Sasso half-turned to her, looking for guidance. She smiled at him, then smiled a wider but no less cruel smile in the direction of the baffled scientist. 'Mister Lyle,' she murmured, 'you die faster than we do.'

Lyle thought about this. He considered all the possibilities at his disposal, all the ideas and plans that might yet save him, and settled on the most rational one. He turned, and ran. It was something he was getting quite good at.

Feng Darin remembered a different time. It was vague, the colours dimmed and the sounds muffled, details fading as time and experience plastered different, fresher memories over the walls of his mind. He remembered cold winters and cold summers, riding across endless steppes in search of water and food, of smoky yurts made of goat skins and twigs, of cowering away from the snow in giant, smelly furs sewn crudely together by the old lady of the tribe, who felt her way from stitch to stitch with hands so worn you could almost see each individual bone in the hand as the skin moved across it.

The memory was distant now. He remembered the Emperor's men coming, remembered first seeing the steel ships being built in the docks, first seeing the sea, first seeing the smoke of London. He had an image of hell in his mind, but no imagination acquired in the mountains could have prepared him for the hell that he saw in reality, as he stepped into the wharves of London. He remembered the looks he would get, a strange man in a strange country, as the people of London looked at his dark skin and scurried away nervously, not used to seeing a Chinese man, and whispering to their children not to speak to him.

He remembered the day Tess had turned to him and said, 'Oi. You a chink, ain't you?' And she hadn't cared. Just shrugged it off, and gone about her larcenous business. He'd been afraid of daylight, until that moment. He'd feared that it showed him for who he was.

Feng Darin looked at the darkness and the fog, smelt the smoke and tasted the ice on the air. Under his feet, Charing Cross Bridge shuddered ever so slightly. He heard the hiss of a train, the burp of a machine, the click of metal on metal, the stamp of a horse's hoof. And just behind it, very quietly, someone muttering, '*Shush.*'

For a moment, just a moment, Feng Darin smiled, which was a rare thing indeed, and drew his blade. He knew what would have to be done and that, too, was cold.

Lyle swung round the corner of the bridge just as something heavy and dark swept over his head, and threw himself down the icy steps at the end, towards the frozen river below. The stones of the Embankment seemed to be coming alive, faces leering up and out of the masonry along the side of the river, bending like a liquid to watch him pass, rippling under his feet. He heard the beat of very, *very* heavy wings on the air and didn't even bother to duck, but threw himself headlong off the stairs, feet slipping on the ice, to land heavily in a snowdrift built up in the hull of a trapped fishing boat. The wharves which lined the river were covered over with inches of ice and snow. Through the fog Lyle saw the phantasmal shapes of ships rising out of the ice, locked in place, forming a small city of streets and alleys. He looked up and saw on the bridge, staring down at him impassively, Sasso, arms raised as if trying to hold the air itself in his palms, on his face an expression which could only be called stony. Around him, gargoyles and griffins and the cherubs off the churches, some large and some no longer than Lyle's arm, swarmed with the biting, hissing sound of aerodynamic practicalities being recklessly suspended. He looked back at the stairs leading down to the ice and saw Lady Diane at the top, a stone cat prowling round her feet. Turning, he saw behind him a pair of stone angels, stone swords raised, and felt sick.

Lyle grabbed the side of the fishing boat and pulled himself up, his feet sliding in the snow that covered the frozen river, as he looked towards Charing Cross Bridge, a vague burning shadow in the distance. He began to run, darting between trapped fishing boats and long barges and crooked steamers. The ice was a blessing; it was something that Sasso couldn't control, and Lyle moved across it as silently as possible, squeezing himself into every shadow he could find, not looking back, *never* looking back, terrified of what he might see. He'd only just begun to realize how big the river was: it seemed to stretch on every side, made bigger yet by the thick ice that had pushed it almost to the very top of the Embankment walls.

Something dark passed overhead, and landed in the shadows in front of Lyle. He didn't stop running but ducked round the side of a boat, feet slapping dully in the snow, and heard the thing move to follow even as he dug in his pockets, pulling out a random handful of test tubes. He swung round another corner, and the giant stone angel was there, serene face staring straight down at him. Lyle threw a test tube at it and ran. The hiss of acid burning through the old stone melded with an unnatural, deep howl that made the stones around the Embankment resonate.

Then the tremor started, not in the ice itself, but either side of the river, shaking the ice free of the Embankment walls in little showers, rocking it unevenly and sending tiny cracks running through it where it was near any stone. Lyle slipped and fell uncomfortably on to his hands and knees, tried to get up, and slipped again. The tremor grew; he heard the sound of icicles crashing, snow falling off roofs, blackened trees shaking, felt the vibration rise up through his stomach, looked round and saw the houses of the Embankment *swaying*, as if they were made of cloth, saw stones cracking, splitting, felt the anger behind the tremors and knew that a very large part of that anger was blindly directed at *him*. He saw the clock tower of the Houses of Parliament crack, little lines spreading through it, cutting through the iron that bound it all together, he saw the glass lamps on the bridge flicker and fade, and thought how odd it was that no one in the area was screaming, shouting, calling out that this was the end of the world, the destruction of the city that Sasso had promised and was now delivering, the end of everything, the shattering of a thousand years of history. Earthquakes, after all, were hardly common in London, let alone earthquakes that made the old churches creak and the stones crack and the past slip away into the heart of the earth in slides of mud, trickles of snow, clouds of dust, centuries of living and dying erased in a single heave of the earth, the end of the city . . .

Lyle crawled, almost on his belly, clinging to the ice as the snow rippled across it in little disturbed eddies and the gutters of the Houses of Parliament creaked and dropped their load of icicles and the iron of the distant railway lines creaked and bent and sung out in metallic distress, until he reached what he judged in the dark and the fog to be the centre of the river, between Westminster and Charing Cross Bridge. He staggered upright and pulled from his pocket a little magnesium sphere, struck a match and watched the sphere blaze into burning white light.

'Sasso!' he screamed out through the roar of the stones. And then, because he couldn't think of an appropriately defiant challenge, added, 'Look over here! Coo-eee!'

The tremors died down, stopped, the last hum echoing away. Lyle held up the sphere, burning through the fog like a lighthouse.

On the bridge, Feng Darin looked up and saw, between him and Westminster Bridge, the small grey shape of Lyle, outlined beneath the blazing sphere of fire. And just beyond it, he saw the too-thick shadows, bunching, moving in, and knew that the darkness tonight was denser than the normal absence-of-light.

On the ice, a shape stepped forward from the crowded blackness as the light in Lyle's hand began to flicker and die.

'It will not save your city, you know,' said Diane Lumire. Lyle didn't say anything, fingers tightening around the light in the sphere, as if trying to trap some of it inside. She stepped forward, moving with surprising ease across the ice. 'I made Sasso, Lyle. I made him; made him love, made him worship me, made him lose everything he had, made him *want* to die, made him stone. He is mine. And he will do what I say.'

'You brought him here? Did all this?' Lyle's voice was strained and quiet.

'I waited a long time to do this. The priest was useful, and so, in your way, were you. You found he was here, told your masters, and they brought the blade. It is the ultimate power, Lyle.'

'Can I just ask . . . quickly . . . are you Tseiqin?'

She hesitated, taken by surprise. Then smiled, and shook her head. 'No. I *was* Tseiqin. They made me stone, and took my power. I had to *make* power again.'

Lyle's eyes flew around the darkness, where now he was sure he could see darker shapes, and knew they couldn't just be his imagination, because he didn't have the imagination to see *that*. 'Selene,' he muttered wretchedly, 'are you left-handed?'

She raised her left hand, marble white, stone cold, and smiled. 'Yes, Horatio Lyle. I am.'

Lyle sighed, nodded sadly, and murmured, 'Come on, then.'

'Do you too want to die, Lyle?'

He smiled grimly at her, as the light winked out in his hand. 'I wasn't talking to you, miss.'

Under the darkness of Charing Cross Bridge, a horn sounded, once, a long, clear note. It bounced against the cold, still stones, echoed its way down the hard path of the Thames and twisted the fog into a new and interesting shape, then went out. A second later, another horn sounded further along the bridge, the dragging, almost sad note clinging to the air even after the call had ceased.

A silence. A deep, heavy silence that still remembered the sound which had come before, and was stirring itself from sleep to wakefulness, a new alertness that sat on the edge of its seat, drumming its fingers impatiently, a tiny little rhythm, *Hark, hark, the dogs do bark . . .*

A clacking sound on the air, out of place, slightly muffled in the night. A spark rising in the distance, growing larger faster, not just one spark as it grew larger, but many small sparks, and trailing tiny wisps of flame as it rose above Charing Cross Bridge, turned luxuriously, looked down at the river, and dived, sweeping down from the sky, bringing with it a ferocious cry, that had been studied at the feet of warriors and kings from the ages. '*Cooeee! Mister Lyyyle! We're comin' to rescue yoooou!*'

And as Icarus dived, Tess bouncing up and down in the back seat waving her bottles of nitroglycerin with a reckless abandonment that made even the distracted Lyle wince, the shadows also moved behind it and below it. From under Charing Cross Bridge, hooves wrapped in cloth to muffle them on the snow and ice, rifles taking aim and breaths steaming in the air, came the cavalry.

The horsemen looked long and hard down the length of the river and, in the darkness, the stones of London seemed to look back. Icarus swept past them, briefly illuminating ten, a dozen, twenty, fifty faces in the fires of its passage, as, with a little whistling sound and a cry of '*Whoopeeee!*' Tess let the first bottle of nitroglycerin fall.

It struck, exploded in white and red and green tongues that

lashed at the ships and shattered the ice behind Selene, twisting it up and out and under, shoving whole slabs deep into the dark dirty water of the Thames, which rushed up hungrily for the surface. As one man, the cavalry charged.

Sasso simply smiled, and waited. He knew that the dead would never die. Neither would the stones.

From underneath Westminster Bridge, hidden in the shadows, the gargoyles shifted their heavy masses from foot to foot, and rose up to meet the cavalry.

CHAPTER 26

Ice

It was the strangest cavalry charge in the already strange history of strategy. It began as a trot from under the shadows of the bridge, light after light being struck, a flame being passed down from man to man, illuminating shiny buttons and large rifles that caught the light in a way which suggested that here was a weapon loved not only for its appearance at the riders' sides, but for its sheer, elegant, deadly mechanical efficiency. Overhead, Icarus spun slowly in the sky, Tess pushing out from its side bottles of oil which shattered and burnt, spilling pools of yellow light across the snow in uneven puddles, melting all around it and burning a hole through the ice, which bubbled and hissed as it was torn away.

The cavalry trotted round the pools of fire as if a floor of ice were the most natural thing in the world, slung their rifles into a more comfortable position and, as if they'd all heard the same silent signal at the same moment, as one, began as one to canter.

In front of them, gliding out from under the shelter of Westminster Bridge, the gargoyles and angels and strange heraldic beasts, ranging from a proud griffin to a comically pudgy hippopotamus, drew up together and, because, as Lyle would have pointed out, the modern scientific revolution hadn't really happened to their lord and master, they formed a line and charged, when all they really needed to do was wait.

Now the ice was creaking, thundering, hammered under the weight of stone that charged across it, and the walls were blackening with more beasts, round-cheeked cherubs flapping along on tiny wings; ancient, oversized generals on their huge stone horses, who'd galloped down from the Haymarket; or the stone dragon that held the shield which guarded the gates to Old London Town; all the creatures that were carved in the city – all the stonework that was alive and watching even *before* another mind gave them movement men could see, that formed part of the character of the city – flooded down on to the river, pouring across the ice in a thick tide that pushed aside the grey and white snow in a series of odd tracks and strange scratches, and made the ice underneath creak. When they charged, the ice behind them was shiny with meltwater, compressed under their combined weight into liquid, proving once again that heat and work did share the same common interests.

The two sides were racing for a head-on collision, and Lyle

was caught in between, pulling himself over the side of a shuddering fishing boat and covering his head with his hands, diving down into the shadows as his heart pounded in his ears, his stomach turned in his throat and his ears tried to migrate to his feet. And still he couldn't get the tune out of his head, the little voice that heard the hammering of the horses' hooves and the thundering of a hundred stone talons, claws, paws, shoes, heels, and he thought, *Hark, hark, the dogs do bark,* a frantic thought that hammered through his mind and whispered, *The city is alive, it's always been alive, always been alert and watching and wakeful and now it's dying and I've only just begun to realize and it's too late!*

He cursed himself in darkness and fear as two armies rushed to meet, in the heart of the city, its main artery, the river that brought the world to the city, the city to the world, spread the songs and the rhymes that told the life of the city to other cities, with the thoughts that sang out in the night, *Hark, hark, the dogs do bark . . .*

Overhead, Tess looked down, saw two dark masses rushing together, like the place where two oceans meet, the centre of each rank charging ahead, the first flashes of the guns as a warning, then a whole volley as each rider raised his rifle to fire, took aim at whichever part of a moving stone wall looked more vulnerable than its neighbour, and fired. The shots bounced off the walls along the river, whined past the bridges and ricocheted upwards, even as Icarus dived downwards, Thomas kicking at lever after lever with his eyebrows dug so deep they almost touched his nose. And Tess thought, *London's burning, London's burning, Fetch the engines, fetch the engines . . .* and, *This is my home! It ain't much of a home, it ain't pretty or nice and it doesn't smell good, but it's my home!*

On Charing Cross Bridge, looking down at the river in flames, Feng Darin saw two dark waves rush together with an unstoppable force and hammer across the ice, the noise growing louder and louder, the ice creaking beneath them, the snow turning to slush, saw them accelerate to a black blur, caught occasionally in the burning pools of oil that ran across the river, saw them collide, heard the scream of horses, the flash of rifles, the rising smoke that blended with the fog, the shudder of grenades, the crack of stone. Looked up further and saw still, on the bridge, Sasso smiling, and wondered why.

Lyle peeked above the edge of his boat and saw the world in flames and smoke and felt, under him, the boat give a little shudder, felt it droop for a moment, shaking as the ice bent. He thought, *Oh dear, this isn't going to end well . . .* took a deep breath, and swung himself over the side, into the middle of the fray.

And Lyle thought: *This is* my *city . . .*

Noise and hooves and stone and claws and rifles were everywhere. Lyle ran almost bent double, focusing on the half-melted space behind the furthest horse, not caring who was friend or foe, just concentrating on that area of open space where he could run away from the pounding in his ears and the claws at his back. The yellow-whiteness beyond was eclipsed by a horse galloping across his path, the rider firing blindly over Lyle's head, a cherub clinging to the rider's shoulder, teeth buried deep through the cloth, tiny fat fingers at the cavalryman's neck. Lyle heard a horse scream and saw it go down, twisting on to one side as a flock of small ornamental gargoyles set upon it. Looking back, he saw an angel drawing itself up, one arm lying at its side, blown off by what force Lyle didn't know, a series of bullet marks in its side. As he watched, the angel, with a puzzled expression, picked up its own arm, thought about it, then brandished it as a club.

Lyle felt in his pocket, pulled out a hypodermic needle, the end corked, and flicked the cork aside. The angel looked at him sceptically, as if wondering what this little creature could possibly contemplate doing with a needle against a club at least half Lyle's weight. It took a considered, lazy swipe at him. He ducked, and tried to scurry under the blow, but the angel spun with surprising grace, as if it was wearing skates on the slippery ice, and brought the club back round towards Lyle's head. He threw himself down, the blow swinging close by, the wind of its passage tickling the back of his neck, and under his hands he felt the ice creak, twist, hum, buckle, and he saw, an inch from his nose, the tiniest little line slide across it, hair-thin; pause, as if considering its next move; then race a few more inches, exploring the new world that seemed to be opening up in front of it.

Lyle crawled after it, hoping no one would notice him, and a heavy stone foot landed on his ankle. He looked back and saw the angel, bringing up the stone arm again, and thought, for just a moment, he saw something else behind the angel's eye, a glimpse of the intelligence that drove it, and remembered, '*I made him; made him love, made him worship me, made him lose everything he had, made him* want *to die, made him stone. He is mine,*' and realized that he'd only found the weapon, not the hand that wielded it, realized how well Selene used people, including, perhaps, himself.

And for a second, professional pride and fear melted in Lyle, and combined into a new shade of emotion, and anger flared up inside him. He twisted under the foot that held him down, raised the hypodermic needle, putting it against the join in the knee of the angel, and pressed the plunger. Acid shot out, searing through stone, giving off a sweet acrid smell that made Lyle's eyes water and dried his throat in a second. The foot that held him down fell lifeless off the angel, who, wearing a surprised expression, teetered for a second, and fell over, crashing into the ice next to Lyle. The crash sent cracks sprawling outwards, widening the hairline marks in the ice, until they were wide enough for Lyle's fingers and he could see, down below, the black waters of the Thames.

He staggered to his feet and looked around, saw a gargoyle, claws raised over the prone figure of a man, raised a test tube and threw it blindly, half-saw it shatter in glass and flames against the stone of the gargoyle, and turned, looking back into the swell of the battle, which had spread like a disease as each line broke and rebuilt, horses and stone figures dancing round each other in a black stain across the white river. And still the stones hummed along the banks of the river and he could feel its vibration rising up through his shoes, and could see the black shapes of stones and statues still flooding in from Westminster Bridge, an endless supply of them, the carved memories of London's history, and he saw *her*, caught for a moment in the light of the burning oil fires, as Icarus sailed overhead, a greenish tube of glass whistling down to shatter the ice, breaking it like the end of the world. He looked towards the safety of Charing Cross Bridge, still untouched, looked towards the battle and

Westminster Bridge, felt the anger and the disappointment and the bitter sense of a world gone wrong, took a deep breath, and ran back into the fray.

Feng Darin was dancing. He fought and danced along the Embankment as the stones rippled under his feet and leered overhead; he danced and ducked and whirled and twirled, eyes vacantly focused on the distant shape of Lucan Sasso, Selene's blade black in his hand. Feng Darin wasn't turning this way or that as the night thickened around him with stone shapes, but spinning his way through the throng as if he were a ghost, trying to write his story through ripples in the fog. His feet hammered out a steady rhythm as he moved inexorably forward, and the rhythm whispered, *Hark, hark* . . .

He moved without tiring, without looking or raising his head. He remembered the wind of his childhood and the endless dry steppes, and he ducked and whirled and *remembered* . . . *he remembered* . . .

Hark, hark, the dogs do bark!

The city blocked out memories of other places, suppressed them beneath the fog and the darkness until all that was left was the city, filling him from top to toe as he danced through the night, weaving and punching and stabbing, and he hardly even noticed the cobbles under his feet or the ease with which Selene's blade pierced stone. All that filled his mind was the dance and the rhythm, that rose up with the streets themselves.

And here, now, was the city, in Feng Darin's head.

Hark, hark, the dogs do bark,
The beggars are coming to town.
Some in rags and some in tags,
And one in a velvet gown.

Because now, just for tonight, Feng Darin was beginning to understand.

And in the throng, for a moment, just a moment, Lyle saw *her*, and she saw him, and perhaps it was just the darkness and the illusions that fire and fog created, but something in his face made her start, and something in his eyes made her hesitate, and for a moment, the utter certainty of a mistress mastering the situation flickered, faltered.

Then she swept away again and a wall of gargoyles swept with her, forming a tight protective knot. But Lyle didn't care, ran after her, raising in his hands a whole array of tubes and bottles and needles and glass baubles and hurling them blindly at anything that got in his way. He charged after Diane Lumire, knowing that she was the one who had made Sasso, made him stone, made him evil, brought him here, broken necks with a twist of her wrist and now she was going to destroy *his* city. He wasn't operating on an intellectual level now; for almost the first time since the baby Lyle had opened his eyes, he was running on instinct, which felt the air move behind him and heard the ice crunch around him and felt the waters rise beneath his feet and kept him moving until he was suddenly ducking under a frantic horse that was trying to rear up from the cracks in the ice that were spreading under its hooves, and out on to the open, dark ice, in front of *her*.

He hurled the first tube of acid at her that came to hand: an angel stepped forward, without a moment's hesitation, and the glass shattered off its front. Lyle thought he saw, behind its empty eyes, an altogether different intelligence, watching him with single-minded menace. He ignored the feeling and kept running, but now the ice underfoot was wobbling and bending, gargoyles leaping inelegantly from slab to slab as the cracks spread across it, worming their way from bank to bank. He half-heard the screams of horses and the clatter of steel as the soldiers struggled to stay either on their mounts or even on their feet. The world was suddenly a thousand little, toppling worlds, each one balancing slippery on the dark water of the Thames, which had decided that today it would like to breathe the air after all, thank you very much, and was trying to crawl its way back up over the ice, reclaiming its territory.

Lyle hopped from slab to slab, sometimes wrongly estimating the jump and landing on an edge, which wobbled and tried to tip him off. A gargoyle lunged at him, but the ice on which it stood simply tipped underneath it, toppling the gargoyle forward, so its claws sailed past Lyle's head and its feet slid out on the ice, talons embedded and screeching like fingers across a blackboard as it slipped down into the cold water. The cavalry were retreating, climbing or swimming or running or riding away from the shattered ice and trying to control their terrified horses, in a confused circle towards Westminster, still firing at the gargoyles. These, rather than risk walking across the ice, were clinging to the walls of the Embankment, swarming across it like fleas to moisture, forming a long, tight circle round the straggling survivors, and then spreading out once more, scattering towards the shadows on Charing Cross Bridge.

Lyle looked and saw her again, Selene, Lumire, the One Who Did It All. She was heading towards the edge of the river, where the ice was thicker, as casually and daintily as if attending a ball. He ran after her, hurling chemical death at anything that got in his way.

Overhead in Icarus, Tess looked down and saw the black mass of stone figures swarming around the confused cavalry, forming a tighter and tighter circle, briefly illuminated by each new flash of rifle fire as the riders circled, confused, hemmed in on all sides. At their backs the ice was shattered and bobbing, mere white specks now on the rising black waters of the Thames.

Tess looked down, and saw, all along the Embankment, more men, desperately trying to work out how steel and lead are meant to break stone, swarming through the narrow streets between Westminster and Charing Cross Bridges, and thought, in a quiet little voice, the voice that she knew would be hers, when all the childish things were gone, *London's burning, London's burning . . .*

And, without warning, there was nothing but darkness and ice between Lyle and Selene. He looked in astonishment at the shattered stone around him, at the broken glass and thick, smelly smoke from a thousand unfortunate chemical combinations now regretting their acquaintance, even as, on Westminster Bridge, Lucan Sasso looked down and saw his love, the woman who made him, the only woman who'd ever rejected him, the woman who was his heart and soul and mind, standing alone, and tried to bend the stones round her, to protect her, dragging the stones across the ice, but Lucan Sasso sees . . . he *sees* . . . the cobbles of Hampstead, the walls of Hackney, the alleys of Shoreditch, the Thames bridges, the streets of Mayfair, the spires of Holborn, the chimneys of Finsbury, the courts of Westminster, and he sees London, stretching out through time and space, a thousand years of stones and lives, so many lives, so many stones, trying to drag him here or here, saying, *I was once walked on by Sir Christopher Wren* or *The blood of kings fell on my cobbles* or *Here we were bought* or *Here we were sold* or *Here died and here lived and here was born and here perished and here fought and here won and here lost*; and though his love needed him and stood alone on the ice, though the stones were his to command, Lucan Sasso *couldn't get the city out of his head!*

And here now is the city, in Lucan Sasso's head.

'Oranges and lemons,' *say the bells of St Clement's.*
'You owe me five farthings,' *say the bells of St Martin's.*
'When will you pay me?' *say the bells of Old Bailey.*
'When I grow rich,' *say the bells of Shoreditch.*
'When will that be?' *say the bells of Stepney.*
'I do not know,' *say the great bells of Bow.*
Here comes a candle to light you to bed,
Here comes a chopper to chop off your head.
Chip chop chip, the last man's dead.

And for a moment, as the world runs out of control, Lucan Sasso finally understands.

CHAPTER 27

River

Diane stood by the walls of the Embankment, head tilted on one side as Lyle approached out of the fog. He stopped a few paces away, looking suspiciously around, eyes narrowed, while from everywhere the cacophony of battle was oddly distant, muffled in the fog, directions lost. Seeing his face, she smiled faintly.

'You think you can really harm *me*? Do you know me, Horatio Lyle? Do you know my reputation? What I am?'

'God help us, I do. This – is all you?'

'Flattery, but I accept it. I am Selene. I make the world what I want it to be. I am very patient.'

'You're a mad bagcase, pardon the technical jargon.'

Lyle looked up at Westminster Bridge, and saw the shadow of

Lucan Sasso, standing utterly still, eyes closed, hands over his ears, as if trying to drown out a furious voice that was raging *inside* his head. He shrugged. 'At the moment . . . I'm cautiously optimistic, Lady Selene.'

She smiled. 'But you don't have a weapon.'

Lyle looked down at his hands. He held one hypodermic, just a few drops of acid clinging to the needle, like ice crystals to a cold window. He didn't need to feel his pockets to know they were empty. He looked up again, a half-hearted smile on his face, and risked another lopsided shrug. 'I might have . . . a plan.'

Selene began walking towards him, picking her way carefully across the ice, steering her way without bothering to glance down. 'I have lived many, many years, Horatio Lyle, if you can regard this existence as living. I have felt nothing, tasted nothing, heard no music that pleased me nor felt anything but lingering cold, even in the sun. The technological revolution seems to be . . . rather dull. It certainly doesn't offer the *power* that is all I crave. In fact, it seems to me to be rather typical of the men who made it, that they will fight their way through ice and death to reach an end, and when they get there . . .' She stopped, within arm's reach of Lyle. He had never realized how intimidating fog made people. '. . . they never seem to find what they're looking for. I was Tseiqin. I ruled the hearts of men. Now I am stone. I rule the heart of stone. It is a death perpetual, and a gift you will not understand.'

Lyle slashed out at her with the needle. She flung her arm up, and to his surprise, the needle drew a line through her sleeve and across the marble-white skin underneath. She grabbed his wrist with her other arm, wrenching it back on itself until his fingers turned blue, her face suddenly made ugly with hatred and pain. Lyle clung desperately on to the needle as the only thing left in his possession. As Selene twisted with a strength he hadn't realized could be created outside a hydraulic system, he saw something staining her arm, where the needle had slashed it. It wasn't dark enough in this light to be blood, nor did it run like water, but rather rose up in the cut across her arm in a slow pool, that clung to the cut like an old scab, and began to dry and change colour almost immediately.

Selene saw his eyes widen in horror and hissed in his ear, 'My blood is clay, the clay of this city, Lyle, that made this city. My heart is stone, my blood is clay, but my mind . . . my *mind* is very much my own.'

Lyle heard his knees creak and felt them bend, then fell on to the ice while she still clung to his wrist. He looked down, saw a hole in the ice and black water lapping hungrily inside it, and felt anger rise up, overwhelming fear. Somewhere, on the edge of instinct, where the mind couldn't function for fear of getting entangled in less practical matters, he felt the air move overhead.

'You killed an old woman and a beggar,' he gasped.

Selene shrugged. 'Life's a short business anyway. They'd already lived theirs.'

She pushed him face-down towards the water, one hand on the back of his neck, until his nose touched the shockingly cold, black surface. A shudder raced down his spine. He tried to breathe deeply, take as much air as he could, but the more he concentrated on breathing, the faster and shallower it became.

Somewhere, on the edge of instinct, where science was always a little bit too practical to venture, he heard the air move, and a voice shout: 'Oi! That's my gov'nor you're drownin'!'

And as Selene looked up in a moment of surprise and horror, Lyle drew one breath that pushed at his lungs and made him feel he was about to explode, and threw himself, head first, into the black waters below.

Tess saw Lyle slip under the waters even as Selene raised her head in astonishment to look at Icarus. She screamed in fury and threw one of the still-hot tubes at Selene. But a gargoyle leapt out of the darkness below and knocked Selene aside, taking the full force of the hissing contraption in her place. As Thomas pulled at the levers, Icarus began sailing upwards again, the world below slowing to a luxurious spin as the machine fought for height. Tess saw the black pool where Lyle had vanished, the water lying still in the firelight, and screamed at Thomas, 'We've gotta go down!'

'What?' Thomas's voice was snatched away by the wind, the faintest shrill cry on the air.

'We've gotta go down! We've gotta help Mister Lyle!'

Tess leant over the side, leaning out until her fingertips barely clung to the edge, eyes fixed on the black waters, and saw that Selene too was looking at the black pool, standing with hands folded neatly in front of her, almost as if at prayer, studying the depths. Tess tried to count the seconds, but seconds were breaths, and then heartbeats, and then the pounding of her head, and then the rhythm of another tube as it burnt out in a gentle *phutphut*, and still she saw nothing, just a blackness below that wouldn't break. She knew that somewhere the soldiers were pushing back at the stone army along the Embankment, that somewhere a cannon had fired, that somewhere below, the world was burning, that it was all ending, the city, the battle, the flight, the night, the dark, the fog, the ice, and still the darkness didn't break.

'Mister Lyle!' she screamed down at the ice, praying for an answer, that it was just a trick. And below, Feng Darin, dragging death behind him as he spun across Westminster Bridge, was woken from his trance as the voice, full of pain and despair, shrilled across the ice, shook the stones, sank into them, another part of London's history, the time the child screamed above the fire and the ice of a battle being won and lost, through the city where the blood of kings fell on the cobbles which here were bought or here were sold or here died and here lived and here was born and here perished, around a shattered river.

And below, next to the still water surrounded by ice, Lady Diane Lumire looked up at Icarus, hearing the child's scream, and smiled. Tess recognized the smile for the cruellest thing she had ever seen, remorseless, without even a cause to justify it beyond selfish personal gain. At least when in the past she'd met villains, they'd bothered to explain *why* they were villains.

Selene just didn't care, and would never, ever understand.

Behind her, near the stairs up to the bridge, the ice exploded, outwards, upwards, as Lyle broke back to the surface.

Feng Darin could almost see his target, Lucan Sasso, standing in the middle of the bridge. But there was now a wall between him and it, stones rising up from the bridge itself to try and stop his advance, and on every side the enemy kept flocking in, scratching and tearing and punching, so that even when he could finally see his foe, he still couldn't reach him!

Down on the river, Selene turned and saw Horatio Lyle pull himself up towards the bridge by the stairs, the water already starting to solidify as it poured off him, tiny icicles clinging to his coat. He crawled upwards, one hand still clinging to the hypodermic. With a hiss of frustration, Selene strode after him. Lyle reached the top of the steps as Selene's hand closed round his ankle, dragging him bodily off the stairs and down on to the ice. He fell the five feet hard, on one side, landing with a crunch and a crackle of the ice embedded in his clothes and clinging to his hair, turning it white. Selene leant down, one hand closing round his throat.

There was a sound like a falling brick shattering soft wood. With a surprised expression, Selene looked down, and then, thoughtfully, pulled the needle out of her upper leg, dragging the plunger back up. A few drops of dirty Thames water still clung to the side of the hypodermic's glass. She turned her gaze on Lyle. 'But you didn't have anything in it,' she protested.

'I took the opportunity of filling it with water while trying to find a way out from under the ice.' Lyle's voice was half breathless wheeze, half chattering teeth.

'But . . .' Selene staggered back an uncertain pace from Lyle, one hand going up to her heart, fingers tightening as if in pain. 'But . . . I *feel* . . . water?'

Lyle crawled away from her, clinging to the icy stones of the stairs. Selene leant suddenly against the Embankment wall, eyes wide, face white, fingers opening, then closing into a tight fist.

She bent, curling up around the point where the needle had gone in, as if in great pain.

'Water?'

'It . . .' Lyle's voice was almost non-existent, his eyes wide and frightened, reality slowly kicking back in and instincts sliding away into their box for another day. 'It expands when frozen. You are very cold, my lady.'

And, as water turned to ice inside her, Selene clutched at the pain in her heart where she hadn't realized she had a heart, and as what little life she had to call her own stopped, Lady Diane Lumire thought she heard – through the closing down of her senses which blocked out all sounds but the ever-unheard hum of the city, the sound that most are too well used to hearing to really notice or care about any more – she *heard* the city, and perhaps even she finally understood.

She slipped, still and heavy, on to the ice.

And Lucan Sasso screamed.

CHAPTER 28

Perfection

Lyle heard the scream, but didn't register it. Cold was burning his face, numbing his toes. He crawled up the stairs from the river on his belly, half-aware of the world around him, but unable to feel it except in the pounding of his mind, which imagined sensations that weren't there. A slow, pinkish warmth was beginning somewhere in the back of his stomach, as if it grew from the spine and spread, narrowing his vision and muffling all sounds in his ears. Instinct said very quietly that this wasn't a good thing, and when intellect growled, it retreated again. Though his mind tried to deny it, Lyle knew that unless he found somewhere warm, he'd soon be dead.

What he found was Lucan Sasso.

The punch threw him down into the snow piled against the

side of the bridge, and sent dull pain coursing through his sleepy nerves. He crawled away blindly, tears rising involuntarily to his eyes and freezing to his eyelashes. The next blow knocked him back against the parapet, which he clung to as if it was his only friend, vision narrowing to a tight point, a sound in his ears like a bubbling volcano.

The hand that closed around his shoulder and dragged him upright had the same iron of Selene's grip, but the eyes that drew level with Lyle's had a tormented, broken fire in them that Selene had never understood. They were the eyes of a man whose mind was not entirely his own, that saw more things than they could cope with, and that could no longer hide the madness burning in the mind behind them.

For a second Lucan Sasso just stood holding Lyle, whose toes trailed uselessly on the ground, as if wondering which death was more suitable. Lyle, all feeling gone from his arms, his feet, his mind, numb to everything except the pain trying to break through the icy barrier that surrounded his senses, didn't fight. He half-closed his eyes, and let himself hear the only thoughts that were left, as the city sang its songs in his ears.

And here, now, was the city, in Horatio Lyle's head.

> *Hush-a-bye, don't you cry,*
> *Go to sleep, my little angel.*
> *Blacks and bays,*
> *Dapples and greys,*
> *Coach and six of little horses.*

And Horatio Lyle understood what he'd always known, deep, deep down throughout his entire life. Horatio Lyle understood that the city was alive, and it was as much a part of him as he was a part of it, and whatever happened, whenever it happened, a tiny bit of him would live, stamped on to the city that he called home.

He opened his eyes and met Lucan Sasso's gaze. For a second, neither moved, neither spoke. It was, thought Lyle, something inexpressible, unutterable. Almost . . . perfect.

And then the cry rang out. 'Sasso! I am for you!'

In a moment Sasso spun, dragging Lyle with him, who flopped in his grip, half-dead already. Feng Darin stood on the bridge, and raised Selene's blade. *Oh, good grief*, thought a vague, slurred voice in Lyle's mind that might once have been his, *what now?*

And Sasso laughed, the hollow laugh of a broken man. '**What will you do with that, little mortal?** I will break you before you move!' His voice was rising in pain and despair. Lyle flinched from it, shuddering, wishing he could struggle but unable to move.

Feng Darin stared at Sasso a long while, then at Lyle, who shook his head feebly, fingers opening and closing in pain. Their eyes met.

Feng Darin smiled.

Feng Darin raised the blade.

Lyle understood Feng Darin, and it was his turn to scream out in despair and fury.

'*Darin!*'

Feng Darin turned the blade with ease and grace, brought it down, and . . .

318

Lyle closed his eyes. He felt the hand that held him let go, opening in surprise, and flopped like a fish on to the bridge, not even bothering to break his own fall. He buried his head in his hands.

The city was suddenly quiet. All eyes that could see had turned to the bridge. Only the gentle wheezing of Icarus, high overhead, broke the silence. Then footsteps, the sharp, heavy steps of Sasso as he advanced towards the shape of Feng Darin. Blood pooled around the fallen man, seeping through the snow. Lyle raised his head and saw Sasso bend down and pull the blade easily from Feng's lifeless fingers, then, with a thoughtful expression, prod the man with a toe. Feng didn't move. Sasso turned back towards Lyle, holding up the blade, the better to catch the light, and saw Lyle's burning eyes fixed on him. He lowered the blade again, surprised.

'Are you alive, little man? Shall I break your heart with the blade, as your friend's heart is broken?'

Lyle dragged himself up, clinging to the parapet of the bridge, which seemed oddly warm under his fingers. He looked down at the cobbles. Water was running away; the snow seemed to be dissolving beneath his feet. He looked up at the sky. Black clouds were racing in from the horizon, as if they'd only just heard about the excitement and wanted to have a look.

'Lucan Sasso was, in his time, a remarkable man,' hissed Lyle, staggering a pace, half-falling, and clinging still to the bridge for support. 'Honoured for his skills and bravery in battle. He was a poet too, a man of culture, and passion. At the time when he was still a young man, there was a lady. Some said she was an Austrian princess, some said she had come even from the realms of the Ottoman, some that she was a Spanish beauty raised in the south by Moors. Her name was Selene.'

Lyle's voice was the only sound in the darkness. He reached a lamp post and used it to pull himself up straighter, feeling the warmth from the light that burned above it. Below, ice began to creak. There was a slow, sucking sound, the gentle hiss of boats slipping out of the melting ice and dipping back into water, the thud of drifting hulls banging against each other, the plop of masonry slipping under the waves.

Lyle's voice grew louder, drowning out another sound, caught by a wind that rose from the river and the streets and seemed to bring with it a strange smell, salty, as if it had blown up from the Atlantic Ocean, and come many miles carrying a new message from another land with it.

'Lucan Sasso met Selene in Rome, and was struck with her instantly. He followed her to Vienna, to Paris, protesting his love for her. She left him a blade, made of a very special stone. He swore he would kill himself with it rather than be parted from her, but she left that night. The same night, on Westminster Bridge, he stabbed himself through the heart with the stone blade. *Here.*'

Sasso was frozen in place, eyes fixed on Lyle, even as the wind rose and gusted the snow off the rooftops, as the water rushed through the river and the darkness seemed to close in around him. Lyle was almost shouting over the wind, tiny flecks of ice flying from his hair, which clattered as it was dragged in the wind.

'Something took hold of Lucan Sasso. He is stone. His heart is an empty space under his skin, his skin is hard, smooth marble, his eyes do not dilate in bright light, the moonlight and the sun-light burn away the illusion of life that is half-real, half-imagined by all who see him, and reveal him for what he *really* is. Do you know what you really are, Lucan Sasso?'

Sasso half-opened his mouth, then hesitated, the blade hang-ing, forgotten at his side. Lyle smiled, even as tears stung his eyes, and his voice was hollow with despair, '*You* are a statue, Lucan Sasso. You never *were* real.'

'I . . .' The wind snatched his words away. Louder, raising his voice. 'I . . . am a god! You cannot tame me . . . I . . . *I* am for ever . . . I am . . . *you cannot tame me!*'

Behind, him, Feng Darin rose up from the shadows and said, very quietly, 'I can.'

And Sasso turned, and saw Feng Darin, the blood still run-ning from where the knife had entered his heart, but slowing now, like clay, and whispered, 'Surely you cannot have *wanted* to die?'

Feng Darin merely smiled, and raised his hand, palms up, towards the sky. Around him, the stones of the bridge rumbled, growled, roared and exploded, drops showering down around. They rose up so tall, a huge stone neck that extended from one end of the bridge to the other to join in an arch across the length of the road and still rose, nearly clipping Icarus as the ship cir-cled overhead; the stones rose up and twisted into new and alien shapes, something coming out of the neck even as the cobbles fractured and tore, ripped out of stone to slide together into a clattering mass, and still the shape kept building into . . . a face. Long and thin, trailing sharp points and jagged, scaled lines. Eyes opened in its depths, peered round, peered down, followed

Feng Darin's gaze, his mind. Teeth of jagged stone grew from its mouth, its nostrils flared, spouting dust. The dragon looked down, and saw Sasso standing small and alone, far, far below, and opened a jaw so wide and so long, it looked as if it could eat Nelson's Column like a piece of spaghetti.

And here now was Feng Darin, in the city's head.

Hark . . .

Hark . . .

The dragon considered the tiny shapes, tiny Lucan Sasso and tiny Feng Darin, far, far below it, thought about it, opened its jaws, and dived down to meet them.

Feng Darin closed his eyes, and the city closed its own in response.

He remembered the wind across the steppes, the free run, the innocent time, the endless sky overhead and the mountains in the distance. He remembered the day he saw the city, and wondered that it took him so long to understand.

As the dragon closed its jaws, Feng Darin smiled, and welcomed it.

It was simply . . . perfect.

CHAPTER 29

Thaw

London, at the end of winter.

Icicles drip half-heartedly into the gutters, waiting for the moment when they can crash off the pipe and call it a day. Meltwater runs down the centre of the streets, sweeping away the dirt before it, and revealing anew the old dirt which had been frozen under the snows. In Heron Quays the coal-carrier looks up as he carries the last sack of black, lumped will-be-soot up from the base of the barge, just a small shape in a city of ships clinging to the side of the river, and sees a hole opening up in the clouds, and wonders whether it isn't time to take the heavy hat and scarf back to the pawnbroker's and redeem the claim on those old waterproofs instead.

In St Mary's Church, Cheapside, the apprentices, knowing a

good deal when they see it, scrub away at the old brass bell of the tower, kicking away the last few shards of ice which cling to it, sending them over the side of the tower to crash down into the street below, while next to them the bell hums a gentle sleepy tune that is picked up by the bells of St Paul's and St Pancras, who whisper to each other,

Blacks and bays,
Dapples and greys . . .

The costermongers calling out in Brick Lane and Chapel Market and Whitecross Street and along Poultry and down Maiden Lane still wear two pairs of woollens apiece, and argue with each other about which is worse – having water coming up through your worn boots that have trodden every cobble in London, or having ice freeze your boots tight shut around your numbed feet. It is an argument that will last until summer burns it all away, in a long time to come.

The drizzle, smelling of salt from the Atlantic that has come a long way with a special message, falls gently outside a tall window, through which warm yellow light spills, eclipsed only by the black outline of a man. For a second the yellow light warming the snow turns red as it catches a glass of port, swirled absently in a crystal glass, and the glass hums in sympathy to the voice that says, in tones of weary resignation, 'Were you aware that Her Majesty's Government funded a reconstruction of Westminster Bridge last year?'

Mr Lingdao relights his pipe and puffs. 'You might almost think the city were deliberately trying to upset you, my lord.'

The drizzle falls on a shed in Hampstead Heath, then runs through its roof. Four shapes sit under the shelter of a wing, eating suet pudding.

Finally one voice says, 'Mister Lyle?'

'Yes?'

'What happened, back there?'

'Back where, Teresa?'

'With the water and the big dragon thing an' how it ate up the evil bigwig an' that?'

'Ah. Back *there*.'

'You ain't tellin', are you?'

'Feng Darin worked out something he could do with Selene's blade. Something very clever, that none of us had really . . . considered.'

Thomas looks up sharply from his helping of suet pudding, and wonders why Lyle isn't meeting anyone's eyes.

'What'd he do?'

'Well . . . it turns out that the blade had this . . . thing,' Lyle waves a fork, uncomfortably, 'which let Feng do . . . things . . . about the city . . . All very unscientific, I grant you, but I'm sure there's a perfectly logical explanation involving . . . oh, I don't know, electromagnetic repulsion and spontaneous ionization in the presence of a magnetic field or . . . something along those lines – not really my field at all – anyway, which allowed Feng to beat the evil bigwig.'

'Ain't it *you* what beat the evil bigwig?'

'No. Just his maker.'

The four go on eating.

*

Down in Cheapside, a bell begins to ring, proclaiming the hour. A bit to the south, rolling past Blackfriars and on towards Westminster Bridge, the river hesitates for a moment, as if listening to the bell, counting the strokes to make sure it is on time for a vital appointment it can't afford to miss and, realizing that it is running late, lingers for a second more to wait for the echoes, then turns and races straight back the way it has come.

The bells ring on, whispering the old, familiar tales to each other.

Hark, hark, the dogs do bark . . .

The turning tide catches a number of ships out in the reeds near the estuary, and pushes them along for a while, towards the wider sea, each carrying a tiny bit of the city in its hull, in the minds of its passengers, who stand on the deck and watch the black smoke of London fading behind them, as they head towards the dawn.

The bells ring on.

London's burning, London's burning . . .

In the high, ancient stones of the Tower of London a door opens and closes. A tremulous voice emerges from the darkness. 'You can't do this to me! I'm an *American*!'

Lord Lincoln strikes a match off one of the hard, rough stones, and raises it, to cast a yellow flame round the prison cell. He looks down at Ignatius Caryway, curled up in a corner, and sighs. 'Mr Caryway,' he says wearily, 'no city in the world will want *you* to be a part of it.'

London Bridge is falling down, falling down, falling down . . .

The match gutters out, letting the darkness and the sound of bells flood back in, like the changing of the tide.

Build it up with iron and steel, my fair lady . . .

'My lord?'

'Yes, Mr Lingdao?'

'Lyle has proven an asset again.'

'Indeed.'

'Some are asking whether he might be more of an asset if he were part of our cause.'

'Horatio Lyle is very useful. But I fear I have doubts regarding his loyalty.'

'How so, my lord?'

Lord Lincoln sighs, holding up one hand to scratch his chin. The iron ring with two cogs counting down the seconds to midnight, or possibly noon, briefly catches the light on his finger.

Iron and steel will bend and break, bend and break, bend and break . . .

'He suffers from . . .' Lord Lincoln's fingers idly trace a pattern in the air, trying to pluck from it the right word. '. . . morality?'

The tide rushes on, busy, busy, busy, places to go, people to see, carrying away the smell and the taste of London, dragging the last sound of the bells with it, which catches at the sails of a ship, sitting far out of the city by the reeds. An alien ship, unusual in these ports, indeed in this climate.

'*Xiansheng!*' barks the first mate to the captain, who nods once.

'*Hao.*'

The ship raises its sails, and it too drifts east, carrying with it, as all things do which have entered the city, a tiny piece of London.

And deep down in its hold, there is a stone coffin, sealed with the sign of a double cog, counting down the seconds to midnight, or noonday, and inside it, something that was once someone thinks:

> *Hush-a-bye, don't you cry,*
> *Go to sleep, my little angel.*
> *Blacks and bays,*
> *Dapples and greys,*
> *Coach and six of little horses.*

And smiles, though it cannot quite remember why.

'Mister Lyle?'

'Yes, Teresa?'

'Where'd Mr Feng go?'

'Back to China.'

'Why? Why ain't he said goodbye?'

'He has many, many clever ideas to have, Teresa.'

And Thomas looks up at Lyle, and for a second meets his eyes, and in his own, small, uncertain way, thinks he begins to understand.

Mister Lyle smiles and finishes his last piece of pudding. He stands up, claps his hands together and says brightly, 'Right! How do we all feel about an investigation of the rate of change of omega with a fixed radius inside a polarized magnetic field when mass "M" is affected not only by inward acceleration "A" but *also* by changing charges Q positive and Q negative and mass "M" is of a soft ferrous or magnetic material?'

Thomas leaps up, smiling brightly. Tess sighs, finishes her last piece of pudding, licks up the crumbs carefully, because you never know when these little things might count, stands up, and goes to Meet Their Destiny. She doesn't know what it is, but at least, for today, it can't be all bad.

And the tide carries the songs that the bells of London sing to each other, when all else is asleep, out to sea.

'Oranges and lemons,' say the bells of St Clement's . . .

It carries a wide variety of other things too, mostly too un-hygienic to bear prolonged exploration. Flotsam from a raft that has hunted for eels and found only stones. A little coal that has spilt from the sacks that colliers carried up from the docks. A few papers that a lawyer has decided really should disappear soon, if trouble isn't to follow. A surprisingly large collection of shattered stone fragments that drift in the dirt along the bottom of the river, nudged this way and that by the turning of the tide. A stone talon. A stone wing. A stone halo, broken forever from the head it should encircle. An arm with cracks down every surface that still clings to the broken and twisted remnants of a black stone blade.

Here comes a candle to light you to bed . . .

Does the city, the eyes and ears and minds and senses and hearts that have made the city and are made anew by it every day, watch the remnants of Lucan Sasso drift out to sea, shattered into a hundred pieces by the force of the city that has risen up to consume him?

Here comes a chopper to chop off your head . . .

Probably not.

It isn't important.

It is said that, when everything else is sleeping, the stones of London Town whisper to each other. The old cobbles of Aldgate murmur to the new of Commercial Road, telling them what a world they have inherited, what a place, what a hunger, pouring out their history, whispering with the changing tide as the Thames rolls gently from here to there and back again, bringing with it little pieces of the world outside, which are quickly lost and consumed in the city.

It is simply . . . perfect.